Prologue

THERE WERE THREE OF THEM, daughters of the Black Trillium. In their full womanhood, they were to be Haramis, the Sorceress; Kadiya, the Seeker-Warrior; and Anigel, the Queen. At one birth they came into the world (which in itself was a strange and unknown thing) and at the moment of their birthing the Archimage Binah, she who was rumored to be the full Guardian of all the land, hailed and named them.

They were, she prophesied, to be the hope and saviors of their people. She bestowed upon each an amulet of amber in which was set a tiny floweret of the legendary Black Trillium, which was both the sign of their royal clan and of the land.

Their country of Ruwenda, though for long generations it had been home to humankind, still held many secrets. A large part was swamp, out of which rose some islands of firm ground. On many of these were ruins, some large enough to

be the graveyards of full cities. The King lived in the Citadel, yet another of these remainders of an earlier day, save that it was still whole.

To the east, humankind drained the swamp, creating polders, which made rich farmland and offered fine grazing for herds and flocks. Ruwenda also served as the major way station for the import of timber from the south, which was needed greatly by their neighbors of Labornok to the north. Other trade wares came out of the swamps themselves: herbs, spices, the scaled shells of water creatures — some as bright as jewels, some so tough they could be fashioned into waterproof scale armor. And most rare of all came things — many so strange they could not be identified — which were found in the ruins on the islands.

The gatherers of these were called Oddlings — the swamp dwellers whom the Ruwendians had found upon their own first arrival and with whom they had no quarrels. Neither wanted what the other desired in the way of territory. Of these Oddlings there were two races — the Nyssomu who were more forthcoming, some taking service even in the King's Citadel, and the Uisgu, shy outdwellers whose chosen land lay farther west in the unexplored swamps. What the Uisgu had to trade they brought to the Nyssomu, who in turn offered it to licensed traders. All generally gathered in the large ruined city known to men as Trevista, which outlanders could reach easily by river.

There was another race within the mires, claiming as their own the more western reaches of the north, and those none would willingly meet. Drowners, the Oddlings called them; Skritek, the learned named them. They were torturers and slayers, and an evil blight. At times they raided the polders or sought prey among the Oddlings, and nothing good was known of their saurian kind.

There was peace in Ruwenda—save for such raids as these—during the childhood of the three Princesses. Men were unaware that a storm was building in the north.

The King of Labornok was old and had occupied the throne for almost the lifetime of many of his people. His heir, Prince Voltrik, was soured with waiting. He spent much time overseas, where he learned different ways and made allies—including the great sorcerer Orogastus. When the Prince returned home, this man of magic was his close companion. When Voltrik did at last assume the crown, Orogastus became his first advisor.

Voltrik coveted Ruwenda—not for its swamps, but for its control of the lumber trade and for the treasure rumored to be found in the ruined places. Once safely settled on the throne, he struck.

The mountain forts guarding the only pass were blasted into nothingness by lightnings called down by Orogastus's magic. Then, guided by a traitorous merchant and with the swiftness of a snake's strike, the Labornoki took the great Citadel itself.

King Krain and those of his lords who survived that battle died horribly at Voltrik's orders. His Queen fell under the swords of those pledged to kill all the royal women, for there was a prophecy that only through them could the invaders be conquered in turn. The three Princesses escaped, each with the aid of her birth talisman—but they did not go together.

Haramis was carried by the witchery of Binah (now old and failing, else no Labornoki would have won foothold in the land) upon the back of a great lammergeier flying northward. Kadiya, with the aid of an Oddling hunter long her tutor in swamp ways, took to the swamps through an ancient passage. And Anigel, with her Uisgu mentor, the old herbmistress

Immu, escaped under cover of the transports of the enemy to the watery city of Trevista.

Each Princess in turn made her way to the Archimage at Noth, and each was set under a geas to discover a portion of a great magical weapon which would free the land.

Their trials were many. Haramis, in the mountain lands, was tracked by Orogastus. He skillfully wooed her, first out of policy and then because he believed he saw in her a fit companion for his own gathering of power. But he was unable to obtain the silver wand that was Haramis's talisman.

Kadiya was led to the lost city of the Vanished Ones and there took up the sword which grew from the stalk of the Black Trillium which had led her there. Anigel, fleeing southward with the aid of the Uisgu, came to the forests of Tassaleyo, where she plucked a crown from the maw of a life-devouring plant. There also she met the Prince Antar, son of Voltrik, sent to bring her back prisoner but already so revolted by the excesses of his father and fearful of the growing power of Orogastus, he would not fulfill his orders, but rather became Anigel's sworn defender.

Kadiya, leading her gathering army of both Uisgu and Nyssomu, joined with Anigel to storm the Citadel. It was Haramis who brought to an end the life and power of Orogastus, by uniting the three talismans into one great and overpowering magical focus.

Haramis refused the crown which was hers by right of first birth, choosing rather to follow Binah as the Archimage, when the dying sorceress left her her cloak of guardianship. Kadiya also put aside her heirship, for there were secrets in the swamplands which called to her, and she knew in her heart that crown and throne were not for her.

Anigel wedded with Antar and joined the two once-enemy

lands. As Queen and King of Laboruwenda, both swore they would rule as one and hold the peace.

Haramis departed for the northern mountains and the knowledge stored there which drew her heart as no living thing might do. Before she went she sundered again the three talismans, taking with her the wand. The crown Anigel set within her own as part of her heirship. Kadiya again took up her sword, the point of which was missing, the pommel of which could unlid into three force-shooting eyes—one the color of her own, one that of an Oddling, and the topmost a brilliant one which had no bodily counterpart.

Kadiya joined her Oddling army and went swampward just at the beginning of the monsoon. She did not know what she truly sought, only that she must seek it.

 RAIN LASHED THE SWAMP. THE waterways flooded, roiled with mud, carried burdens of uprooted trees and brush. Vines writhed in the water like serpents, and true serpents were belly up and tangled fatally among reeds. Some of the monstrous growth swirled out making temporary traps to catch flotsam, to the danger of any craft daring to attempt upstream travel. The pounding of wind deafened all sound except the roar of rain and water.

Yet there was travel against all odds. Even as much as those who knew the swamp feared their world gone wild, this one season they had dared it. An army had come out of the mires: clans had drawn to clans, peoples to peoples.

There had been such a battle as even the ancient songs had never pictured. Evil had struck with a power of fire and sorcery beyond knowledge, and had gone down to a defeat of charred ashes. Now those who dared the streams and rivers felt only an overpowering need to turn their backs upon that battlefield, to withdraw into their own places. Victory had been theirs, yet the shadow of what had happened was like the storm clouds above.

Their number shrank constantly during the journey. This force and that took to side ways, peeling away to seek out their home islets or the lake villages of the clans. The Nyssomu went early since their holdings lay the closest. Their distant cousins, the Uisgu, rode in shallow skiffs drawn by those who were both fighting comrades and aides—the water-dwelling rimoriks, even their great strength taxed by the fury of the waters. They disappeared more and more into half concealed tributaries which led to their fortresses, still unknown to those not of their kind save a few far venturers, none welcomed.

Though the fast diminishing army fought hard to leave the past behind them, there were gruesome reminders of what horror had held sway here. Trussed in one patch of mud burdened reeds were the remains of a human, one of the ill-fated invasion force.

The girl, swinging her paddle violently in one of the foremost skiffs, looked away hurriedly. Some Skritek had feasted there—satisfied the abominable hunger of his kind upon the flesh of his one-time ally.

Skriteks—many now must be on the run before the storm fury. They knew only too well what would happen to any of their kind who had survived the defeat of the invaders within reach of the victors.

The small party left had pushed on now into the Thorny Hell, a place of dread in which the innermost heart of fear seemed trapped in the tangle of thorn-sprouting growth. A sense of peril appeared to cling in leprous patches to the trunks of dead trees.

Those who ventured here because it was the straightest path to their destination did not attempt to see beyond the bristling curtain which walled the river on either hand.

The rain formed shrouds across the open water which shut out much of the view ahead. Bowed head and hunched shoulders could not help. Kadiya—who had once been a Princess housed in all the soft life known to her kind—endured, even as she endured the weight of the sheathed weapon which dug against her ribs when she swung to the paddle's need. The same stubbornness which had brought her an army held. Kadiya could not and would not turn aside with any of those who continued to urge her to shelter with them. Nor could she have remained at the Citadel, now cleansed of the evil which had struck down those of her house. Payment had been taken. However, she was not yet free...

Once more that weight resting upon her was greater than all that the storm could hurl at her, stronger than any floating trap she and her companions fought their way through.

Why did she feel this driving urge, this pressure which was sometimes close to frantic? She felt she was being moved by a will which was not her own. The first time she had fled there had been red death, fire, the end of all the life she had known. Now... now what drove her?

Drive it did—through the very maw of the storm. Islets on which they tried to camp were only sinks of mud and water-heavy brush. There was no real shelter. Sleep was only a temporary end to an exhaustion that left the body one great ache. Still each time she roused she was quick to settle once more into hazardous traveling.

At least the storm kept their drenched world free of some dangers. No voor cruised above, no scale-armored xanna arose from murky paths with sucker-encrusted limbs to threaten them. Those plants which had their own vicious weapons were curled in upon themselves to outwait the floods.

On the seventh day they came to the end of the river road. Now there was only their single craft left to nose the sticky mud of the bank. At least here the thorns did not repel.

Kadiya threw her pack ahead to a mound of earth which looked stable enough to hold it. Reaching out for a trailing vine, she used it to drag herself ashore. Then she turned to face those who had accompanied her without complaint and wearily raised one hand in salute.

Many things had changed in the days just past, but old Oaths were still honored. No matter how valorous they had been in a battle which had wrenched their world out of the hands of the Dark, no man or woman of the Oddlings would venture beyond this landing into a long-forbidden land—none except Jagun, the huntsman who had taught her the swamp ways and was now swinging ashore in her water-filling tracks. Oathed against this he had been, but that Oath was lifted by her own belief and act.

Yet those others watching her now, their great yellow-green eyes unblinking as if those very stares would hold her, were plainly loath to let her go.

"Light-bearer." One of the two women warriors raised her hand in entreaty. "Come with us. You have carried our hope." For a moment her eyes sought the heavy burden at Kadiya's belt. "There is peace—the peace which we have won. Let us shelter you. Seek not this place which is not to be seen..."

The girl pushed back a sodden string of hair dangling from under her xanna-bone helm. She found that she still had the power to summon a smile.

"Joscata, this has been laid upon me." Her hand went to the bulbous hilt of that talisman which was also a sword. "It would seem that I cannot rest until I have fulfilled yet another duty. Let me but do this and I promise I shall return with a full heart to you all—for such comradeship I wish more than all else in the world. The choice is not yet mine to make. I have something still to do."

The Nyssomu looked beyond the girl's shoulder to the drenched land. On her face there was a shadow which might have been set by fear.

"May all good go with you, Farseer. Firm be the land for your footing, clear the path to where you must trod."

"Swift be your boats, comrades," Kadiya replied as she hoisted her pack to her shoulders, "quick the way. If fortune wills I shall see you again."

Jafen, war speaker of the clan who had brought them here, still held the tie rope. "Lady of the Sword, remember the signal. There will be always a watcher. When you have done what you must do..."

Slowly Kadiya shook her head, then blinked her eyes against the stream of water the gesture dislodged from her helm. "War Captain, do not expect a quick return. In all truth I do not know what lies before me now. When I am free, then surely I shall seek out those whose spears were a wall against the Dark."

Memory struck for a moment. It was as though not a Nyssomu faced her but that awesome figure she had seen but once before, who had come to her when she had been a hunted fugitive with despair nipping at her heels. And because of the courage born from that meeting with the mysterious presence in the garden of the lost city, she now felt the flash of memory as a spur, urging her on.

The five left behind did not push off but held their craft steady as long as she and Jagun were in sight.

...————————————————————————...

.   .   .

Luckily the mud slime in which one could not find steady footing did not last. There were sometimes pools across their path that Jagun depth-tested with the butt of his spear. Their pace was necessarily slow and the way was long.

There was little shelter. Game was scarce and the provisions which made up the larger part of their packs were fast disappearing despite all their care. There came the time when they went without food for the night and were no better off in the morning. However, under that gray sky the rain had mercifully slackened, and Kadiya at last caught sight of the huddle of ruins ahead.

It was the Place of Learning—the stronghold of the Sindona, the Vanished Ones. She paused. Would the old magic touch her once she passed through that broken semblance of a gate? She began to splash toward it—then remembering, she glanced back.

"Jagun?"

His face was set as if he were battle ready, yet he was following. Looking to neither side, he marched as one does to a danger which must be faced. The age-old Oath put upon his people: even though she had loosened it for him when they journeyed this way before, did it burden him still?

He did not answer but he came on. There was a great burst of wind driven rain, as if the monsoon itself would bar their passage at this last moment. Then they stumbled forward, through the wreckage of the gate, falling to their knees from a last blow of the wind.

But . . . the beat of the storm was gone! They might have passed under a roof, though the sky was open over them. In the air hung a heavy moisture, more like a morning fog. While before them—

No ruins, no tumble of age-struck stone. Kadiya had seen the transformation work before, passing in the opposite direction. Ruins without to the eye; within, a city silent, deserted, yet unpitted by years. Streets stretched empty before them. The buildings bordering them, though half clothed with the green of vines, showed no crumbling. Just as the Citadel in which she had been born had survived time without decay, so had this place though all other sites the Vanished Ones had left behind were tumbled stone.

Jagun's pack thudded from his back to the pavement. He muttered something as might one who lived by natural laws and did not welcome a confrontation with what put those in abeyance.

"This is a place of..." He hesitated as if he could not find the proper words.

The clouds were darker. Night was overtaking the storm. Kadiya was on her feet. Twilight, or black night, she was now so close —

"This is a place of Power," she said, and her words seemed softened by the mist which was growing stronger. "And I have something to do."

She did not turn her head to see if he would follow, nor did she linger for any word of agreement. Instead she hurried onward. To either hand the intact buildings loomed. The curtains of vines which draped them took on a darker hue in the twilight. Windows like great lidless eyes watched her from behind those living screens. No flicker of lamp, flare of torch gave honest welcome. Still she felt no alarm, no fear that anything here lay in wait.

From street, to square, to street, she went to find that which she knew was the heart of this place. She rounded a mist-veiled pool to come to a stairway. There she stopped, both hands gripping the sword she wore but had not drawn. On either side, mounted on each rising step, were life-size (or perhaps larger than life-size) statues, facing each other so that none could pass between them unseen.

The artist who had carved them had given them a kind of shimmering life as if each were bespelled. Men and women in company, they were surely representations of the Vanished Ones. Each countenance differed from the others so that one could well believe they were portraits of the once-living.

Kadiya slipped off her pack, then drew the sword. This she held by the pointless blade. As if the gesture assured her right to entrance, the girl climbed the stairs.

Gaining the columned platform above, she paused. There was the second stairway which she sought, leading downward to a garden which was not of any world she knew. Here fruit and flower shared the same branch. Time vanished: There was no past, no future, only the moment in which she moved. The mist was nearly gone. Even the twilight lingered, as if night had no place here.

Sparks of light danced in the air. They were many-colored, as if jewels had taken wings. From flower to flower, swelling fruit to fruit, they wheeled and spun. She had never seen their like elsewhere in the swamplands.

With a sigh Kadiya dropped to the top step. At that moment all the weariness of her travel settled upon her. She raised her hand to push off the helm which suddenly had taken on an intolerable weight. It fell, to clang on the white stone, and she frowned at the noise.

Her hair was plastered to her mud splattered cheeks, or lay in lank strings upon her mail clad shoulders. It held the darkness of peat waters. Swamp smells were strong about her body. The fragrance of the garden seemed a reproach.

Across her knees rested the sword. The three eyes which formed the pommel were sealed, closed as tightly as if they had never been opened to loose raw powers. Kadiya slipped her hands along the blade. Once her touch had awakened tingling life, but that was gone now. This was certainly what was meant to be.

Though she caressed the sword, her eyes were on the garden. The one who had come to her here, who had sent her into battle with the Dark to learn for herself a little of what she was, or could be, would that one come again now?

No. Instead the twilight was slowly dimming at last. Nothing moved save the gemmed flyers. With a sigh, her shoulders slumped, Kadiya arose and went down step by lingering step into the garden.

The thick turf which covered all the open land between shrubs, beds of flowers, and twining vines was broken in only one place. Where that patch of earth was visible there seemed to be also a hovering luminosity.

Kadiya stumbled toward it. She stooped and, with both hands clasped tightly over the ovals which held the eyes, drove the squared-off blade tip of her talisman into the spot of bared earth. The blade entered, but not easily. There was strong resistance which drew heavily on her already taxed energy. But the sword stood erect when she moved back a step, a strange new growth in this place of comfort and peace.

Her hands went to her throat to clasp that other symbol of Power which she had worn from birth—the amulet of amber with a tiny embedded flowerlet within it. Kadiya waited.

She had returned this sword of Power to the place from which it had grown. It did not change as she had thought it would. The girl tensed, her shoulders straightened. She loosed hold of the amulet to sweep back the lank locks of hair and fully clear her sight. Nothing moved.

Kadiya cleared her throat. Though she spoke aloud, her words sounded deadened, far off.

"All is finished. We have completed that task which was set us. The evil is vanquished — Haramis is Archimage. Anigel reigns over both friend and those who were once foes. What would you have of me?"

The answer? Was the unchanging sword to be her only answer? Was she, in the place which knew no time, showing her old impatience? Resolutely she spoke again:

"I was told when I was here before, by that one who met me, that this is a place of learning. My . . . my need then seemed great, for I was going up against all the forces our enemies could range against us." She paused and sought for words anew. "Now also my need is great. What would you have of me? What lies in my future that I must give in return? Haramis has her learning and her desired power, Anigel her kingdom. If I have truly earned a future, what is it to be? I have had no answer, but I have been drawn here for some reason. Give me answers, you who shelter in this place, as once before you showed me the way!"

Still nothing moved save the glowing things. Night had darkened, but a pale light encircled the planted sword.

Kadiya half reached for it, then snatched back her hand. She must understand more first. Turning, she climbed the stairs to the top refusing to look back.

Weariness was now trifold, and with it she felt a sense of emptiness and loss. It was not that she had left her portion of Power behind, but more as if some other will had walled her out, stepped between her and knowledge.

Yet in her remained a core of that stubbornness which had

never accepted helplessness and would not now. There *was* a purpose behind all this, of that she was certain. And that she intended to discover. If not then, in days to come.

"Lady —"

At the foot of the stairway of the Guardians by the edge of the pool, stood Jagun, holding her pack with his. He held his spear point down as one did when approaching an Elder or Clan Captain. But perhaps that gesture was not meant for her but rather for what had once abided here.

Kadiya went down, her step firm. She held her helm in her hand, and there was still the dagger in her belt, even though she had left the sword behind. There was no danger here to threaten the body, of that she was sure. There was something else, though. What it was, she must learn for herself.

"Trail master." She gestured to the building beyond the pool. "Here is a choice of shelter and we are surely made free of it."

 EVEN THOUGH THE CHOSEN BUILD-
ing was the snuggest shelter they had
found since leaving the Citadel, there
was no way of making a fire and the damp
clung. Between the roof and the stairs
stretched the now black mirror of the
pool. The darkness within the empty doorway was daunting
enough so that Kadiya hesitated just within, trying to see even
a little of what might wait there. She decided that the sense
of awareness which she had slowly developed during her travels through the mires was too uncertain to be really trusted
now. She felt no subtle warnings, but that was no assurance
that there was nothing waiting here.

Jagun had been pawing through his pack. Though Kadiya
could claim farsight, dark was always less thick for the Oddling. He drew out a tube a little shorter than his forearm. With
this in hand he went out again into the open.

All Kadiya could sight there was a shadowy tossing of the brush growing along the edges of the pavement. Then there came a dagger point of wan light. Jagun had found, and was prying forth from its refuge under a leaf, a glow-grub. Another and another was stuffed methodically into the tube. When he returned he carried a rod which diffused a feeble but very welcome light.

A quick survey showed that they had found a room barren of everything but four walls, a solid pavement and a roof which was certainly storm proof.

With stiff fingers Kadiya pulled at the buckles of her shell armor. The odor of her wet hair, of her slime-stained body was an offense. Much as she had always sought the swamplands, this uncleanliness was something she had never accepted without faint disgust. Once free of the armor, her under jerkin pulled loose from its clammy grip on her body and she felt a fraction more at ease with herself.

The fastenings of her pack were also hard to force; the woven reeds had tightened. Kadiya broke a fingernail to the quick and spit out a fiery word.

By the limited glimmer of Jagun's improvised lamp she was able to separate a strip of woven reed-pith towel. There was the pool waiting without but she did not intend to visit that by night. Instead a soft patter beyond the door suggested a more beneficial rain was falling. Discarding the rest of her sodden and too well worn clothing, she deliberately ventured forth. A handful of leaves gave her something with which to scrub and she used that fast fraying vegetation well.

She had long ago sacrificed the lengths of her heavy hair for the wearing of the helm. Now, since it fell no farther than her shivering shoulders, she was able to wet it thoroughly, run her fingers through tangles, and do the best she could to bring it to partial order.

There was a chill in the rain and she ducked back into their shelter to use her scrap of towel vigorously. A clean under jerkin was a luxury which she savored as she laced it at the throat. For a moment she thought of what she had once known in the ladies' bower at the Citadel — all the comfort which was now Anigel's. Then Kadiya shook her head, as much at her thought as to swing her hair loose.

For the first time Jagun spoke. "You do not wear the sword." His large eyes reflected the glow, even seemed to have a faint radiance of their own from where he sat cross-legged, his hands within his pack.

Kadiya flicked out the towel, shook her still wet head.

"It — it was not received," she said. "I set it in the place from which it grew from the Archimage's stalk. There came no change. No change. . ." she repeated, and then added with more force, "How could that be, Hunt Master? Has the prophecy not been fulfilled in full? We women of the House of Krain brought forth the Great Weapon of the ancients. Voltrik and Orogastus are dead. Their army has sworn Oath to Antar, and, since he is Anigel's chosen lord, also to Ruwenda which they sought to rend and destroy. The Skritek have fled back to their own loathesome holes. I have seen my younger sister safely crowned and happily, as she deems, wed; my elder sister go to her place of learning, her choice of power wielding. Yet my geas still is not laid."

She had dropped to her knees so that her eyes were nearly on a level with those of the Oddling. Now she studied him as if she demanded answers.

"Tell me, Jagun, why is the reward for a task well done now denied me?"

"Farseer, who can understand the ones who built this place? They have been gone hundreds of hundreds." He gave a quick glance right and left and then back again. "They had powers beyond reckoning — their life was not ours."

"True. They have been long gone . . ."

Jagun was nodding. "The Great One Binah was the last of their blood, choosing to stand as Guardian here when they left. Now time has taken even her."

He pulled out the last of their dried root cakes and broke it carefully in half, holding one piece out to her. Though she was faint with hunger (realizing that the more when she saw the remnant of food) she did not immediately bite into its tooth-cracking hardness. Instead she turned the small block around in her hand.

"Jagun, tell me of the Vanished Ones. Oh, I know what our own records at the Citadel have to tell — did I not search those just before we came hither? — that this land was once a great lake, perhaps even an inlet of the sea, that it encircled islands that were the dwelling places of another people, neither Oddling, nor of my own race.

"Legend has it that they were mighty in powers we do not know and that for long they lived in peace. Then we are told of a great war in which weapons such as we cannot dream of were turned one against another — though perhaps when we witnessed what Orogastus called up against us we saw in part those dealers of death. These rent the very substance of the land and the waters were drained away, cities were left to fall to the perils of time. But where did they go, those Vanished Ones? Certainly they did not all die in the hellish ruin they wrought.

"Yet, who were they? Remember, Jagun, the first time we came to this place we followed the pointing arm of a statue hacked free from a coating of dried mud. You had a name for that statue: Lamaril. Tell me, Hunt Master, who was that Lamaril?"

Kadiya did not know why she chose that question out of all those which now seethed in her mind.

Perhaps she should ask concerning that veiled one who had spoken to her at her first coming. Had that been—the thought came sudden and sharp—another Vanished One like Binah who had chosen to remain?

Drawing upon her memory, now Kadiya thought there had been something illusionary about the encounter. It had had none of the reality of her meeting with the Archimage. Her perplexity now brought another query from her.

"Sword Bearer," her companion's tone was formal as if he now addressed a Speaker, the ruler of a house clan, "none of my people have dared to enter this place. We are Oath-bound against it."

"Not you any longer, Jagun. The talisman freed you." The girl remembered those words which had come from someplace outside her understanding to heal his despair when he believed himself forsworn. Again she repeated them:

"Bear no soul burden."

For a moment he was silent and his eyes were not on her but rather sought the grub lamp, as if he were reading there some message in the manner a wise woman would scry from a filled bowl.

"You ask of Lamaril. Yes, my people have legends also— but time broken, hard to understand now. He was a warrior— a shield Guardian against the Dark. It is said that he stood alone at the end against one of the mightiest of the evil ones, that he won a battle for the Light, but then died. Also he was one who favored my people, so at his going we did him all the honor that we might.

"Farseer—the Vanished Ones made us, Nyssomu and Uisgu both. We had been as those that still come and go in the mires, mindless, without memory of yesterday or thought of tomorrow. With the aid of the Vanished Ones we became true people. Their knowledge of life force, life flow, was very great, enabling them to do that which can hardly be believed in these days. Because we were formed by their powers from lesser creatures we have striven to keep alive what we remember of them. But the sources of their power were always closed to us, for we were as children not to be trusted with a sharp-edged dagger. When the Dark threatened, those who had summoned us out of the mires spoke. They set the Oath upon us that we would not seek what they wished hidden and ordered us into hiding lest we be hunted down by the evil."

"But who were they?" Kadiya asked that of herself rather than Jagun now. "I have looked upon those statues which stand guard across the way. I saw the likeness of Lamaril on the trail. In some ways they might be of my own kind, yet in others they differ."

"No word passed among us from Speaker to Speaker has told of what they were before our people arose from the waterways at their command. I do not think them kin of yours, Farseer. As to whether they all died in the war with the Dark ... no. Some are said to have survived and withdrawn to another place, perhaps the one from which they once came."

"This Dark—oh, I know that such a name is given by my people to great evil such as Orogastus loosed upon us—from where did *that* arise?"

"Farseer, there is darkness in the heart of your kind, in Oddlings, perhaps in all living things if we knew how to measure or discover it. The Vanished Ones were not all masters of the Light. They may well have had their Voltrik, their Orogastus. At least the war legend hints so — although the name by which that evil was known has not come to us.

"Even as the Nyssomu and the Uisgu were lifted up by the Light to be thinking creatures of life and hope, so it is said that the Skritek were formed to do the work of evil, and were left masterless at the end to be ever a plague for our land."

"Yet there was that one who spoke to me — though I did not see the Speaker clearly." Kadiya dared now the most compelling question. "I have heard that there is an essence in all beings which is loosed by the death of the body. Was it such an essence that I met here? Or can it be that Binah was not the only Guardian who remained? Jagun, I must know!"

She thought regretfully of wasted time. Haramis had always sought out the old books and records of the Citadel, but from early childhood Kadiya had been impatient of such things. The need for action was strong in her; even now it made her shift uneasily as she bit into her ration. She thought of the garden beyond. There was food in plenty there, fruit far better than this which was like ashes on her tongue.

The Oddling had not answered. In herself she knew what must be done — in the morning she must go searching for more than food. Many things had been discovered in the time-devoured ruins already explored by Nyssomu and Uisgu. What might have lingered undisturbed here in a place where exploration had been forbidden?

Choking down the last crumb, the girl reached for the grub rod.

"Give me the use of this for a space, Hunter. I wish to know what manner of lodging we have chosen this night."

He nodded but made no move to join her as she crossed to carry the light to the nearest wall. Yes, she had not been mis-

taken; in spite of the gloom, she had sighted something here.
Now she held the tube closely to the stone, moving it slowly.

There were paintings on those walls — mostly of flowers, but
here and there of some fanciful creature — so time-dimmed as
to be hardly visible. It was oddly conceived: she might be
looking out from a window into the garden. Flowers and fruit
on the same branch, and, in the air above them, flying things
of slightly more brilliant hues which appeared to leap out of
the stone when even the very soft grub light touched them.

As she moved along Kadiya saw intricate detailing which
invited further study. But nowhere was there any represen-
tation of a living creature save those flyers. The artist or artists
who had worked here left no portraits of themselves or of
those who might have commissioned such scenes.

Kadiya reached the corner and turned to view the second
wall. Halfway along that was an opening and here the floral
patterns gave way to curves, broken lines — writing? She
thought there was a suggestion of such, but she had no key to
unlock it. Some of those lines she traced with a finger, as if
by touch she could solve their mysteries.

Then another dark doorway was before her. She swung the
tube into the gap. The glimmer was too faint to show what
lay beyond. Perhaps in another place she would have disliked
the fact that the opening held no barrier which could be closed.
Here she had not the slightest feeling of uneasiness, though
she did not go through.

There was another section of writing and then a second
corner faced her. This wall was the one in which the entrance
to the outer world was set. Again there were pictures, but not
of a garden in rich growth. Rather she was looking upon water. It did not have the dark dullness of a swamp lakelet, nor
the yellow traces of a river, nor was it the mirror pool. No,

this was painted a glistening silver-blue, and far out from a bit of shore indicated at the bottom of the wall was a shadow of what might be an island.

No boat troubled the surface of that clear water, though the curl of waves was indicated and Kadiya was sure it was no mere pool. Could this be a scene of that famed lake-sea which had once been?

The fourth wall was in contrast to the other three. What the glimmer picked out there brought an exclamation from her. Seeming ready to step down from that surface into the room was a row of strange creatures.

"Jagun!" Kadiya summoned the hunter who had been unrolling their sleep mats, playing no part in her explorations. "Jagun, what are these?"

He padded across the floor to join her and Kadiya moved the light tube as close to the painting as she could.

"These . . . I have never seen such before."

"I do not know, Farseer."

Was she overreacting or had she heard a trace of sullenness, even evasion in that?

"There may have been many things here in the old days which are unknown in the here and now." He wheeled and went back to his preparations for the night.

The pictured figures stood on their hind legs in a human-like position, and they had upper appendages which resembled arms, save that the "hands" were collections of formidable claws. Their bodies followed the general outline of a warrior's shield, wide at the top—shoulder level—tapering down to a much narrower space between their legs. The heads were set upon those wide shoulders as if they lacked necks. The shield-shaped bodies were serrated across the forepart into plates, each of which appeared to be, in turn, formed of small scales.

The skillfully used color of the wall painting gave a gloss still to some parts of those bodies, an iridescent sheen such as Kadiya had seen on the wing cases of insects. They were a greenish blue even to their heads which were shaped very much like a drop of water about to fall from the lip of a jug—the wider part dividing two very large ears set well apart on either side of the upper skull, the narrower portion forming a snout. The eyes were small but the artist had somehow set into them a gleam of red which now caught the grub light and gave startling life to the whole countenance.

Strange indeed, yet there was nothing alarming about them. Their claw hands were spread wide open before them as if they reached for an offering gladly given, or else ready to greet a friend. There was something wistfully appealing about them.

Tentatively Kadiya touched the forehead of one of the group, more than half expecting she might feel a texture other than stone. But that came from the skill of the artist; they were but paintings.

"Farseer!" Jagun's summons was peremptory. "It is time to rest—not to go gazing at walls."

Again the girl felt that it was that wall and what had been painted there which made him uneasy. Because of that half-suspicion she longed to know more. However, he was right: fatigue made her body heavy. She rubbed her hand across her forehead—that dull ache she always felt when she had driven herself too long nagged at her. Kadiya went back to the place close to the door where Jagun had chosen to set up camp.

This time there was no drone or rattle of rain, no seepage of storm to turn discomfort into real misery. Kadiya placed the tube between their two sleeping mats. This was the end of the trail—at least the trail she had seen in her mind until this night. The pressure which had urged her away from the Citadel was gone. Still, as sleep overtook her, the last thing in her mind was the memory of the sword she had left defiantly wedged in ground reluctant to receive it.

Kadiya awoke suddenly as she had often done during the past days while they threaded a swamp concealing enemies. She was aware of some change; her trail-heightened senses had alerted her from sleep.

Through slitted eyes she viewed her surroundings. The glow rod had nearly finished its light—the grubs were going into hibernation having been so long removed from nourishment. But she could still see Jagun, and the hunter had not moved.

Now Kadiya called upon hearing. There was a silence in this place which was deadening, divorced from all the night sounds of the outer world. She could pick up the quiet hiss of her companion's breathing—nothing else. But the girl was sure there had been something to waken her.

Their earlier talk of an essence which might linger behind the dwellers who had once been —?

There was certainly no hint of Skritek stench, though she was well aware those killers could move with noiseless stealth when they wished. No. Her body still inert now Kadiya strove to adjust to another form of seeking.

Yes!

She sat up abruptly, thrusting aside the edge of the sleeping mat. It was there! Like a horn call to action! Yet she did not reach for the armor she had discarded—though she did buckle on the belt with the empty sword sheath, the dagger still pendant.

Emerging with caution from the building, she looked across the pool to those pale gleams which marked the statue Guardians of the stairs. Slowly Kadiya moved toward them, a struggle between hard-learned caution and eagerness in her. The inborn desire for action won.

Up those stairs she went, halting on each to view, right and left, the motionless sentinels. Somehow their features were clearly visible in spite of the gloom — as if there was life buried within.

Kadiya stood at last among the columns looking back across the pool and the city of vine-smothered buildings beyond. Light!

From old conditioning her hand swept instantly to dagger hilt. Certainly there — to her right — she had seen a flicker of light!

The radiance of that half-misted figure she had met here? Impossible — yet...

THERE WOULD BE NO PARTY OF Nyssomu or Uisgu here. The Oddlings might explore other ruins for the "treasure" which could be traded in their market at Trevista—but not the remains of a city Oath-forbidden. Nor in the aftermath of a war which had pulled all the swamplands into action would there be at this early date hunting parties such as were sometimes employed by the more venturesome of her own people.

The war! Those of Labornok who had drenched the land with blood had even dared to invade the swamps. Their General Hamil had won almost to this city. Could there have been stragglers from that force, driven and harassed by Oddlings, threatened by the very nature of the country they did not understand, cut off here?

Or someone—some*thing*—else? Kadiya still clung to the memory of that veiled presence.

The night was going now — she could see more as she studied the city spread out from this viewpoint. If there were others here then it was best that she learn what she could of them, and as quickly as possible.

Kadiya sped down the steps, located a cross street leading in the right direction. As she entered that side way the caution she had learned through the past months curbed her first rush. Slacking pace she looked for cover ahead.

Here the buildings were set flush with the street and even the growth of vine curtain, so profuse elsewhere, was strictly limited. She did not follow a straight path. Instead she wove from street to alleyway, down that narrow strip, to street again, always hoping she was heading in the right direction.

The heavy mist which took the place of storm-driven rain within these walls thickened and curled, slowing her even more. Every few strides Kadiya paused with her back to the nearest wall and studied the way before her, paying close attention to any rags of fog which might conceal movement.

Luckily her sodden swamp boots made no sound on the pavement and she continued to use hunters' caution, all she had learned from Jagun, a master of such craft.

Another way here, even more narrow. It was so walled by buildings that its length was twilight dark. Neither wall along it showed any break of window or door. But about two thirds of the way along a loop of vine twisted down two stories. It had almost the look of a noose trap, save it was in no way concealed. The girl approached it one step at a time, listening — and also striving to enlist that other sense of which she was not entirely sure.

During the time she had worn the sword talisman she had always been aware of a warning. However, that weapon was no longer at her command. The Oddlings possessed senses of their own as danger alerts. Those worked well in the swamp mires. But within a city? These walls and buildings were alien—even to she who had been born and bred in the Citadel, also a remainder of the far past.

On impulse Kadiya closed her eyes, strove to quest outward with thought. She had done so once with some success as a guard against the presence of the Dark. Could it serve in another way?

Answer came as light as a brush of soft feathers against her skin, save that passage was from within, not without her body. Kadiya's breath hissed—she had hardly expected an answer—but there was no time to muse on what had happened, to question or examine. Instead she strove to hold to the feeling as if she might fasten, by some turn of a wrist, a hook within the jaw of a fish. Not that she wished to draw that feeling near her. No, rather to guide herself toward its source.

Pushing away from the wall Kadiya opened her eyes—only to learn that her intent hold on that elusive guide had brought her shaving-close to disaster. For the vine noose uncoiled in a blur of speed to whip through the air. The girl threw herself backward, stumbled, and went down bruisingly hard on one knee.

A vicious jerk brought a cry as the end of that lash tangled and then swiftly vised a grip on her wild mop of hair. The pain was intense as the vine dragged her forward. Kadiya felt as if her scalp might be torn from her skull.

She had her dagger out, and—though she could not see much of that which hung from above holding her prisoner and in spite of the agony her efforts caused—she twisted and turned, to stab and cut above her head. At times her blade met resistance.

Tears of sheer pain wet her cheeks as the thing continued

to pull her upward. Now her feet barely touched the pavement as her captor strove to swing her aloft. Before her dropped a second rope-like strand. Kadiya sliced at it. Her weapon sank in; the vine, half cut through, recoiled against the stone wall.

Perhaps this had some effect on the line which kept her prisoner. The upward pull seemed to pause as she sawed furiously at her hair. The keenness of that blade was her salvation, for it sliced through those tautly stretched locks and she landed facedown on the pavement.

Without trying to regain her feet Kadiya wriggled forward, the flesh of her palms grating painfully on the harsh surface.

There was a swishing sound from above. She made a last plunge which she hoped would take her out of reach of the thing, skidding across the way until her shoulder struck against the opposite wall.

A sensation of vicious rage struck like a spear into her mind. But in its way that attack aided her, for it was the anger of a hunter baffled by prey.

Kadiya pulled herself up against the wall, facing the direction of the menace. The long rope thing lashed the air at her, coming once or twice close enough to fan air against her cheek. Frantically she edged away.

The aura of hot rage was a new kind of pain. She shook her head from side to side, limp and panting. She was at least beyond the reach of the thing.

Now she knew an anger in return. She felt betrayed by that feeling of peace which had seemed to enfold her since she had entered the city. Was that part of a trap? Moments ago she had believed that there was no threat from these empty buildings and walls about. Now —

Breathing hard, she closed her left hand tightly about her

amulet as her right held ready the dagger. Then she called upon what small power she had learned she possessed.

The Dark had its own betraying emanation — just as the Skritek gave forth their foul body odor. She had met the Dark and she would not forget that scent which only an inner sense could know. Yet here and now she could pick up nothing of such a foulness. There was a smell, yes. That she could identify as issuing from a thick ooze dribbling from the cut vine. Sap — or blood?

In the swamp there were plants which were a danger to all living things. They were not born of evil magic, but their very nature offered peril. Here in the city there was lush growth wherever the ground had been left uncovered to root it. Those vines she had seen elsewhere had wreathed and covered many of the deserted buildings.

This thing, its one portion still twisting snake-wise, could well be of a similar species, rooted on the far side of the wall. However, if it were a hunter — such as those swamp things she had seen — how did it continue to live here where there appeared to be no other life?

Kadiya wiped the stickiness from the blade of her dagger by drawing it across her travel-ragged breeches. With her other hand she gingerly explored the aching crown of her head. Several wisps of hair came loose, their roots bloody.

The flesh on her knees was raw. She was still shaking from her ordeal. Prudence argued that she return to their camp, to seek treatment for her wounds and any knowledge Jagun might supply.

As she stood there she had kept loose that mind sense. The rage of the attacker still threatened — she could also pick up an undercurrent of pain as if the wound of the injured member fed that hate. However, that feather touch, that which now she identified as a summons, still called.

There were too many unanswered questions. If she could gain only a few answers, then she must. With the grim intent which had ridden her on her quest for the sword talisman awakened once more in her, Kadiya made her choice to go on.

The gray light of the day was strong enough now for her to see well ahead. She stepped from the mouth of that alley into another wide open space.

Though the buildings here were not tall, they were imposing. Their forewalls were not smooth but thickly patterned with deeply incised designs, especially about the doors and windows. There were patches of vegetation from which came the heady perfume of flowers. As Kadiya emerged into the open there came a scurrying and the swift flight of some creature not much larger than her hand. So there *was* life here.

She kept well away from all the greenery as she made her way into the middle of the square where there was the basin of a fountain. To her surprise water still played there, arising in feathery plumes from two separate points to meet in the center before beginning a combined descent.

Kadiya stumbled onto the wide rim about the basin and fell rather than sat on a bench which encircled it. She rested the dagger close enough to be snatched in an instant, then leaned forward to plunge both hands into the water.

To her vast surprise the liquid was not chill but warm, as if it had lain under a summer sun. She puddled it in the palms of her hands and raised it to her face. It had a faint spicy scent.

Daring to use it she washed her arms and her abraded knees, then gingerly bent her head forward so she could pour handfuls over her bloody head and hair. The water was very clear; she could see the bottom of the basin clearly.

Flecks of light glinted there even though there was no sun

to seek them out. She leaned over and scooped one up. Out
of the water came a chain of finely wrought metal. She recognized it as one of the strange treasures of the past which
had ever puzzled her father's smiths at the Citadel. It had
neither the yellow-red of gold, nor the cool sheen of silver, but
seemed rather to be fashioned of thread drawn from a blue-
green gem substance and woven into a cord.

As Kadiya held this high, water dripped from scores of pale
silver stones set along the chain, and those too gave off flashes
of light. She stared at her find entranced. For all of her life
she had heard stories of treasures to be found in the ruins,
and she had seen artifacts (mainly broken), which lucky traders had brought from the fair at Trevista. Those had always
been pieces and bits with only hints of what form they might
once have held. This was entire, perfect.

When the girl straightened it out she saw it was formed like
a bib, made to extend from the throat down collar-wise across
the breast. Her mother had had jewels, some so fine they were
brought forth in reverence only for state occasions, but this
overshadowed all such.

There were other glints in the water. Kadiya held the necklace and looked farther along the basin. Here was wealth beyond any reckoning she knew. Beauty, riches exceeding all the
stores of the Citadel, beyond even the imagining of her people,
if all those sparks equalled even in part what she held. Kadiya
turned the necklace around and around, bemused by it. The
drops seemed frozen water holding all the range of rainbow
light.

Deep inside her a question formed. Why did this treasure
lie here — so discarded?

The leaping spray of the fountain was warm against her
skin, yet Kadiya no longer felt refreshed. Her uneasiness

dampened her wonder at the find. Suddenly she loosed her hold on the necklet, allowing it to fall back into the depths from which she had drawn it. She did not try to fish it forth again, nor reach for any of the other pieces she could see.

The ways of the Vanished Ones were not those of her people, even though those statues had forms like her own. Two seasons ago it had been her turn, much as she had been impatient with ceremonial customs, to attend the first sowing of the polders. It was a duty each woman of the Royal blood took in turn.

There she had made the required sacrifices to fortune, fertility, and the fields to ensure good harvests. She had been escorted to a pool of water not as clear as that which leaped and dashed here, but at least not too stained with the matter of the swamps, and there she had ritually taken from her arm a cherished band of twisted gold—for the offering must be something of value to the giver—to toss it into the pool before the Spring Maidens of her escort had thrown thither their flower garlands. So she had paid dues to some power, though no one explained what that power might be, nor why it must be appeased by treasures.

Kadiya stared at the basin. Was this just such a place of propitiation as that polder pool? Did what lay within it now represent petitions for good fortune? She arose slowly. Be that so or not, she would take nothing.

With the coming of full morning the haze had gone. Still, the insistent feeling which had brought her this far had not lessened. She wheeled about to face the buildings which surrounded the fountain. These were far more ornamented than any she had seen elsewhere.

To explore them all...

That thought did not have time to daunt her. Even above

the splash of the fountain she heard what sounded clearly — a chime as sweet as if from crystal bells. Drawn by that she rounded the basin to approach a building where a columned overhang made a shadow.

As Kadiya approached she could see a doorway. It was open without sign of barrier. This, too, was flanked by a statue on either side. However, these silent Guardians were not wearing forms like her own. Rather the twin sentries were copies of the creatures in the wall painting — those oddities Jagun had not identified.

Unlike the statues by the entrance to the garden these had none of that odd sense of buried life. Grotesque as they were, Kadiya was sure they had not been erected to inspire any dread. She stood surveying them, one and then the other, when she became aware of something else.

From the darker interior beyond the doorless portal there drifted a scent. In the Citadel on great feast days they had lit tall lanterns which burned a spicy oil. Here was a hint of that same odor. Had such a lantern been the source of the light which had set her exploring? If so, that beacon would require more than one lamp, set higher in the building, or she would not have sighted it. No Oddling ever used such.

Kadiya ventured forward, very glad that her boots made no sound. Her hand was at her dagger hilt. Involuntarily she drew the weapon as her second stride carried her into complete darkness. Her head swam with vertigo and queasiness; she feared entrapment in this place of utter darkness.

The dizziness got worse — she fought it with movement. Kadiya threw herself forward, bursting from the curtain of blindness into a gray light where she had the power to see again.

Before her opened a great hall. What awaited her held her motionless for several gasping breaths. This was a place of formal elegance, far richer than the audience chamber of the Citadel. She looked for a dais, for a throne.

There was movement as if shadows came and went, though what or who threw them remained invisible. But shadows . . . colored! She blinked and blinked again. When she tried to focus on one of those very tenuous forms, to see it clearly, the wisp fled or flickered out. Still from the corners of her eyes she could catch glimpses of what might have been a company in festival garb gathered in stately and formal patterns.

Again the chimes sounded. This time the tinkle of notes echoed from the tall walls of the room. Somehow Kadiya was emboldened by that sound. As the echoes died she dared to speak:

"Great Ones—" She had resheathed her dagger. One did not stand before overlords with bared steel in hand, whether those she could half see be only shadows or not. "Great Ones, if I have judged aright, there has gone forth a summons. I have come."

DID THOSE SHADOWS SHIFT, SEEM to gather in two long lines, opening a path before her? There came another and louder singing of the crystal notes. Down that only partly seen space which had been left open, two small, strange figures which had the firmness of real bodies moved.

They were only half as tall as she. The first was partially shrouded in a wide shawl or scarf draped about broad shoulders, one piece muffling its head, the other end trailing on the floor. Hand-like appendages protruded from this covering to clasp a rod with a wide loop at its top. Hung in that were crystal bell-like drops which sounded at each step the bearer took.

The companion of the bell ringer was the same size but obviously wearing a garment intended for a very much larger being. Sleeves had been rolled back, and a high standing collar served now as a cowl, hiding its features as completely as the scarf veiled those of its fellow.

In its two claw hands it bore a lamp with a flame which shot from a spout at the fore. From that wafted the fragrance she had scented, as if it were fed by oil distilled directly from flowers. The oversized garment trailed behind it to form a heavy train.

Both the scarf and the robe were alive with color, covered by glints which echoed the rainbows of the crystals. Neither appeared to regard the shadows. Yet as they passed along that aisle, some of those seemed for an instant to take on great substance — though never long enough for Kadiya to be sure of what she saw. There was a solemnity in the approach of the two. They might have been children dressed in their elders' robes of ceremony, attempting to mimic rites they had once witnessed — with the same serious attention the original priests or priestesses would have shown. There was nothing alarming about them for all their oddity of appearance. Kadiya slowly relaxed as she watched them in wonder.

Plainly they were intent upon her as the goal of that formal advance. She wondered fleetingly how they could see through the muffling about their heads. To address such as these as "Great Ones" . . . no, that did not seem right.

The girl gave a greeting as she would have to an Oddling Speaker, setting both palms together and inclining her head.

"May the day be fair, the harvest and the hunt good, the waterways clear to your going." She spoke in the Oddling trade tongue, hoping that perhaps she would be understood.

The creature vigorously rang the bells three times more, then held the rod steady to still the chime. There followed a chittering which was certainly no Oddling speech, rather sounds she had never heard before.

Kadiya was at a loss. She must find some way to communicate with this pair, but how?

Jagun had instructed her in hand signs which were used in the swamps when there was a need for silence — as when an Oddling force lay ambush for the Skritek. The girl flexed her fingers, then moved them in the simplest of those gestures — one meaning a truce.

The ringer of the crystals responded with a vigorous shake of his instrument. Did that short, loud chime mean acceptance? The creature half turned, making a beckoning gesture.

Somehow Kadiya had no feeling of fear or uneasiness, only a growing curiosity. The lamp bearer had also turned about with a swish of robe, freeing one set of claws to jerk those folds from entanglement. Kadiya followed them down the long hall, taking care not to tread on the trails of the ill-fitting garments.

That of the lamp bearer, she noted as she drew closer, was so badly worn that only bands and swirls of what might be metallic thread held it together. Once it must have been a thing of splendor, truly a royal robe of state perhaps even from the days of the Vanished Ones, now put to some ceremonial use by these others.

As she advanced, those eye straining shadows began to fade, and by the time their small procession had reached the end of the huge chamber there were left only fleeting wisps like tatters of fog. There was no light save the lamp, and the walls vanished in dim obscurity. Kadiya slowed pace a little as her inborn distrust of the unknown which lay in all swamplands stirred.

In the wake of her guides, she passed through an archway in a wall into even deeper gloom. The chimes rang out and she caught other sounds: a scraping, a skittering, even the thud of what might be shod feet, a fluttering. . .

Out of the dark, the light of the lamp picked out a head — then another. Kadiya was startled. The long snout, the large ears, were covered by what did not seem skin but rather an overlay of iridescent scales. No statues, no paintings, these were the living models of the creatures which had been depicted on the wall.

Their skin might be scaled, even armor plated in places, but it had no resemblance to that of a Skritek. Nor was there any stench, though sound and some of the limited radiance of the lamp betrayed the fact that a number of them crowded about her. Their beads of eyes were fixed on her and Kadiya felt that they were viewing her with astonishment equal to her own.

The greeter who bore the lamp now set its burden down on a table. Straightaway, as if that had been a signal, there flared other points of light. Within moments a number of other lamps clustered near the first or bobbed about that board, bringing fuller sight to Kadiya.

The table itself was low as if meant to serve creatures of the size which milled about it now. Some of the plated bodies were nearly bare save for necklets or belts, gem-set to catch the light; others wore scraps of ancient clothing.

Into the full light of the table lamps stepped one for whom the others made quick room. Its body was not muffled by any worn-out robe, though it did wear loose about its wide shoulders a length of cloth. On it were fastened, in no regular pattern, brooches, spread out necklets, and other bits of jewelry as precious in appearance as the necklet of the fountain.

This newcomer beckoned Kadiya closer, and two others hurried out of the shadows dragging a bench which they placed before her side of the table in overt invitation.

The others were busy also. Platters appeared out of the further gloom, mostly piled with such fruit as she had seen in the garden. The dishes themselves were of crystal, some engraved in patterns, or fashioned in fanciful shapes — such as birds with outstretched wings, their backs hollowed to hold the fruit, or the shells of some of the swamp creatures, even curves of many petaled flowers. None she could see were chipped or cracked. Here was treasure any trader would give close to his life to garner.

In addition there were two goblets of the precious green-blue metal. One was set down before her, the other to the hand of the creature wearing the much-bejeweled scarf.

Another came forward to pour from a tall ewer. The liquid did not have the ruby tint of feast wine, but looked rather like pure water.

The creature who apparently had been appointed to share this meal with her — perhaps a feast of ceremony — raised the goblet and made a small gesture in her direction, not unlike proposing a toast. Kadiya, having seated herself opposite after a pause in which she defeated caution, followed that example, fitting her action to the other.

From the muzzle of her host a black tube-like tongue shot into the contents of the goblet, sucking instead of drinking. Kadiya took a mouthful. Water, yes, and yet there was the faint suggestion of a fruit flavor in it.

Having drunk, her host or hostess pushed toward the girl one of the flower-shaped plates on which, embowered in its own leaves, was a ripe ogarn, a delicacy seldom seen at the Citadel. Kadiya picked it up with a nod of thanks and bit into its plump side, savoring the juice and pulp, noting that the other diner bored into its fruit with the tip of that elongated tongue.

So encouraged Kadiya ate her fill of fruit and then part of a dish which seemed to be a soft mush, scooping this out with fingers as best she could, since there were no signs of spoons or other eating utensils about.

There was a constant clicking around her which she took to be speech. Certainly this language was beyond her understanding. Questions seethed in her mind, frustrating to her hard learned patience.

Then, light-swift in stroke, words formed in her mind.

"We have watched and waited long, Noble One. Now is the day of great joy as it was dream-promised—you have returned to us!"

The creature which had shared her meal met her eye to eye. Kadiya did not doubt that the mind message came from it. Mind-sending was rumored to be part of the old magic, spoken of only in the legends. She had achieved a small portion of such Power when scrying with her sisters. But this was like true speech though totally silent.

Kadiya did not know how to answer. Did one think out what message one must convey—form word pictures in one's mind? And the message itself . . . She had not known these beings existed. Who and what were they? Whom did they take her for?

"I am Kadiya," she spoke slowly, as one feeling a passage in the dark, trying to shape the words in her mind, "daughter to King Krain who was from the Citadel. I was one upon whom was set a geas, that of finding the Great Talisman of the Black Trillium in part—so that the whole might be used against the forces of evil. In this place I found that talisman and we used it well."

Kadiya centered effort on building a mind picture of the orb pommeled sword now standing in the garden from which she had first taken it. Then she changed that picture to the one of the trillium stalk from which it had grown.

"Now I have come to return that thing of Power to the Will which granted it."

There was an increased stirring among those surrounding the table. She sensed astonishment tinged with excitement. But also she somehow knew this was not what they expected from her.

"You are . . ." The mind picture which was transmitted to her resembled the mist-veiled being who had dispatched her to battle, something also akin to the statues on the garden stair. A Vanished One! Did these strange small beings equate her with those ancient and awesome holders of the High Power?

Kadiya shook her head. It was important that she did not claim anything of that, allow them to believe that she was more than she truly was.

"Those Great Ones were of the long ago." It was almost too difficult to translate the concept into a mind picture. She was not sure that she could. But surely these creatures must know it had been generations, hundreds of hundreds, since the city had been alive with those who had built it. They must see that there were differences between one bedraggled girl in swamp worn clothing and those statue people.

There was a long moment of silence. Even the movements and sounds made by the crowd were stilled as she continued to hold eye contact with the leader.

"Were you not awaited, you would not have come." The answer seemed ambiguous. Kadiya could only guess at the meaning. Were there wards upon the city which would have barred any chance visitor, as the Oath barred the Oddlings? Would they have shut her out had this meeting not been intended?

Intended? Was this the beginning of the answers she had sought since that moment when the planted sword had remained unchanged? Had that strong pull which had brought her across the swamp, even through the monsoon, been meant to bring her to this meeting?

"We have waited long," the words continued in her mind. "Dream search has been made many, many times. We have striven hard to seek those who must return—"

"But I am no kin of theirs!" she countered swiftly.

"Were you not accepted you would not walk these ways." That was a flat statement and Kadiya sensed that no argument of hers would change it. But what did these creatures want from her? She had chosen the swamp as her own domain, but had another Power had a hand in that?

"I am Kadiya," she said again. "I am no kin, share no blood with those who ruled here. Though it was by the favor of one"—she thought of the Archimage Binah—"that I first found this place. I am of another people who entered this land long after the Vanished Ones had gone. The Oddlings I know; they have been my battle comrades. The Skritek I know, and they are the enemy. Tell me, Speaker, who are you? For what people do you speak?" She gave him the premier title known to the swamp folk, not knowing how else to address one who must be a leader.

Again there was a silent pause, broken this time by a stir of those in the company, though there was no change in the position of the one fronting her.

Then came an answer in part:

"This one is Gosel of the Hassitti, those who were to wait."

Kadiya acknowledged this with a courteous nod.

"Those who were to wait," Gosel repeated, "for so was the bond laid upon us when the Shining Ones departed for their own place. Dreams have been sent us, many dreams through the seasons, and in them each we saw again what had been and received that promise of what would be: that we should not be alone, even though we could not follow their road which was not meant for our kind. We have waited for the coming of the promised one — but it has been long and lone . . ."

If thought could vanish in a sigh, then this did. Kadiya felt a little of a vast need long unfulfilled.

"I am not one of those who left you." She must drive that truth home. She must destroy at once any hope these might have that she was one of the city people come again.

"You are one brought to us," Gosel returned stubbornly. "Surely you came by the will of the Great Ones or you would not be here. Therefore the Hassitti are to be again dwellers of the courtyards, heart-friends, even as was."

"Friends, I will gladly claim you," Kadiya answered. She held out her hand across the table as if in guest-welcome.

So their hands met palm to palm. Instantly Kadiya was aware of a flood of warmth, of welcome and good feeling such as she had seldom known. There was something about these Hassitti which was disarming, which drew her even as she had always been drawn to the Oddlings and the swamplands, yet this was even more intense.

"We have kept all which we could, safe held for your coming," Gosel said with the eagerness of a child who wished to please an elder. "Come with us, Noble One, to see how the Hassitti have striven to follow all the needs of duty."

So she was escorted from that room of feasting by Gosel, the one who carried the crystal bells, and now a host of lamp bearers. In company they went from chamber to chamber.

There were the remains of rich furnishings, skeletons of chairs and tables, fashioned in a greater size than those she had always known, even as Gosel's table had been lower. The walls were painted. Some showed scenes she longed to study closer, but her guides impatiently pressed her on. One chamber was fitted with many shelves and on those were stacked boxes of metal, some touched by rust.

At Gosel's direction several of these were opened and their contents displayed. It was a strange mixture of objects. There were more of such gems as lay in the fountain basin or used to adorn the rags the Hassitti wore. Also there were rods with bulbous encrustations on their sides, and rolls of what she thought might be the cured skin such as was used for the inscribing of formal documents among her own people. Again she was given no time for touching or lengthy examination.

Several rooms were so crammed with things that one could only look in from the doorway. The lamplight did not stretch far enough to let her see what objects this clutter might conceal — save that many pieces were big and bulky.

Kadiya began to believe that either those who had once dwelt here, or perhaps the Hassitti in a desire to preserve all that was left, had emptied other buildings to transport their contents here. It would take her days to make sense of it all, if that could ever be done. Still curiosity bred excitement and she felt that stir of blood which made feverish the hunter of treasure. Here was such a find as the Ruwendians had never known existed.

They came at last through the maze of rooms and hallways into a courtyard. Here was another fountain in play and the fresh air of the outer world.

For the first time she could view clearly all those who had accompanied her. Most of them wore some kind of drapery, scarves heavy with bits of jewelry, or a few long tattered robes. Their own scaled skins gave off an irradiance similar to some of the jewels they wore, glinting green, blue, red, orange in the daylight. They were all of a size, standing just to the height of her shoulder. There were no smaller ones suggesting offspring among them.

Now those who had carried lamps blew them out. They broke apart from the tight escort group, some pressing forward to bend heads and protrude their long tongues to suck up the fountain water.

Though there was no sun overhead, Kadiya was suddenly aware of the passing of time. Jagun would have wakened, found her gone, be seeking her. The hunter had skills which would aid him to follow her through the city, since she had not tried to conceal her passage. But there were dangers such as the vine which had attacked her, and certainly she must not allow Jagun to remain in anxiety about her.

She could identify Gosel by scarf ornaments and now she went to the Speaker, striving quickly to form a mind picture of the Nyssomu hunter.

"My battle comrade—he will be seeking me."

"Already the swamp paddler has come," Gosel replied calmly. "He is safe caught in the maze. Is it your will that he be free?"

Were the Hassitti and the Oddlings enemies? Kadiya remembered Jagun's reaction to the wall drawings. Had he known of the Hassitti but for some reason wished to keep them secret?

"He is my good friend! Let me go to him!" There was the sharpness of an order in her voice.

5

HOW MUCH DANGER DID JAGUN face? Again her impetuous lack of thought had drawn another into trouble. Would she ever learn? Though the Hassitti could scuttle at a swift pace, Kadiya was impatiently pulling ahead of Gosel, needing at last to slow to allow the smaller creature to catch up with her.

They were followed again by a stream of Hassitti. The cackle of their speech was echoed from the larger walls as they went — not reentering the building in the direction from which they had come but along a lengthy corridor, the roof of which had been inset with transparent squares yielding a dim, greenish light.

The passage curved and Kadiya was sure they were angling back toward that outer square where she had found the fountain of jewels. But they did not emerge there. Rather the curving hall became a ramp slanting downward. The lighted patches on the roof disappeared.

Though shadowy dusk crowded in, it did not seem to affect any of the Hassitti. None of them carried lamps yet went confidently ahead. However, Kadiya was uneasy and her own pace slowed. Her companions had shown her only good will but their welcome might have been a sham. They had admitted that Jagun was somehow captive. Had they so easily also ensnared her because of her recklessness?

The down slope ceased and the pavement underfoot ran straight. Kadiya stumbled, for the dark was almost complete, and she knocked against one of the Hassitti. Her free hand was caught in a grip of rough-coated claws. For a moment she tried to free herself but a hard jerk availed her nothing.

"Great One—we take you. It is safe—"

Kadiya felt herself flush in vexation. She had so quickly and easily betrayed her unease. One faced the unknown with at least a shell of composure.

Still there were no lamps. Now she strode hand in hand with this scaled alien through a blackness so solid to her sight that it was as if a pocket of tangible darkness had entrapped her.

Her guide pulled her toward the left leaving her no recourse but to follow. The chittering speech of the others had ended, but the girl heard the constant scrape of clawed feet on stone.

Then—light ahead, such a burst of it that Kadiya's eyes could not take the explosion of raw color. She put her hands up to shade her eyes and tried to peer between the shelter of fingers at what waited ahead.

A giant fire might be filling a space as great as that audience hall which must now lie far above. Yet the shooting flames were not vertical but horizontal, sweeping from left to right in constant movement. Also they were not just red and yellow. There were crackling passes of blue, purple, green, and brilliant eye-punishing white. They would flicker, leap, hold steady for a moment and then be gone.

The Hassitti had drawn her out on what seemed to be a ledge, as far as her light-dazzled eyes could tell. Before them those lightning strikes of violent color skimmed, leaped, swung above some huge space which was below the level on which they stood. Though many times one of the spears of that strange conflagration would soar into the air, none of them approached, or struck near the ledge. Nor did Kadiya feel any sensation of heat.

"It is the maze." Gosel's explanation formed in her mind.

There was no pattern to that furious play of light beams. Were not mazes supposed to be a collection of pathways which led into one another, or into dead ends, unless one knew the secret? Sheltering her eyes as well as she could Kadiya strove to distinguish such pathways. There was only that light in constant searing motion.

She turned on Gosel. "Where is my comrade? What have you done with him?"

The Hassitti made a gesture at the place of colors.

"He is there."

Caught in *that*? Kadiya's hot anger brought her two steps nearer to the edge of the ledge. But how could she find him?

"Get him out!" She snapped an order.

Gosel's hands moved in a gesture which plainly suggested helplessness. The Hassitti was looking at her oddly. Now it dropped forward, the scarf swathed head turning at what must be a painful angle in order to still see the girl.

"Great One, there is no way—"

That light burnt away sight instead of flesh. Jagun, whose people were bred in the murky swamplands where frequent mists curtained much of the land, what must be his present torment? If she suffered now from those lightning-like flashes, how much worse it must be for him.

"There must be a way!" Kadiya said to herself and her bared teeth aimed the comment also to the Hassitti.

"Great One," Gosel answered, "the ways are closed save to those with the Power."

Power? Her hand went to the amulet at her throat. She thought of the orbed sword. Two powers—keys to this?

But first she must know, be sure that Jagun *was* here, gain some idea of the direction in which she must search. Kadiya opened the pouch at her belt and rolled into the palm of her hand a hollow reed slightly over finger length. It had been made for Nyssomu use, but she had employed it successfully before. She would do so again. The girl handled it delicately as it was so small. Lips about the one end, fingertips just so on certain patterned holes along the length.

Kadiya blew a series of notes not unlike the tinkle of the crystals which the Hassitti used. There was no roaring from the flames which laced the space before her. Could that call intended to alert another hunter carry to Jagun?

She sounded the flute again and varied the sound with notes which increased the summons. There was silence from the Hassitti. Were they sure that she had failed?

For the third time she blew the call.

Faint— Yes, she was sure! There *was* an answer.

She had already discarded her first plan for venturing into that maze. Could it not be that she could draw Jagun out this way, bring him to her even as one hunter called another to join on a fresh game trail? They had done this during the past fighting, gathering in squads of Oddlings to join a central force when it was necessary.

Kadiya held that call steady, resenting the need to halt now and then to flip the moisture from the tube. But she was sure that each time an answer came it was louder.

Again the summons sounded. Her eyes smarted from the constant assault of the raw color before her, but she could not shade them now. Tears gathered as she strove to look into that maelstrom, to hunt for a glimpse of Jagun.

The flute notes rose and fell. How long had she called? Her fingers had stiffened into the pattern of the holes. Now, deep breath. Once again —

Out of a band of scorching orange staggered a black figure which did not belong in that sea.

Kadiya thrust the flute into her purse and threw herself belly down on the ledge. The Oddling was below, weaving back and forth as one drained of blood or so wearied that his body resisted his will. Kadiya wriggled forward until her head and shoulders projected over the edge. She felt a heavy weight on her legs and glanced back to see through the mist of her strained sight: two of the Hassitti had stationed themselves to hold her body safe against the stone.

"Jagun!" Kadiya raised her voice and reached down.

He was reeling, his head hunched forward so that he stared at his feet, perhaps his only protection against the clash of color.

"Jagun!"

He half fell, to come up against the barrier which formed the foundation for the ledge. He raised his head and looked up to her. His eyes were mere slits and from them dribbled thick drops of mucus. His hands raised to link fingers about her wrists, while her grip tightened in turn. Now she began to edge back giving all her strength to drawing the Oddling up and out of that trap. Claw hands had seized upon her, were aiding her efforts.

She was well back from the edge now and Jagun's head

and shoulders were rising into view. Hassitti scuttled forward, grabbing at the Oddling. Kadiya felt the strain end as they pulled the hunter to safety.

Jagun lay unmoving, facedown, and she hurried to roll him over. His mouth gaped open and he moved limp in her grasp. Fear struck Kadiya. Somehow she hoisted him up, both of their backs to that swirling maelstrom, his head resting against her shoulder. She was not even sure he was breathing now. What torment he had undergone in that maze she could not guess — Oddlings might even find it fatal.

"You — " She looked to Gosel. "What have you done?"

The Hassitti was at her side, muzzle pointed down toward the Oddling as if sniffing.

Did the creature even understand? Kadiya strove to find a pulse in the Oddling's neck as she steadied him against her. There was the sharp scent given off by his kind at the height of fear.

"Get him out!" The order was more for herself than the Hassitti. But how? Though Jagun was smaller than she, he was no lightweight and the long passage they had followed to come here was more than she dared attempt while carrying him. Carefully she laid him back upon the pavement and then turned and grabbed at one of the trailing shawls worn by a nearby Hassitti, jerking it from the creature's shoulders.

Kadiya flapped that down on the pavement. Her own eyes burned and smarted, but she was able to do this much. Spreading out the shawl she lifted Jagun onto it. The length of material was thicker in her hand than it looked. She had reversed it so that the many fastened ornaments were now on the bottom side and she was able to move Jagun onto a fairly smooth surface. Taking her own belt she made the hunter fast, pulling the shawl around him as far as it would go and then securing it. That done she gathered up the end of the length she had left loose.

There was not enough of the stretch to allow her to stand upright. However, what she could do she would. Only now claw hands caught that drag for the improvised travois she had made and Gosel mind-spoke:

"We will take the swamper—"

"You have done this to him!" Kadiya flashed. That warmness of feeling which had been with her since she had first seen the Hassitti had vanished. Trust them with him now? Not while she still held hope he was alive.

"He came without peace words. He is Oddling, not Noble One, and the maze was made to catch comers who are not of this place," Gosel returned. "We can help him—if the Noble One wants this swamper, we will aid."

Four of them had fallen in about the wrapped hunter and now their claws caught in the shawl roll and lifted. Kadiya retreated a step. They were swinging him up off the ground in a way she could not have managed, and they had already moved toward that opening through which they had come into this place. Now she felt the scrape of rough scaled skin on her own wrist. Gosel was beside her, urging her on. She followed, but kept her still punished eyes as well as she could on Jagun and his bearers.

The journey back was long. Some of the Hassitti left to scurry on at a faster pace. But the rest remained, for Jagun's bearers changed at intervals. During each halt, Kadiya tried to find some sign of life in their charge. At the second such test there was a faint stir of breath against her hand.

"Jagun?" She mind-sought as she had done with the Hassitti.

A whirl of color, punishing pain—and through that something else which bit sharply at her. He had been concerned for her. It was fear for her which had brought him into this.

Kadiya fought now to reach his scattered thoughts. "It is well, warrior. I am here, there is no danger..."

That might not be the truth but she was going to hold to that as long as she could. Then she heard the scrape of feet and two more Hassitti joined them. One of them had lengths of what looked like large, half pulped leaves, and the other carried a flask.

These burdens the girl could see clearly for another trailed them with a lamp which swung on chains. Once more their fellows made room around Jagun. Kadiya refused to give way, kneeling beside the Oddling. He was visibly breathing, but his eyes were closed, seemingly caked with a yellowish discharge.

The Hassitti carrying the leaf lengths laid them carefully beside Jagun as the one with the lamp leaned forward to give better light. Their companion snapped up the cover on the flask.

Into the underground musty smell of this deep way spread something Kadiya knew well. This was the very breath of the garden — that perfect place of serenity and peace. Claw fingers doubled and scooped, bringing up a greenish jelly, and the scent of healthy growing things was strengthened.

Dropping to the floor, the flask bearer swept those burdened claws back and forth across the shortest of the leaf lengths, coating it thoroughly and thickly.

It was the first of the newcomers who took command of the operation now. This one was so shawl-bedecked that the creature seemed at first to have some trouble in freeing its hands as it reached for the laden leaf.

"Tostlet comes to aid." Gosel flashed that to Kadiya almost as if he expected her to refuse their attendance of the Oddling. "She is learned in healing."

A wisewoman-healer? Why not; each race no matter how different must have those taught to aid. Though the girl still could not tell the difference between male and female as far as the Hassitti were concerned, she had come to believe Gosel was male.

Tostlet poked a claw into the mass on the leaf. She apparently approved the preparation, for she picked up the length, and, with infinite care, placed it over Jagun's eyes — or rather the whole upper part of his face. He struggled against the belt which held him on the improvised stretcher, as if he would push it away. However, Tostlet with the aid of another raised the Oddling's head and bound the coated bandage in place with the rest of the leaves which they slit into usable strings as they worked.

The lamp bearer again leading the way, the party began once more the long journey to the upper regions. But not before Tostlet had spread a dab of the jelly on a remaining bit of leaf and held it out to Kadiya.

"For the eyes, Nobel One," she urged and the girl did make use of it, dabbing as she went. The whirls of light which had continued to flash before her at intervals faded, as did the smarting. She was sure that, had she been caught in the midst of the maze, she might well have gone blind from the fury of those beams around her.

At length they came into the upper reaches of the city, out into that second courtyard with its fountain. It seemed to Kadiya that the day was darker. Was it her sight suffering even though her eyes no longer hurt? What would it mean to be without sight, lost forever in the darkness? Her thoughts shivered.

Jagun was set down by the fountain. His head turned from side to side now and he was moaning.

"Dark—hurt—I thirst—" Those words, even in Oddling speech, she knew. Kadiya hurried to the basin, cupped her hands to scoop up water. There was a touch on her shoulder. Someone who stood beside her held out a goblet as richly begemmed as that from which she had drunk the guesting draught.

She dipped it, filled it, and was instantly on her knees beside Jagun, his head braced up against her as she held the edge of the goblet to those lips beneath the leaf mask.

"Drink, shield brother." She used the Oddling speech as best she could, though none of her race could form the sounds fully.

Jagun obeyed. Again he tried to move his hands and Kadiya, still holding him up, gestured to the nearest Hassitti to loosen the belt. The hunter's hand groped upward through the air until his fingers fell on Kadiya's wrist and tightened there.

"Farseer"—this time he spoke in the trade language—"is it you in truth? Are you, also, caught in this place of many heat-less fires?" There was an urgency in his demand which she was quick to respond to.

"Comrade, we are free of that place. Once more we are under sky. Drink: this is water, clear as it seldom is afar from the isles."

Drink he did, then both hands went to the bandage across his eyes. But Kadiya caught the nearest and held it still.

"Not yet, comrade. This is healing for the lights."

He turned his head a little against her shoulder. She saw his flat nostrils expand as when they were on the hunting trail, as if he could sniff out any intruder.

"There are others here." He used the trader tongue and his voice had dropped to hardly above a whisper.

"There are those who brought us both forth from the place of lights. They call themselves Hassitti."

She could feel the instant tension of his body.

"Hassitti—"

Then she caught the mind speech and Gosel was there. Could Jagun "hear" that also? It seemed as if the Hassitti expected him to.

"We are those who wait, swamper. We wait even though your kind would have none of waiting and went forth on paths of your own choosing!" There was accusation in that.

"Hassitti." Again Jagun spoke the name aloud. "But such are of the Dark tales—"

"Swamper!" There was rising anger in that. "Never did we hold with the Dark! We were of those who served, who were left in trust! When you went off to your mud and murk, we remained."

Jagun turned his head a fraction more so that his bandaged cheek touched Kadiya's breast.

"Farseer, take into mind the pictures of these so that I may see."

She lifted her head a little so that she could stare straight at Gosel, building a mind picture of this one who appeared to be the leader of these creatures.

"Soooo . . ." Jagun made the word a hiss, "the very ancient tales are then the truth. But how can that be? For it was said that such went with the Vanished Ones who had an odd taste for their companionship and would never have left them behind."

"We chose to stay." Mind speech answered him. "For we were of the last ones, those whom the Guardians knew. And—" For a moment Kadiya was wracked by a feeling of such pain and longing that she nearly flung up an arm as she would have warded some blow.

"And, when those who closed the way and held against the Dark finally fell, we were left. We knew that it could not end that way. Greatness does not die, it can rise again. See, did we not have the truth of that, for here is this Noble One returned even as we dreamed it!"

"Jagun"—Kadiya tried to settle him more comfortably—"the Hassitti believe that I am one of the Vanished Ones, though I have told them it is not so."

"You have come to us"—Gosel looked straight at her—"and the dreams were true. What is there to be done, Noble One, that you have returned to your people?"

Kadiya remembered the sword still planted in the garden. There had been no release of that burden upon her return. What then was to come?

6

 THE GRAY SKIES OF THE STORM season still hung over the city, though the fierce rains and winds did not beat within. More of the Vanished Ones' magic, Kadiya thought.

She stood at an upper window looking out over the somber rows of buildings, though here and there the cloaking vegetation softened outlines and curtained walls. This was not the palace of the great hall wherein she had first faced the Hassitti, but rather a tower behind that hall to which she had been escorted—and to which Jagun had been borne at her insistence.

There were furnishings of a sort here. Plainly it and the two other rooms on this story had been a living suite for someone of rank, and the Hassitti had worked to maintain it as best they could.

A bed, oddly shaped to resemble a half shell (perhaps even

its material being formed of the crushed substance of such)
stood on a round dais. There was a short legged table with
the same opalescent gleam. By that was a pile of mats covered
with richly stitched cloth, much faded but still intact. Lamps
with shell shades stood lit to battle shadows at the far side of
the room.

The paintings on the walls were here all of a shoreline so
finely depicted that were it not for three windows which gave
upon the real world, Kadiya could have believed she looked
out upon moving water. Along its edge birds waded and beds
of reeds grew all abloom with golden spikes of flowers.

There was a large chest also. This had been eagerly flung
open by two of the female Hassitti who had been among her
guides, to display folds of glitter studded fabric. In one small
section lay necklaces, arm bands, and other gem-set wear.

Olla and Runna had insisted that this was all to be Kadiya's
and they had shown disappointment when she did not immediately take the opportunity to change from her worn travel
clothing into such proffered splendor. The girl had brushed
aside their suggestions, far more intent that Jagun be estab-
lished as comfortably as possible on a pallet of mats where she
could keep him under eye.

It was only a short space ago that Tostlet had lifted the
bandages to inspect the Oddling's eyes. Moments later, Jagun
roused to look at Kadiya with the joyous exclamation she had
half feared she would never hear:

"King's Daughter, I see!"

He had clutched forceably at her arm as she knelt beside
him, drawing her farther down. There was such joy on his
face as she had never witnessed before.

"It is well, oh, Farseer, it is well!"

Tostlet came in, a cup in her claws. "Let this one drink."

She offered the cup to Kadiya almost as if she believed that Jagun might not accept it from her. "Drink, and sleep, for now only sleep is needed."

Drink he did, as Kadiya gently pushed him back on the mats, his eyes already closing. They still looked swollen and the flesh about them was puffed.

She waited until she was sure that he was asleep and then she sent the Hassitti away. If they had indeed entrapped Jagun in that place of punishing light, at least they had been willing to nurse him once he had come forth. Her anger was gone. They might well have been only obeying some archaic pledge when they sent Jagun, or allowed him, to enter the maze. She could not fault them for that, not now.

The maze itself awed her. To have set such a trap was far beyond any learning she knew. Perhaps even Orogastus at the height of his power could not have wrought a like defense. And how long ago had it been set and empowered? If the Hassitti had not put it to use, had it been left so even from the days of the Vanished Ones?

Kadiya rubbed her hand across her forehead. So many questions, so many puzzles. This day had made her more and more aware of how ignorant she was. Haramis was Archimage. Magic was Haramis's concern, not hers. Perhaps instead of seeking mysteries in the mountains her sister should have come questing in the swamp mires.

Wearily she left the window. It was night and all the fatigue and terrors of the day had worn her down. She came to stand once more beside the chest Olla had left open. On impulse she plucked out the first of the folded materials lying within.

It shook out in brilliant glory as she held it, the ends dripping to the floor. Dripping because it was overlaid with a myriad of crystal drops, some of which chimed together softly as the folds moved at her touch.

The garment was not unlike those tattered robes Kadiya had seen on several of the Hassitti, except this was pristine in its glory. It might have been fashioned yesterday. The sleeves were long and full, gathered in by crystal bands at the wrists. There was a complicated fastening partway down the front where cords wove back and forth around knobby buttons of crystal.

In color it was white, yet the folds, as Kadiya turned it to examine it closely, showed touches of other faint hues, as might be found in iridescent interiors of shells. She held it up. Long—it had been meant for someone taller—yet it was plainly wearable, not about to fall to pieces if she did choose to don it.

Making up her mind, Kadiya folded it over her arm, and, after another glance to make sure all was well with Jagun, she went into the next chamber. As in the outside fountains she had seen, a clear stream of water issued from the mouth of a carven fish-like creature into a basin fully large enough to hold her body.

Kadiya laid the robe to one side, tugged at the fastening of her scale mail. Then she caught sight of a figure to one side. Startled, she had dagger in hand before she realized that she was gazing into the largest mirror she had ever seen, one reaching from floor to roof. That miserable creature she faced there was herself. From the wild mass of her tangled hair, ragged on top where she had freed herself from the serpent vine, to her water soaked boots, she looked worse than a polder laborer at planting time.

Quickly she discarded her swamp-stained clothing to settle into the bath. The water was warm, even as it had been in the fountain. Kadiya recognized the purpose of a row of boxes on a wall shelf at hand level, one of the pleasures she had known in the Citadel after a long day swamp exploring with Jagun. Here were stored squares of thick moss which, when squeezed and wrung in water, left herb scented suds in her hands. Kadiya washed away the traces of slime which had soaked through her clothing and darkened her skin, and then attacked her hair, though the suds stung in those places on her scalp where the vine had pulled.

There was a towel of woven reed waiting and she dried herself vigorously before she lifted once more that royal robe. Clothing of state she had known all her life, had had to wear under protest at times. But in all the treasures of her mother's wardrobe there had never been anything as fine as this.

It was too large; she had to take up her belt, clean it as best she could with wet moss and wipe it dry in order to gather those crystal laden lengths close enough. The sleeves she had to roll well up, and even though she tugged much of the rest up through her belt the skirt trained out on the floor and threatened to trip her. Kadiya turned again to survey herself in that revealing mirror. And made a face at the reflection.

Against the clear white her face and hands looked coarse and dark. There was nothing to be done for her ragged hair except to hope that it would grow out. Such finery did not become her. Yet, looking down at the discarded clothing on the floor, she could not bring herself to shed the glory of the robe and redon her own.

In fact she did not even want the fine stuff she now wore to brush against it. Still to leave it here in a tangle would not do. She would have to find a way of cleaning it, of somehow sewing the tears, ridding it of all the staining.

Kadiya drew the garments together and carried them at

arm's length back to the outer room, laying them on a mat in the corner. Surely Olla or Runna would be able to show her how to deal with them.

Scattered mats of a soft cream-yellow were protection for her bare feet. But the heavy belt across the fine stuff irked her and she went again to rummage in the coffer, bringing forth a scarf of what seemed to be silver, beaten silk-soft, which she twisted into a girdle. Her dagger she transferred to that. For too long she had lived with it close to hand to discard it now.

There was a soft murmur of sound from beyond the slatted curtain which formed the door. Hassitti—she could pick up their mind patterns, even though she did not try to delve into their thoughts.

"Come." Sweeping the length of the robe to one side so she could move, Kadiya watched Olla enter bearing a tray with silver plates, and behind her Runna carrying one of those lamps which gave forth the spicy smells.

They both ducked their long-snouted heads in her direction as they padded across to place their burdens on the table.

Olla motioned to the table and then to Kadiya, her chittery voice like that of a grass insect, low and somehow cheerful. Kadiya obediently took her place (with some difficulty because of the bulk of the robe) on the mats. It was Runna who hastened to help her spread out that entangling skirt, while Olla uncovered two bowls and poured water into just such a goblet as those Gosel and she had used.

Again the food was fruit and a bowl of thickened soup-like substance, but this time they had provided her with an over-large spoon. Kadiya found it good and she ate heartily, smiling and nodding her thanks to the Hassitti.

There was a curious dream-like quality to all of this. Kadiya ate and drank. The spicy smoke from the lamp made a floating wisp in the room as the dark increased and the smaller shelf lamps did not banish growing shadows. When she had done and the tray was borne away by the Hassitti, Kadiya went to sit beside Jagun. He was sleeping quietly but to be this close to him brought back reality.

The girl slipped fingers back and forth where the robe covered her crossed legs. Certainly it was real to the touch, just as this room appeared to be entirely solid.

Yet she was uneasy. It was as if she had stepped into some action of which she knew no detail at all. Before, her mission had seemed concrete: to visit the garden and rid herself of her portion of the Great Talisman, then to discover — to *learn* — as the mysterious veiled one had promised at their meeting. But learn what? She could not now even begin to guess.

Mage powers? No, those were for Haramis. Establish a swamp kingdom? She reached for no crown, was no rival to Anigel. There was an emptiness within her which she must learn to fill. But with what?

At no other time had one of her kind been made so free of the mire lands. Nyssomu and Uisgu had come to battle at her summons — or the knowledge that she had raised the ancient strength had brought them. The mires and their ways she knew as she believed no one else of the Ruwenda blood could claim — even the most venturesome of traders.

Yet this was a land of secrets upon secrets. Perhaps even a lifetime could never make one entirely knowledgeable.

The Archimage Binah had kept to her tower at Noth — yet she must have known much. If in truth she was one of the Vanished Ones chosen to be Guardian here — then all the past would be open to her, that tattered past the Hassitti strove to hold together.

Kadiya closed her eyes slowly and with determination. She

had been able to communicate with Gosel, know at least the surface thoughts of others of his kind. Now, she wanted what she had come here to find: that One who had promised her learning.

Just as she had tried to govern her thoughts to reach the Hassitti, now she strove to build up the mind picture of that figure which had been largely a pillar of mist, to call —

Kadiya tensed, but she did not utter the cry which had almost reached her lips. She cut thought, shivered, her hands going unconsciously to cover her ears.

In her ignorant reaching she had touched something so dark, so full of menace that it was like a blade rising to her throat. She opened her eyes.

There were shadows in plenty. She made herself face each quarter of the room in turn, search for the smallest hint of source of that threat. But there was nothing. Only Jagun cried out and his hands beat up into the air as if he warded off an enemy. Yet he did not rise nor open his eyes, and Kadiya thought that he must still sleep, that what she felt must have reached him as a troubling dream.

Dream! The Hassitti had mentioned dreams, suggested that they had been guided by them —

Only so far had her thought traveled when there came a sound from the doorway and she recognized Gosel by thought pattern as she might have known him by face.

"Noble One!" His mind send was imperative.

"Come."

He had bundled up his trailing shawl so that he might move the faster as he burst through the door curtain.

"Noble One!"

To Kadiya's surprise and discomfort he dropped before her, one hand reaching out, but not quite touching her robe's edge.

Fear had come with him, she could feel it. On the mat bed Jagun rolled his head from side to side and gave a low sound which was not quite a moan.

"There is a stirring—" Gosel stared up at her as if the very intentness of his look could wring from Kadiya some answer he needed.

"Quave has dreamed," he continued after a moment. "Deep dreamed. There is evil on the move—though where and how the dream did not reveal. But Quave is sore disturbed. Noble One, use the Power and tell us what comes and what we may do!"

They would not listen, they still thought that she was of the Vanished Ones. How could she make them believe she had no such powers?

"Gosel." Kadiya tried to order her thoughts, to make them clear. "I have told you—I am not one of those you think I am. My race has no great powers. . ." She thought of Haramis and corrected herself. "Most of us do not, and I am one lacking. A geas brought me here—who laid it upon me and why I do not know. But—" She bit her lip.

"When I was offered a crown, Gosel, I chose instead the mire lands. Perhaps I did so believing that most of the Dark had departed out of the swamps when we dragged down Voltrik and Orogastus. Yet I made that choice and I hold to it.

"In this place you have showed me a storehouse of knowledge which I believe runs far beyond that my people ever dreamed of—yet it is not *my* knowledge. I have wielded Power—but it was by the will of something which stood outside the person who was Kadiya, daughter of Krain. You must not be deceived. I cannot summon up thunderbolts, nor wrest the very winds into my service. I cannot raise demons, nor call upon any strange life to form guards for you or any of this land.

"However, what I can learn, what I can do, that I shall."

He was standing now, his head turned a little to one side so that the lamplight drew a queer shadow against the curve of the shell bed.

"Quave dreamed, Vasp dreamed, Thrug dreamed, and before them there was Zanya, Usita, and Vark and more, back and back — Those who once were shall come again. And what more should bring them than such a stirring as Quave has shadow-seen this night? Only one who was meant could come here. You have been before — you were seen. But then we knew also that the time was not yet.

"Now we ask it of you, Noble One: stand between us and what will come."

Kadiya sighed. She had done her best. And it was perhaps true that she was doomed now to failure — but her old will stirred in her. To think of disaster was to call it into one's presence. If the Hassitti would not accept the truth she must do the best she could. But without knowledge of just what she faced she was doubly at a disadvantage.

"What manner of evil stirs?" she asked.

Gosel shook his head. "It was not made plain to Quave — only that it is old and dark. It has lain long in slumber —"

"Those who once dwelt here had records. If this thing was old, could those not be searched?"

There was a quick eagerness in the Hassitti's answer.

"That can be done, Noble One. It is true that one needs a lamp to search out what must be found. Also, the dreamers will try again! This very hour they shall try!"

With a swirl of his drapery he was gone.

Kadiya had drawn her dagger. The reality of that cherished weapon was an anchor in this world of dreamers and shadow threats. The records she had seen in one of those rooms crammed with the memorabilia of the Vanished Ones—could the Hassitti read them? She was sure that such a task was beyond her own talents.

"Farseer—"

She turned quickly to Jagun.

"What may I do for you, comrade?"

She saw his wide mouth shape a half smile. "It is rather, King's Daughter, what I may do for you. These skitterers with their dreaming and their hoarding of what they themselves do not know—do not let them draw you into standing for them."

"What do you truly know of these little people, Jagun?" she questioned.

His smile was gone. "Farseer, very little. Until I saw them for myself I believed that that knowledge was of the same stuff as swamp mist—or even less. They are from the fashioning of the Vanished Ones, even as were we of the Kin—and the Skritek—but they were said to have gone with the Great Ones into the unknown. They were thought to have had no real life apart from those others, whereas we were given the swamp mires to hold and rule. They are not of our kind any more than the Skritek—though they are not of the Dark as are those."

"You have dreamed also, hunter."

He was silent for a moment, and turned his head a little away from her.

"Yes, I dreamed." She saw him shiver. "Though I cannot remember it now. Perhaps all this," he made a motion with his hand, "is a place of dreams. Farseer, we would be better out of it."

Kadiya shook her head wearily. "I might say well to that —
save there is the sword. It remains, and while it does I am not
free to go my way. But you are not bound, Jagun."

Now he looked straight at her and she felt shame for those
last words.

"Comrade," she hastened to say, "I would not have you
away except by your own choice."

"Which I have made long since," he answered.

KADIYA HAD LEFT ONE LAMP BURN-
ing. Even in its subdued glow she could
see some reflections from the patterns on
the robe she had discarded in folds across
the end of the bed. Within that shell hollow were not the sleep mats she was used
to but rather a fluff of stuff she decided must be culled from
the seed puffs of mak reeds, and into this nesting apparently
the occupant was supposed to burrow.

She lay with her wrists crossed behind her head and tried
to face squarely what might lie ahead. This was a blind seeking, unless she could find something in that mass of records
she had only glimpsed when the Hassitti had taken her on the
tour of their storage rooms.

She had never been a delver into old records, even if they
were inscribed in words she could read—which she greatly
doubted. This should be Haramis's task.

Haramis—

Kadiya's hands went now to the amber amulet at her throat. Cupping it in both her palms, she closed her eyes and tried to reach her sister using the mind speech. There was no touching, no sense of anything beyond. She had had only a small hope that there would be.

Yet the amulet fed a warmth to her hands, down her arms, into the very heart of her body. Kadiya, clasping the amulet tight against her breast, no longer struggled to use that which she did not understand. Instead her thoughts drifted to the garden. In the morning she would go there—

She awoke as suddenly as if she had been aroused to sentry duty. The lamp still shone, a beacon against the night. Kadiya fought her way out of the puffy fibers of bedding which had arisen like waves around her.

Crossing the room, she discovered that even in that short time the Hassitti had dealt with her traveling clothing. What could be cleaned had been; what could be mended was. She could bear to wear it again.

The summons which had brought her out of sleep still rang in her head. Pausing only for a moment to assure herself that Jagun slept, she crept out of the room.

There was a faint radiance from below as if another lamp had been left there. She descended the flight of stairs to ground level. There was a solid door—the first she had seen— but it yielded to her push and then she was out in the night.

Once more she held the amulet in hand. Even as it had guided her moons ago to Binah's tower, so now was it aglow. That spark of light within wreathed the tiny Black Trillium, waning and waxing as she swung it carefully this way and that.

Binah's birth gift was of the magic of the Vanished Ones.

In this, the heart of their territory, she believed it could be trusted anew. Obeying the impulse with which she had awakened, the girl moved off through the mists of the night. She divided her attention between what she held and what lay about her, remembering very well the vine trap.

Though she could see but little as she went, Kadiya was certain she was beginning to retrace the ways which had brought her here. And she was not surprised when at last she stood again before the garden stairway with its silent and motionless Guardians.

Then she was among the columns, looking down to where the sparks of insects wove patterns between bloom and bloom. The perfume seemed stronger than even the spice lamps of the Hassitti as she descended the inner stairway. One of the sparks, a vivid blue-green, swung toward her, hovered for a second or two over the amulet as she held it outstretched.

"I have come." Kadiya spoke aloud. She had moved to stand beside the sword which still stood planted and unchanging.

Yet—something *had* changed. Ever since the blade had come again into her hands after its service as part of the Great Power, the lids had appeared locked tightly in place over the three eyes. Now they showed slits as if about to lift.

Kadiya shrank from touching the talisman even as she knew that she had no choice. She stooped and closed hand about the blade just below the pommel. It came loose easily from the earth, as if it leaped of its own will into her grasp.

A burden she did not want, yet one she must bear. Kadiya held it up for a closer sight. Yes, the eyes showed slits. Hurriedly she sheathed it, having no desire to awaken the Power which lay within. There was no feeling of any threat here; she could not believe that danger lurked now.

However, she was not rid of that geas-born burden.

Kadiya retraced her way as far as the steps. She sat there, watching mist flow in the garden. Though near middle night, she was able to pick out bush, tree, plant. Once more, longing a pain in her, she held out both hands to all which grew there, all that might ever come...

"Tell me—let me know what wills this? Binah set one geas upon me. Who would use me now?"

There was a rustle, a swaying of branches she could only half see. Spark flyers shot toward each other as if they were frightened and would face the danger in a body. Kadiya held her breath for a long second, sure that the one she had met before would appear.

But all she could see was the passing of the wind in the branches, the clustering of the sparks. Then those broke apart, whirled each on its own chosen path as if what had disturbed them was gone.

Anger rose in her, that same anger which she had known in the past when she had met with frustration. This was like standing before an open door and yet being barred entrance.

Kadiya trailed back to the outer columns. Mist seemed to have thickened since her previous passage. She could see the forms of the Guardian statues only as shrouded figures. Yet as she descended the steps she faced one and then the other— even holding out the amulet, as if its still steady glow could reveal more clearly those watchers. Once she went closer to a form at her right, reaching out to lay fingers on the chill body.

There plucked at her the belief that these statues had a meaning, one which she must master. If she were only not so ignorant! That inner dull anger was turning against herself.

With the sword again in hand, Kadiya found her way back through the silent city, once more ascended to the tower room. She had seen no Hassitti during her travels and thought that perhaps they had some quarters of their own in which they slumbered. Did they also dream?

As she once more took to the bed she drew the sword from its scabbard to rest it beside her. The eyes had opened no farther; neither had they closed. The Power might slumber, but it had not gone.

If any dreamed the rest of the night Kadiya was not among them. In spite of her taking once more the sword, she was oddly more at peace with herself. Jagun was on his feet again, sharing (to the unspoken but nevertheless clear disapproval of Olla and Runna) her morning meal.

The treasure house, or more exactly, the room in which she had seen the many books and reading rolls, was foremost in Kadiya's mind. If she knew more of the past perhaps she could sift out better what was needful in the present.

"Our Speakers have their time weavings," Jagun remarked when she told him where she would search. "Some of the villages possess very old rolls. But only the Speakers can weave and thereafter translate those. Such knowledge seems to come by birth—for when a hatchling is of a proper age it is tested. What to some remain a locked mystery is for others a storehouse of knowledge."

"What of you, hunter? These woven histories, are they clear to you?" Since the Oddlings had their way of preserving the past, perhaps it was based on some form of learning their mentors the Vanished Ones had used. If so, Jagun's help would be invaluable. Somehow she doubted she would find much aid among the Hassitti, for Kadiya had the impression that they had relentlessly saved much they could not understand.

"No, Farseer, my knowledge lies in other directions—the

ways of the beasts, of the swamp growth, of the seasons. I
came to that knowledge, for, as a hatchling, I was put to pren-
ticeship with Rusloog who was one of the greatest swamp travelers my village knew. Some other things I have learned from
your people since I dwelt in the Citadel and served the King.
But of these ancient mysteries which have to do with memories
and weaving—do not expect much of me."

Kadiya pounced upon that. "You say 'much.' Then you have
a fraction—"

Jagun squirmed a little and reached hurriedly for a goblet,
drinking down its contents as if he needed time to consider.

"Farseer, the Speaker of my clan is one who wishes always
to know more. When I was a swamp runner and a hunter of
old things, she showed me what to look for among such finds.
I can recognize some of the old signs. That is all."

"But that is something!" Kadiya put aside her emptied bowl
of mush, licking her spoon for the last particle. "There was
much I could have learned. But I did not like the hours spent
in the mustiness of the library any more than I relished those
I was supposed to spend in the ladies' bower seaming up pretty
cloth pictures. Haramis had the learning, Anigel the clever
fingers; I had the swamp."

The room of stored learning was daunting. Kadiya had
merely glanced into it from the doorway when the Hassitti
had swept her through their storehouses. When she had asked
to be brought here for a second time three of the small people
had formed an escort, two of them bearing lamps.

To search would be a massive task—the worse because one
would not know exactly what to look for. The lamps from the
doorway showed only a portion of the chamber. What shelves

the girl could see clearly were crowded with record rolls —
some in casings, some without — left to the ravages of time and
perhaps insects. There were piles of boxes against the walls
under those shelves. Sharing the already crowded space were
massive books such as she had seen several times brought back
by traders and eagerly taken by her father even though their
contents might be unreadable. The covers of these were slabs
of wood and some were bound about with metal clasps.

Where to begin — and what did she really seek? Not the mysteries of magic and strange lore which had been in Haramis's
keeping — rather the history of those who stored these records.
They had magic but Kadiya wanted to know more of them, of
where they had gone and why. Something told her that the
dreamers who prophesied an evil to come were tied with what
had been, that the present was growing out of the past.

The Hassitti made no attempt to enter the room. They chit-
tered angrily among themselves when Kadiya took a lamp
from one and handed it to Jagun, reaching for the second for
herself. They moved, almost as if they would bar her way with
their own bodies; but when she strode purposefully on they
drew to one side.

She held the lamp high. Jagun went on to the nearest wall,
his own light picking out scrolls, boxes, and the dull metal
fastening on books. Her light was limited — just enough to
show her that there was a table not too far away (its top near
covered with scroll boxes), before it a chair thickly carved
(dust lying white in the carvings).

Here was a work place. Kadiya swung her lamp lower to
illume that surface. There was an empty hollow among the
boxes, directly before the chair. Yet a wink of light there
caught her attention. A small tube of metal stood upright in
a pot. A single strip of parchment, now nearly as dark as the

surface on which it lay, was uncurled next to it. The worker here might have been called away in the midst of a task.

Kadiya swept a finger across the surface of that parchment, carrying away a film of dust. There were marks to be seen — weaving lines such as those which enhanced the wall of the first building they had entered.

"Jagun," she summoned the hunter, "what do you make of this?"

The hunter peered down at it, then ran one finger along beneath the top line, as if tracing its path would supply a clue.

"This," he reported a moment later, "is a sign for mountains."

Kadiya was surprised. The mountains to the east and the north had once formed the impenetrable defense for Ruwenda until Orogastus's magic and the treachery of men had breached it, loosing death on the only world she knew. Haramis had gone to the mountains to learn her powers, had returned to them by choice to hone and augment further what she had learned.

Kadiya had seen the heights only at a distance when she had visited the polders. There were inhabitants of those sky reaching lands, but none had ever contacted the lowlanders, nor had men intruded upon them.

"What else?" she demanded eagerly.

Jagun chewed his lower lip as he held closer his own lamp. Suddenly that jerked as if from an uncontrollable move of the hand which held it.

"This!" His voice was urgent. He stabbed a finger down on another point — one in wavering line which showed no individual words or letters. "Evil . . . great evil. A warning!"

Once more his finger traced the line and then he shook his head. "Farseer, there is no more that I can read."

"Someone was writing here," the girl mused aloud. "It was of importance, I am sure. Then it was left laying openly . . . on purpose? To warn any who came after? Mountains and evil—a foreseeing? Orogastus had his hidey-hole in the northern mountains. He was a gatherer of strange learning—he would even have gathered Haramis, had she willed, because she might hold knowledge of things new to him. A forewarning against Orogastus?"

But to foresee so far into the future—was such a thing possible? Kadiya had doubts of that. Therefore there had been once other evil in the heights, one so strong that even the Vanished Ones must record a warning of it.

She turned on Jagun. "Mountains—you can read that sign. Let us look for it here first."

Such a small clue—how long would it take? And even if they found the proper sign could it have a meaning if they were not able to read more than that one symbol?

"Farseer," Jagun said slowly, "you wear again the sword of harsh justice. Perhaps that may afford us a search tool."

Surprised, Kadiya put down her lamp to draw the sword, taking care not to slip a hand over those slits of eyes. Eyes were for seeing—and that top eye had the Power of the Old Ones. On impulse the girl swung the sword pommel out over that strip of writing which had been so long lying here.

"Sssssaaaa . . ." Jagun hissed like a sal-snake.

Kadiya kept firm hold on the sword. It had not resisted her grip but the top eye had come fully open. A spot of light from it reflected on the long strip.

Parts of the weaving lines were changing color though the hues were not sharp. There were greens with the darkness of likan pads, traces of red which might have been the swirling of blood drops on water, a blue, and there was a touch of violet becoming purple-brown, like pool muck.

A weaving of which she could make no sense at all. It no longer even resembled any writing that she could imagine.

Jagun's large eyes were opened to the fullest extent.

"Speaker's records!"

"You can read these?" Kadiya was still hopeful. If this was Oddling script, surely Jagun must know something!

He now stood, hands spread flat on either end of that strip, his eyes intent.

"Place of the Sals," he said slowly. "Guard . . . danger . . . mountains."

"Place of the Sals," Kadiya repeated. "Where does that lie?"

He looked up at her and there was an expression close to awe on his face.

"It was once a village, but with the coming of the great-great rains it was taken by the river. Those who dwelt there — they who survived after the churning of the waters — built again elsewhere. Farseer, you have seen their place — It is the village of my clan!"

She remembered well her visit there, that place where the long houses were built on piled platforms out in the lake. It was far, close to the Golden Mire, down river, back through the Thorny Hell.

Kadiya glanced at the surrounding litter. Perhaps this script was not the only thing which could be unlocked by the eye. Lamp in one hand, sword in the other, Jagun helping to unroll scrolls, and open such books which looked as if they might be forced, she circled the table, held out the pommel over those records piled closest. But there came no result, nor could she see any familiar symbol. Jagun protested that he could do no better.

A stir from the door shattered their intent search. Gosel appeared and with him Tostlet. Both of them held their tattered drapery close to their small bodies lest they bring down some of those piles between which they threaded a way.

"Noble One." The thought brought Kadiya's full attention. "Quave has dreamed again. There is a coming of the Dark. Summon forth your Powers that nothing can reach here."

Kadiya fronted the Hassitti squarely.

"Gosel, I have no true Powers. This"—she held up the sword so that he could see the three orbs on the pommel— "served my people well, through me. Yet I do not know from whence its force comes, or if I can summon it at will. To test it in open battle when I am so ignorant is to play the fool. This is all it has done for us today." At her gesture Jagun picked up the strip on which the script was so changed. "My battle comrade tells me this is a recording of his people, but he is not one taught to read such. What can you read in this place, Gosel?"

The Hassitti stared at her.

"Noble One, we are not those chosen to record. We"—his clawed fist indicated the room—"have brought hither all which we have found for safekeeping, but what may be among this we do not know."

"Your dreamer," Kadiya said, losing what had been a very faint hope. "What has the dream brought?"

"Dark and dark, Noble One." Tentatively Gosel reached forward toward the sword, though he did not put claw to its surface. The lid of the eye at the top was up, it was almost as if that orb was studying the Hassitti.

Gosel stared back. And then, to Kadiya's surprise, both of his clawed hands came up, touching the Hassitti's own elongated face between the eyes.

"Noble One," his thought reached her. "This is a thing of Power which we do not know, save that it is such that leads one to the doing of strange and great things."

Now he turned his head a fraction to view the strip Jagun still held.

"If that was what it showed to you, then, Noble One, you must know its meaning."

Kadiya could have hissed like Jagun in her exasperation. She had no answers for all her searching, only more and more questions!

Very well, they had a message which had been left behind, translated by the aid of the one thing she was sure carried with it what her people might term "magic." This mentioned a long-ago village, storm-drenched into nothingness, then re-born as Jagun's own. If nothing more concrete could be dis-covered here, why waste time searching through these unintelligible records of another race and people, having to listen to constant warning of dark dreams?

She could take their find to Jagun's home. Surely they must have fuller records, something more helpful. Mountains, dark forgotten villages—if there was any sorting out to be done it should be by action. That was Kadiya's way of life. They must take their find to where it could be translated into useful information.

8

ONCE SHE WAS DECIDED UPON the journey, Kadiya had to withstand the arguments of the Hassitti. The little people were rooted fast in the city and they seemed unable to think of anyone voluntarily venturing out of it. She faced warnings and pleas which ate at her patience. Once or twice she wondered if the Hassitti might even take steps to detain them — perhaps using some trick such as the maze of light.

However, Kadiya continued to draw upon her store of hard learned patience, insisting that she must go. To her surprise she was suddenly backed by the dreamers when she sat in council with Gosel and the other Seniors.

Quave was the leader of those sleep sages, a Hassitti whose eyes were not bright buttons but rather veiled by a cloudy film as if he used other means of sight. He was treated with great ceremony by his people. When he came into the meeting one of his attendants carried a bowl, not of the metal Kadiya had seen elsewhere but rather fashioned of some age darkened wood.

After Quave had settled in the seat Gosel hurriedly quitted, the bowl was set on the table before him. He seemed to huddle there with his head lowered, looking into the bowl's depths where a dark liquid was cupped. His next move was so sudden that Kadiya was caught by surprise. The Hassitti's paw shot out from beneath the edge of the thick shawl draped about him and the claw digits caught at Kadiya's wrist where the girl's hands lay on the board.

That grip was tight enough to jerk her forward and Quave raised his head so that the seemingly blind eyes fixed on her.

"Dreams have come." Quave's words were sharp in her mind with a demanding note. "Noble One, if you cannot dream—then look! Call upon that which you need for your purposes!"

Need for her purposes? Kadiya's thoughts were not in clear order. She needed knowledge of a kind which was not common, which in the very depths of her she dreaded. Who might have such knowledge? There were wisewomen among the Oddlings—and there was Haramis!

She stared down into the bowl, fastening her thoughts upon her sister, striving to picture her in those depths as she had seen her last at the Citadel.

"Haramis—" she called the name aloud even as she also sought with the inner thought.

There was no stir of liquid in the bowl, but its dark surface grew brighter from a spark in the very center, the dim radiance spreading out toward the edges from the heart of light.

The picture was not clear. Walls seemed to flicker in and out of being. Along those she thought she could see books and scrolls stored, though kept in neater order than the room she had searched here. There was a table on which clustered flasks and jars, a pile of parchment sheets. She who sat before those, pen in hand, was even less visible than her surroundings.

"Haramis!" Kadiya drew upon her will and energy to make contact with her sister.

That shadow which was Haramis suddenly raised her head as if summoned, turned a little so that Kadiya could now see her sister full faced. Lips moved in that face, the eyes peered as if the other strove to see through some barrier.

"Haramis!" The whole scene wavered and rippled as if the liquid mirror in which she viewed it was disturbed. Then it was gone.

"Who is this Weaver of dreams you strive to summon?" Quave loosed his grip on Kadiya.

"My sister, she whom the Archimage Binah chose to take her place as sorceress and Guardian."

"She is of great Power, this Haramis?"

"Of us all she holds the Power the strongest," Kadiya answered. "I can wield this," she touched the sword cautiously, "but I am not learned in the ways of magic. That is why I must discover all which I can. I have no dreams to warn or guide." She tried to erase the hasty tone from her voice, to make Quave understand her real helplessness and through him these others.

For a space of several breaths the other did not answer. He made a small gesture with one claw and the attendant who had brought the bowl picked it up again.

"This is possible," Quave's reply came at last. "We are not those who deal with strengths as the Noble Ones knew. If you believe, One Who Has Been Dreamed, that you must seek knowledge, then you indeed prove that you are of the Ancient

Ones—forever did they so." He pulled fussily at his scarf and then looked to Gosel.

"If this one must venture forth, then let aid be given. There is that arising which will cloud the sky far darker than any storm we have known. Noble One," now he turned to Kadiya, "there was evil in the past, and those you know fought it. Evil arises again. Be careful in your seeking, step lightly on any trail, and be ever ready with your eyes and this thing of Power. Lately I, too, have dreamed. I think that something begins to shadow us so that we cannot detect our danger."

He arose and bowed his head to Kadiya. Feeling the force of personality in this dreamer, the girl inclined her head in turn.

So there was no more disinclination on the part of the Hassitti to help them. Jagun displayed satisfaction over that. They would once more face the fury of the storm and the trip down the Upper Mutar, daring again passage through the Thorny Hell. However difficult it would be to travel through the almost constant storms it would be better to go now than to wait for better weather, for the force of wind and flood would keep a-den many of the dangerous inhabitants along the way.

They would need a boat and supplies, the latter easier to assemble than the former. But at Kadiya's questioning, Gosel produced a strange, skiff-like transport which could be used over both slimy mud and the river water—or so Jagun pronounced, having inspected it carefully.

The Hassitti had had other visitors through the years—or rather at a much earlier time there had been unlucky explorers entrapped in the ancients' defenses. Those had been victims of the city but their gear had been harvested by the Hassitti to be puzzled over and then stored after their usual pattern of preservation.

Jagun admitted that the skiff-boat was unlike any he had seen but some features of it pleased and excited him. He was eager to try it out — or perhaps simply eager to leave the city entirely.

They gained food supplies easily enough. The mush the Hassitti favored could be fire dried. Fruit was pulped and put into sealed jars. And Tostlet supplied a number of packets, trying hard to make Kadiya aware of the value of each for both health and healing.

Outside the gate, the lowering clouds were dark on the morning they started. The skiff had been fitted with draw ropes which Kadiya and Jagun manned as a team. The Hassitti massed at the gate to see them out but the thick curtain of the rain soon hid all but the bulk of the ruins.

As all hunters, Jagun had an inborn and well-fostered sense of direction. He moved confidently forward, though burdened as they were, their speed was hardly more than a walk.

Kadiya had replaced some of her clothing which the rot of the swamps had ruined, using woven stuff from the collections of garments the Hassitti hoarded. She discovered to her satisfaction that in the most part her choice had been good and several of the materials she had chosen were actually waterproof.

They had some way to go before they could reach the Mutar. Rainy season though it was, Jagun was continually alert. Kadiya watched also for those perils which were rooted, as well as the ones which crawled and leaped through the slime path they needed to take.

She was as ready with a short spear she had found in the treasure chambers as was Jagun with his blow pipe when they were warned by a sudden sickly odor. The thing which wriggled out of the mud just before them was scaled, bearing twisted horns on a head which seemed too large and heavy for its many legged body.

Kadiya feinted, drawing the creature to the left, giving Jagun a good shot at one of its bulging eyes. They had played this game before, though the prey was new to the girl.

With a dart protruding from its eye, the thing twisted and yellowish ooze dribbled from its half open mouth. Kadiya struck the second blow straight into that mouth, giving her spear a twist inward. The thing jerked its head back, snatching the spear out of her hold, but it no longer snapped at them. Its many legged coils beat into the slime and it churned up mud to hide its dying body.

When it had subsided to only quivering, Kadiya and Jagun cautiously approached to free their weapons. But he also drew his belt knife to strike at the root of the nearest fang, prying and working loose from the jaw first one and then another of the fore teeth of the thing. Wrapping these in a large leaf, he stored them in his pack. Kadiya guessed they would become formidable heads for water spears.

Other inhabitants of the mud gathered to feed on the dead monster but these they had no trouble in avoiding as they left the patch of writhing wet ground behind them.

They made camp that night on a scrap of higher ground where a mat of reed could be trampled to form a flooring for a shelter, the roof of which was the skiff. There could be no fire in this muck of mud and wet. For all her fatigue of body Kadiya was unable to settle into the nest of beaten reeds overlaid with a travel mat.

"Jagun—" She knew that the hunter had not gone to rest either for she heard the faint crackle of the reeds which betrayed restless movement. The rain had paused for a while, a respite not to be counted on. "How came your people to set up this far village of yours? You have said it is an outpost of Nyssomu land. Was it because of this long-ago flood you spoke of?"

"Why we came north, King's Daughter? Well, that is a tale worn thin by many seasons. It is said that our clan was always caught by a desire to see beyond. More of us are hunters than is common in other villages. We have a custom of far travel. It was that which brought me first to your father's court. There I chose to stay because I was curious about your people and what led them to do this and that which were not of our customs. I became a hunter for the court as you know—"

"Yes!" How well she could remember other days, and the time she had first seen Jagun. He had with him two inton kittings to whom he had taught simple tricks—simple and yet enough to amaze all who watched him exhibit their learning, for intons were shy and very seldom seen.

"There were Issa and Itta," she named them out of memory. "Then you guided the traders into the Dark Ways and they brought back many ral shells and the skins of voor."

"Which triple fingers count of my clan mates could as easily have done," he replied. "But there was also this. The Speaker of my House, as I said, is interested in strange knowledge. To her I sent much I had learned in the Citadel and during my wanderings. For this we were given clan credit so that those of my close kin stand well at the Great Speakings.

"This I did gladly for to me also there is a need to learn what many have forgotten or never have known. Now I have even more to add to the records." Kadiya detected the satisfaction in his voice.

"These Hassitti—their dreamers—speak of great evil." She mused.

"Farseer, the swamp is a ruin-broken land and it was formed so by ill design. That evil walks in it is as natural as the formation of seeds on a whittle vine. We have had our taste of what evil can do; we know that trouble may rise again —"

"Those of Labornok?"

"There is a Queen now of your land and that land and she shared your own birthing, Farseer. Also she was one who helped to wield the great talisman."

"And Orogastus is dead. Also Voltrik," Kadiya said slowly. "Haramis is Guardian — but she has gone afar. Binah chose to dwell in Noth, which was part of the mire lands, but my sister has gone to the mountains. And it is in the mountains that danger lies. . . . Jagun, in all your wandering have you ever looked upon the western mountains? Who or what live there?"

"Farseer, your wondering is like mine. No, I have never been that far into Uisgu land, which laps the mountain bases. Nor has any hunter of my clan whose records I have seen. Now, seek sleep, King's Daughter, the first watch will be mine."

Reluctantly Kadiya settled herself, but she was thinking of Haramis and that half cloaked sight of her sister which the Hassitti dreamer had shown her. Haramis had spoken of the Vispi, rulers of the snow and ice of the heights and for the most part invisible to any venturing there. Did Haramis have one of those to be her companion and support even as Kadiya had Jagun, or was she alone? Kadiya shivered. To be alone . . . that she could not have wished for Haramis. From childhood she herself had sought swamp ways. In the stricter confines of the court she had always been impatient that she was not in some fashion what she was meant to be. The Oddlings were her friends far more than the courtiers. Now a small spark of thought stirred. Would she ever find the mires lonely because she was not of their breeding? It was a question which had never troubled her before.

The rain had begun again; its steady drum against the skiff over their heads was loud. Stirring restlessly on her swamp scented bed Kadiya tried to push away thought. At last the blankness of deep sleep came.

When Jagun awakened her she sat, the sword balanced across her knees, staring into thickness of falling water. There could be no detection by eye in this dark, nor even by ear, with the constant sound of the rain. Awkwardly she loosed that other sense she had learned to use, mind searching for signs of life about them.

There were the flickers of small things, not intimidated as the larger populations were by the rain and mud traps. All Kadiya could gather from those fleeting touches were sensations of hunger and the need to fill protesting bellies; the completely centered mind of a predator hot on the trail. Otherwise the world about might have been devoid of life.

The girl became aware slowly of something else. The trillium amulet she had worn since birth was warm. When she drew it out from under her waterlogged jerkin, she saw a small gleam in its heart, a circling of pallid light around the opened flowerlet caught there. On impulse she raised it, touching it to her forehead just below the banding of her braids.

Certainly there was heat there. Something else too: a pulsing. That trapped inner flower might be breathing as would an animal. There had been life in her talisman before. It had served as a true guide when she had sought Binah. If she only knew more about what aid it might give! Haramis was the one with Power—she had fashioned the talismans using all they had won into such a potent weapon. Kadiya ran her hand along the pointless blade of her sword, careful not to finger the three eyes. This was her Power and she had killed with it. Must she do so again?

It was still a cloudy, twilight dark when they started in the morning. Jagun tested the footing ahead with the butt of his spear, striving to mark those treacherous pockets of mud which could engulf the unwary, and it was necessary to make many detours. This day they slogged doggedly ahead, not troubled by any peril save what the countryside itself might offer. In Kadiya's amulet the light continued to glow, a beacon against the gloom of day and thought.

When at last that journey to the river was finished, with near four days of hard travel behind them, Kadiya drew a deep breath of relief as she followed Jagun's orders helping to launch the skiff.

The current ran swift from the storm. Jagun had shipped a long steering oar and kept strict watch. Having no need to paddle, Kadiya crouched near the bow, widening her mind sense as far as she could. Life—there was enough of that— but she picked up no trace of anything really threatening.

They had put ten days' travel from the city behind them when they came to that lake which surrounded the long pier which supported the houses of Jagun's clan. The waters of the lake were much higher than Kadiya had seen on her first visit there. Much had changed with her and with the outer world since that day when she had dared to break the custom. As a fugitive with a price that cried aloud for her capture, she had sought out the Nyssomu in their own place, come to appeal for help against a common enemy. Yet, save for the water now washing higher against those platforms, all appeared as it had then.

As before, their arrival was announced by hidden sentinels.

The whistle of greeting seemed still to echo as the craft in which Kadiya rode bumped the pile-supported walk of the center longhouse.

Again four of the Nyssomu women waited, seeming insensible of the rain which washed the painted patterns from their cheeks and slicked their robes against their bodies. Two of those women Kadiya recognized. What would be their greeting now?

Jagun bowed his head. "Greetings, First of the House. Safe may all be in the sight of Those Whom We Do Not Name."

The Nyssomu woman eyed them for what seemed to the weary Kadiya to be an inordinately long moment before she made the formal answer:

"This roof be over you, hunter, and you, King's Daughter, who comes to us again."

Kadiya replied first with the gesture of respect she had learned long ago in Trevista when she had first taken to swamp running.

"I, Kadiya, wish all within well." She fitted her muddy palm into that which the woman held out to her.

The Nyssomu smiled. "Well be with you at your coming, King's Daughter. We have heard of what you and yours wrought afar, bringing down a great evil. We were battle kin there and so shall we be peace kin here." Then her smile vanished and she stared up into the girl's eyes as if she could read there some message.

"There is trouble in your heart. This kinhold welcomes you, who have chosen to come to us. All guest rights be yours."

The women who stood at each door in the long hall bowed as the First of the House led Kadiya to the room she so well remembered. Its luxury, though strange, was much cherished by one just out of the mud and floods.

Kadiya bathed, remembering that other time when what these friends had offered had in a small way eased her sore heart even as their lotions and oils had eased her body. She had fled blood and fire and such monstrous cruelty she would not have thought possible. Her world had ended in a single day and night and there had been nothing to hold to except her will and the need for vengeance.

The soft fistful of soap, which she dug out of a shell set conveniently near, stung her scalp where the hair had been torn but that was only a small discomfort. She relaxed in the water and allowed all the peace and comfort which was Nyssomu-born to flow into her again.

She swathed herself in one of the fringed robes they had ready and combed out her wet hair with a fishbone comb. The scent of the bath petals clung to her still damp skin and she was grateful for this small escape from the swamp smell.

The six clan heads who formed the Council of the First gathered as they had upon Kadiya's first nervous appearance before them. She settled herself on a cushioned stool to face them. A younger woman brought the hosting cup and each drank in turn, Kadiya very careful to drop to the floor the customary libation.

"King's Daughter, I have seen you bear trouble with you as a burden. But there has come to us no tale of armies astir — not since the return of those of us who were a part of the victory when that dark overmountain king and his evil mage strove to grind us underfoot. You wear that" — she pointed to the amulet on Kadiya's breast — "and carry that" — and now the finger indicated the sword the girl had laid down at her feet. "Both live. Thus, we are not yet done with trouble, after all. What new king arises to ravage our land?"

Kadiya hesitated and then decided that the story would best serve in its entirety.

"No king crosses our borders, Speaker. My sister Anigel wears the double crown of the two lands now and rules in outward peace. However, there is a warning that evil has not yet done with us — or else there is a new force of the Dark come to test our strength, one spreading from the mountains."

So she began the story of what had happened since she had left the Citadel driven by that inner pressure to travel to the garden of the sword.

9

WHEN KADIYA SPOKE OF THE Hassitti there was a stir among her listeners. She who governed the household interrupted:

"King's Daughter, you speak of legends."

"Legends who live," Kadiya returned firmly. "Ones who consider themselves Guardians of all left by the Vanished Ones."

Now there was a faint murmur among the Nyssomu women. One, Kadiya thought, not of denial but of wonder.

She plunged swiftly on to the adventure of Jagun in the maze of light and saw the First shake her head.

"Traps! So would they serve us, who were hands and feet in far places for the Vanished Ones! That is not to be accepted!"

Kadiya paused, then continued. "Lady of the House, I believe the little ones were not the setters of such traps. Rather those were in place ever since the Vanished Ones withdrew. It is the Hassitti claim that they are the Guardians and protectors of all which High Ones left behind. Indeed they seemed to have done their best to be so." She described the many rooms with the stacked treasures within. Thus she came to the claims of the dreamers and again she was interrupted.

"These claim to catch dreams! And dreams that you say are dark warnings. Danger from the mountains. But did we not just fight a war with some who came over mountains? Surely they have not so risen again?"

"Other mountains — not to the north, but the west," Kadiya answered. "These dreamers of theirs are carefully listened to and believed."

"And you seek knowledge of these mountains from us, King's Daughter? Why? Our folk have no dealing with the heights beyond the mire lands."

"I have come because of this." Kadiya opened the pouch of protective silis skin which she had retrieved from among her belongings before she began her tale. Now she unrolled the strip of patterned weaving which the orb of the talisman had revealed.

For a moment it seemed as if the First had no wish to touch it. Then, as if forcing herself to some duty she disliked, the Oddling accepted the strip to spread it wide across her knee. One of the others seated near her arose and moved quickly to view it over the First's shoulder.

Those lines which the orb had drawn into distinct view had not faded into obscurity and could be easily seen. The First ran a fingertip along them, as if touching the substance would make the message they bore even clearer.

· · · ———————————————————————————————— · · ·

Then she looked up as if to consult eye to eye with that other who had joined her in inspecting the find.

"First," it was that other who spoke, "the weave pattern runs true. This is Nyssomu."

"But," the First objected, "surely Old, Old. That which it speaks of is far seasons behind us. In my mother's mother's day it was already near forgot. Weaver, do we have a match for this record?"

Slowly the other nodded. "Yes, there are three patterns like unto it. Two of which it was needful to reweave during the last season of dry because they were so old they were like to vanish.

"There was such a message — that evil abode to the west but that it was fast held there and such safeguards set upon it that the mires need not stand to arms against it. The Vanished Ones set those bars. This one" — she looked to Kadiya — "speaks of one of their other safeguards being still a mighty trap. They had Power such as we cannot equal.

"The Great Old One, Binah, had Power. You have touched that Power, King's Daughter — or some part of it — for yourself. One of your heart's blood, your sister, holds Binah's place. Still none can equal what the Vanished Ones used and knew. We do not reach for such Power. It is not in us to call upon that which is not born within our kind. In all the long seasons since the Vanished Ones went from us, we have only studied to hold our own people safe as we might. We have lived by the old Oaths, and this place from which you have just come has been Oath-closed to us. Perhaps that was because among us there might be born some so ill-minded and reckless as to wish to reach for what was not theirs.

"If evil stirs" — she had moved a little before the First, and there was a sternness about her—"perhaps it wakes because there has been overmuch of the old Power summoned during the moons just past. This sorcerer Orogastus who dabbled in things which were forbidden, using the very fires of the air for his weapons—how do we know that he did not overset some balance of old, loosing what was thought to be forever laid?"

The First raised her hand and her companion was silent.

"King's Daughter, you have given us much to think on." She smoothed the strip of weaving with the palm of her hand. "We have our records, kept as well and securely as we can hold them. Because of this—this dreamer's warning—because of that which you hold, unable to return to its source"—she pointed to the sword—"we must believe that there is indeed a stirring. You are given host-right here and kin-aid in what must be done. Though we are a people who do not raise spear or send dart easily, yet neither do we close our eyes and ears against warnings."

"First, I give to you thanks. For some things it takes many hands. What you have offered is good to hear," Kadiya replied.

The women had risen and now they uniformly moved hands and head in a formal gesture. Led by the First they filed out of the chamber. Then there scurried in two young Oddlings who motioned for Kadiya to come with them. They ushered her into what she thought to be a hosting chamber for a visitor not of the kin.

There food awaited her and she ate heartily, savoring the tastes of dishes which she had learned from her early childhood ventures into the mire with Jagun to enjoy. This was far different from the soft mushes and pulpy fruits the Hassitti had given her and she relished the crisp crunch of tender laka-reed roots.

When the young maid came to take away the tray, she indicated the piled reeds of the mat bed and raised invitingly

. . . —————————————————————————— . . .

one end of a well-woven grass blanket into which had been entwined the fragrant dried stems of flowers supposed to give good rest.

Kadiya settled down on the mats and was about to draw the blanket up about her shoulders when there came a soft call from the other side of the door curtain. When Kadiya answered it was not the maid returning, rather the older Oddling whom the First had addressed as Weaver and who had taken part in Kadiya's interrogation.

The Nyssomu held both hands well away from her body as she carried an artifact. A stiff reed had been bent and worked into an oval. Within that was a weaving of an irregular, open pattern of string fiber—like a crooked web. From one side of the oval there dangled two reed cords which had been colored, one green, one blue. These were not equal in length, but the free end of each was bound about a tuft of feathers—these of a metallic brilliance even in the subdued light of the room.

"Have you seen this, King's Daughter?"

"No, Weaver. What is this thing, one of Power?"

"Indeed of Power. This is a dream web, a catcher set to protect against evil visions in sleep. Since you have been told such are about, we shall be wise and set these aloft."

Holding the dream web in one hand the Weaver reached so far overhead that she needed to stand on her toes to touch what she sought. She pulled down a near invisible line to which she hooked her "protection" so it hung free and twirled about, the feathered strings fluttering.

The Weaver eyed it critically, gave a small tug to one of the dangling lines which set it spinning again. Then she nodded briskly as one who finishes a good job.

"Sleep well, King's Daughter. You need not feel the evil touch of black dreams now."

Before Kadiya's thanks were half uttered the door curtain dropped behind her. That lamp which had been left on a stool top flickered low and Kadiya lay back under the fragrant covering. There was a twitch of shadow against shadow in the dim light of the room. The dream trap was still in slight motion. She wondered what the Hassitti dreamer would have to say about this. It would seem that the Nyssomu were not as willing to open themselves to meaningful dreams as were the dwellers in the city.

Whether it was the fatigue which settled so heavily upon her that pushed her into the depths of truly dreamless sleep, or whether the protection worked, Kadiya did not know. She slid into a place of warm and welcome darkness and was content.

Where the library Kadiya had explored in the city had been a labyrinth of seemingly unsorted materials, the one she visited with the Weaver in Jagun's village house was a model of neatness and a place of activity. The Nyssomu woman who commanded that activity made no move toward explaining much to her visitor and Kadiya quickly decided that the record weaving was one of those guild-like mysteries jealously preserved by those engaged in them.

The looms were small and table mounted, much like those she had seen used in Trevista for the production of scarves and ribbons. There were three here, two of which were in use. The balls of spun reed and grass fiber dyed a number of colors were in large spools to hand. Instead of shuttles the Weavers used long threaded needles to set lines which followed no pattern Kadiya's eyes could detect.

By the third loom lay the strip she had brought and next to it a larger spool on which a section of material nearly as wide as the ancient strip had been wound.

As the two younger Oddling women kept on with their work the Weaver herself brought Kadiya to that middle loom and began to unwind, with infinite care, the enspooled ribbon. A puff of motes arose as the coils reluctantly yielded to her gentle pull and Kadiya believed that this was a record which had been in existence for some time.

Though the shutters had been tight closed against the intermittent beating of the rain, there was enough light from lamps which swung from the beams overhead for Kadiya to see the lines of different colors twine and separate, become circles or patches at intervals.

The Weaver unwound but a portion of the length. Then she reached for the piece from the city and held it in one hand next to the weaving she had loosed in the other.

"This is the work of Jassoa who was Weaver a hundred seasons ago. It is excellent work which has held well against all aging. Here there is an account of the storms which overflowed our home site then. Also there is something else . . . that there came a rumor from the Uisgu that they feared a certain evil which dwelt upon their borders because there had been a shaking of the mountains. Wind and rain had brought about a slippage of ground from the heights—"

"Would that be considered evil drawn by intent?" Kadiya interrupted and then added swiftly, "Your pardon, Weaver, I am too quick for proper manners."

The Weaver, whom she had thought far more dour than the First at their earlier meeting, smiled a fraction.

"King's Daughter, an eagerness to learn cannot be bound

always by the proper ways. No, to your question. A slippage which was storm-born would not be an attack by evil. However, if that spillage opened a closed path or door it might well be counted so."

"A path or door," Kadiya repeated, "in the mountains to the north range — the Vispi? My sister has dealt with those and to good purpose. Do they also range beyond the Uisgu?"

"I do not know," the Weaver returned. "The Uisgu in all the dealings they have had with us have never spoken of such peoples. However," she had turned her attention back once more to the strip of weaving, "after this there came no further warnings of trouble."

"Are there any other records of what the Uisgu feared?"

"The Uisgu may have their own records. When they share with us it is only to warn of a danger all the mires may face. They have sent only this." She was rewinding the spool of woven records.

"And those mountains beyond the Uisgu, is there much known of them?" persisted Kadiya. She was beginning to realize more and more how very little she knew of the swamp world — she who had valued herself so highly because of her contacts with Jagun and what seemed now her very limited journeying here and there. Her wartime ventures had taken her far beyond anything she had known or guessed existed, and now it seemed even that had been very little with which to push back the boundaries of ignorance.

"We record what we know of the mires, of the lives of our peoples," the Weaver answered her. "What are the mountains to us? The Uisgu are our kin but we meet with them only for trade or in times of great peril."

She had taken up the rewound spool to replace it with others which stood in ordered rows on the shelves arrayed on

three sides of the room, but at that moment there resounded
through the air—

—Or did it come by ear? Kadiya's hands had moved involuntarily to shut off that wailing. Though she so stoppered
her ears the volume of the cry was in no way reduced. It was
a mind cry then, so harsh and high-carrying it was like a blow
to the head, leaving her wavering dizzily.

The Oddlings in the room had made the same ear stopping
gesture and now their faces twisted in pain. This could not be
any freak of the storm without.

Kadiya straightened as the sound died away. She had hand
to sword and was at the doorway, the Weaver hardly a pace
behind.

"Trouble comes," she heard the Oddling woman mutter.

There was already a crowd in the hall without, more and
more feeding into it from every family room and pressing onto
the wide platform beyond, where their boats were tied. All of
them, Kadiya noted, had taken up arms. There was a forest of
spears, blow pipes ready to hand among male and female alike.
Only the younglings were herded to the back, sent once more
into cover by impatient slaps from their Elders.

Nor was this longhouse the only one so aroused. Kadiya
could see the same massing of inhabitants before all the others
which formed the village. Some of the defenders were dropping off into their light skiffs, riding the turbulent waters of
the lake toward the shore.

She saw Jagun joining one of the groups waiting to dis-
embark and pushed her way to his side.

"What is it?" she demanded, raising her voice to be heard
above the hooting and calling of the others, all speaking the
mire language now.

He did not even turn his head, rather watched for a chance

to take his turn in one of the craft. So she caught him by the arm for fear he would disappear before she could get information.

"One comes. There is a death message!" He freed himself with a sharp jerk.

Kadiya knew better than to try to follow him into the boat he had chosen. She was too heavy of body, too lacking in training with Nyssomu weapons to be of aid at present.

The First and her Council of women were now well to the fore of the open space, none of them paying any attention to the rain which was once more blowing in heavy gusts. In each of the craft already launched, at least one of the boaters was hastily bailing.

To Kadiya's surprise the boats setting out from all the houses scattered. A number headed for the river opening, but others made for the shores all the way around the lake. And when the first of those reached the mud banks they slid their craft up onto the land and wormed themselves away into the brush. Save for the boats still in sight, the shore in a few moments was bare of life.

Kadiya was well aware of the Oddling ability to make of their waterlogged country a defense. There were enough fighters loosed now in that wilderness of the mire to ensure that any force striving to come to the lake heart of the holding would not find that advance an easy one.

Skritek? Kadiya could not think of any other possible enemy. If some small band of Voltrik's men was lost still in this wilderness those survivors would not be in any condition to offer any attack. But Skritek were more noted for their ambushes, slyly worming their way into occupied territory to cut off a small body of Oddlings. She had never heard of any of the "Drowners" attacking a village—except under the push of

Voltrik's men during the dire weeks just past. This was not their way of fighting.

The girl moved closer to the First and her Councilors. There had come no other sound to outscream the storm. The sheets of water sweeping across the lake were like curtains which veiled the shores at intervals. And those Kadiya mistrusted. It could well be that the Skritek had learned new tactics from the invaders and some unusual leader among them was now putting those to the test.

The flotilla of boats which had made for the end of the lake could hardly be seen under these conditions. There were always sentries on duty, not only near the lake but along the stream beyond, as well as a gateway of brush which was normally pulled across that stream as a concealing curtain.

She was straining to see more of those boats, even her vaunted farsight troubled by this need, when there came another of the sounds. This was not so shaking — or perhaps having endured it once she was better able to stand up to it now.

There was movement among the women near her. One of them reached the side of the First and handed to her a curled shell large enough to be used as a horn. Putting it to her wide mouth the First gave breath to a series of hoots, loud as any bugle call but not unlike some of the Nyssomu speech.

Another mental cry and the First made answer. From the far end of the lake two of the house craft swung out into better view, between them a third in which, as they came closer, Kadiya could distinguish two huddled figures.

As soon as she was able to sight the bedraggled and sodden cloaks which weighed them down she knew them for Uisgu. And the very fact that they had come here meant that no small trouble brought them.

Though there was never any dispute between the two Odddling races, neither was there much intercourse. The Uisgu were far more of the wild than the Nyssomu, shy of mingling with those not of their race or caste. Before the war she had seen only a few of them in Trevista, for no matter how far in the mire lands they might range they did not approach any holdings of the humans, using the Nyssomu as their go-betweens.

That these two came here now was a matter for surprise. As the escorted skiff drew in to the house where Kadiya was, she was even more astounded at the nature of the party. The one in the bow of the tiny boat flung back her cloak and raised her head. As all her race she was furred except on the face and that fur had been sleeked so tightly to her body that she looked as if she had been dipped in some dark dye.

The face paint, which was also a matter of custom for those of her people, had been almost washed away, leaving only some faint smears here and there. Her companion was a male — quite young, Kadiya thought — well muscled and from the way he handled the oar of the boat, one who had been travel trained.

The escort boats drew one to each side. Jagun commanded one, Kadiya noted as they nosed in to the platform. The Uisgu boat did not move to tie up, almost as if those aboard were not sure of their welcome.

Once more it was the First who gave voice. Not through the agency of the horn this time, but calling out clear enough to be heard above the beat of the rain, though Kadiya could not understand the words she uttered.

Now the Uisgu craft did come in. The male threw a rope which the nearest Nyssomu caught. The boat was hauled carefully in so that the Uisgu woman was able to reach the platform, where one of the waiting clansmen was quick to give her a hand.

She did not stand straight, rather bent a little forward, and there was swiftly passed up to her by her companion a staff which she grasped to steady herself.

One of the boatmen who had escorted her made a swift report and again the First sounded her horn. Then she held out a hand to the Uisgu as if they were clan sisters and led her into the shelter of the house. Her Councilors, Kadiya with them, followed quickly after.

The Uisgu boy shouldered a journey pack of some size and fell into step with Kadiya, glancing at her in wide-eyed surprise. One hand raised and he made a queer gesture Kadiya had seen before. Just so had the Hassitti claws moved when they met. Hassitti, Uisgu—what had those two in common? Another of those endless questions to plague her.

 THIS TIME IT WAS THE UISGU woman who was established on the stool of the questioned visitor while Kadiya slipped in to stand behind one of the benches on which her interrogators were seated. Though she had been offered rest and refreshment, the Uisgu had refused it impatiently and asked for audience with the First at once.

Not only that, but she had insisted that the Firsts of the other five clan houses which made up the village be summoned, too, and it was only while waiting for their arrival that she accepted food and drink.

The youth who was her companion also had slipped into the Council chamber and now squatted a little behind Kadiya, his pack before him, hands resting on it as if the contents were so precious that he must take extra precautions to see it safe.

Perhaps to make sure all would understand, the Uisgu woman used mind speech.

"This one is Salin of the House of Safor of the Clan of Segin. I am one who sees — " She added to her mind speech a hand gesture which was echoed at once by the First of this house.

"There has come such a darkness that has not been seen in hundreds of seasons. This thing kills in a way of great horror. For it we have no name or memory. Thus I come hither, that I may ask your Weavers of past thoughts to seek the nature of this creeping terror. Learning what it may be, perhaps my people can take battle measures against it."

"This thing of which you speak, of what manner is it?"

"Of this kind." Without turning her head the Uisgu snapped her fingers. The youth quickly dug into the pack bringing out a shallow basin of that same blue-green metal which Kadiya had seen the Hassitti use.

Into the shallow depths of this he poured a measure of clear liquid from a fish skin bag and then, on his hands and knees, advanced to place the basin at the feet of the Uisgu where she fronted the First.

The latter moved forward on her bench, leaning so that she could see into that container. The Uisgu closed her eyes. Her breathing became slow and deep and there was utter silence in the chamber. Kadiya realized what was in progress. There were foreseers she had seen in Trevista who had "read the water" for petitioners. Some proclaimed they could even see a little into the future by such means, others merely that they could show what was happening in another place at the same time.

Within the basin the water began to move as if stirred, forming a miniature whirlpool. As it swirled so, it darkened, no longer transparent.

Now the color of a peat-dark swamp pool, the water ceased to swirl. The Uisgu held her hand over the basin, well above the surface of that now-quiet pool, and her long fingers twirled and twisted. Her head was well back upon her hunched shoulders and her large eyes were closed.

Then her hands fell limply to her knees. There was movement again on the surface of the basin's contents — not a swirling this time but rather a seeming flicker of light on the dark surface.

Kadiya edged forward until she could see clearly what picture grew into life there. They were looking down, as if they were as winged as a quim, upon a section of open and solid land, such as were to be found in hillocks of the swamps. These were usually the foundation for ruins. But this was rutted by furrows, and there were signs of a harvest of pulin.

But the wholesome remains of that were being absorbed by a spread of yellowish-green growth shot through with lines of blood red. And the thing appeared to pulsate as if it crawled over the wholesome land like one of the giant slugs of the Golden Mire.

There was something disgusting, utterly alien in that thing. Kadiya swallowed, tasting the rise of her own bile. This had no place in any sane world meant for the abode of human or Oddling. But the worst was not that undulating carpet which lay poisoning the soil: it was the body which lay to one side, curled about itself as if striving to ease some last torture. The victim was plainly Uisgu, yet on the arms which were tightened about bent knees there showed patches of the same green-yellow as the thing on the ground.

The picture in the basin grew larger. They hung now directly above that body and Kadiya saw that those arms and legs so tightly clasped together did not hide the fact that into the chest of the victim had been driven a hunting blade.

Then the water containing the picture came to life, swirled vigorously and settled. They looked at another scene. This time swift running water lapped another island in the murk. There again was the foul yellow-green—this time in splotches, as if spilled out of some giant container. And those splotches grew wider even as they watched.

Another picture, in this a skiff was adrift. Beside it, belly up, floated one of the rimoriks with whom the Uisgu lived in companionship and who drew their boats at full speed when journeys were necessary. Across that bloated belly was a splotch of yellow-green, while in the skiff itself lay an Uisgu.

This was not a static scene. Even as they watched the Uisgu in the craft moved slowly, causing the skiff to dip dangerously. The passenger now displayed his left leg, which from ankle to hip was plastered with the now familiar stain. As they watched he brought out with very apparent difficulty a fish-cleaning, sharp-edged scraper. Then with a last burst of effort he brought it up to slash open his own throat.

The water swirled, the picture vanished; but all those who watched, Kadiya was certain, had seen something which really happened.

No new picture formed. Instead the Uisgu woman's eyes opened, and she changed the angle of her head so that she could squarely face the Nyssomu clan Firsts.

"So it is with us, wisewomen. This evil spreads across our land as if some monster strides, leaving foul death in every footprint as it passes. There is no hope for any life the yellow poison touches. We lost one whole clan because they strove to help a hunter who staggered home beset with the infection. Now any who fall prey to it take their own lives that they may not carry it to others.

"Weaver records are known to be many and cover hundreds

of seasons. Our own have no mention of such a thing nor how it can be fought, but it spreads and this land is threatened. I ask of you, what message can you give me concerning this?"

The Weaver had arisen and come to stand looking down into the now dormant bowl where the darkness was slowly ebbing.

"This is not of my knowledge and I have been Guardian of the storage looms for twice sixty seasons, Sister in Power. Yet you are right, many records are stored here and to seek through them can be done."

Kadiya, with some of her old impetuosity, came closer.

"Farseer," she asked the Uisgu, "from what direction does this foul evil come?"

There was a trace of frown on the Uisgu's face. Her eyes swept Kadiya from head to foot and back again. There had never been ties between her people and the Ruwendians of the Citadel. Could there also be lack of trust?

On impulse Kadiya held forward the sword so that its bulbous-eyed pommel could be clearly seen. In doing so she swung it over the basin. And—

One of those slitted eyes opened—that of the Oddling. It appeared to stare straight at the Uisgu wisewoman.

Her small body tensed. One of her hands rose a trifle from her knee. Then she stared at Kadiya. "Holder of Power"—she made that Hassitti-like gesture even as had the youth—"so once more you walk the land. What brings you in answer to this?" She pointed to the basin.

"I do not know. But tell me, wisewoman, does this spread from the western mountains, this trail of death?"

The Uisgu blinked. "Power bearer, it does."

"And toward where does it appear to head?"

"Toward the Skritek lands."

The First of Jagun's clan spoke. "Weaver, a search must be made."

However, Kadiya had something more to ask. "What lies in Skritek lands that would draw such an evil?"

The First's mouth twisted as if she would spit. "Who knows of the Skritek—they are a black blot of vileness in this world. Did not those enemies who came upon your own people, King's Daughter, seek to enlist them in their armies? Were they not people of that Sorcerer who ravaged the land? That some new evil Power would seek them out—that can well be expected."

Then she spoke to the wisewoman. "Sister in Power, your way has been long and you must be greatly wearied. Let you be at rest while the records are searched. Be sure what help we can give you shall receive. If this plague spreads, let your people come to us for shelter. As against Skritek so shall our spears and darts be united to face this."

The record room was ablaze with a number of lamps. Under the glow the table had been largely cleared and several stools had been brought in so that not only the Weaver and her two apprentices, but also the First and Kadiya were given space there. The Uisgu Salin and her escort had been fed and were now sleeping off the effects of their hard journey.

It was the Weaver who, with deft touch, unrolled strips of the records. Some she dismissed at once and gave to her assistants to be rewound, but three remained on the table. The fourth piece was that which Kadiya had brought from the city of the Vanished Ones.

The Weaver used a fingertip to trace out lines of blue-green, touching now and then on a spot of red. Kadiya fought down growing impatience. She thought of those other records stored hit or miss by the Hassitti. Would it now be necessary for her to return to the city and see if she could puzzle out more there? Her lack of knowledge was a frustrating barrier. She had no skill in reading those archaic symbols. Nor did she believe that any here could do any better. Haramis?

When Haramis had taken the Archimage's cloak about her shoulders, she had also assumed the Guardianship Binah had held so long. Therefore this plague in the swamplands would certainly be a concern for her.

Kadiya reached for the amulet of amber at her throat. Once it had been a key to communication with her sister. Could it so serve again?

There was silence in the room, save for the scratching of the Weaver's fingernail across the record strips. The girl cautiously edged back a little from the table, taking the amulet tightly in her grasp, closing her eyes, concentrating as best she could on a mental picture of her sister as she had seen her in that gloomy room.

"Haramis!" Her unvoiced call carried a note of command. "Haramis..."

It was as if a gauzy mist hid the one she would reach. She pushed toward it, only to feel as if she ran face-on into a barrier.

"Haramis?" There was nothing. A door might have been firmly closed between them. Yet she sensed this loss of communication was not of Haramis's doing. Did forces stir now which were greater than any her sister could command? Kadiya squeezed the amulet as if to wring out the answer she needed.

"Ah..." the Weaver's finger had paused at last. She turned to her nearer assistant.

"Bring the roll of Lysta, that of the fourth season!"

The Nyssomu girl arose and went to the far wall of the room. Her fingers swept along a shelf tight packed with rolls, one of which she brought to the table. The record had been sown into a transparent cylinder of fish skin and this the Weaver slit with care, using the same caution as she unrolled it inch by inch. Two of those watching her sneezed and Kadiya's nose prickled from a scent she could not identify.

"That is word from very long ago," the First commented. "Was there some hint of such an evil before?"

"Not of the plague, no." The Weaver spread her fingers wide to keep the tough roll flat as she leaned forward to peer at its surface.

What Kadiya could see of that surface did not resemble the other woven rolls about them. There were lines in the fabric, yes, but they were not regular, instead they spiraled horizontally.

"In the fourth season of Lysta's weavership there was a raid from Skritek territory. So serious was this invasion of our land that Uisgu and Nyssomu banded together to meet them. There was a clan march from this village which followed to here"— she tapped the roll — "well within Skritek holdings. They captured a Skritek Caller of Blood.

"In the guard was one of Power who could read the thought spears of the Caller. And this he learned: that within the heart of their foul land there is a place of blackness, like perhaps unto a door. Something in that time had issued forth from there ready to turn upon us. But the evil will was not strong enough to last—rather it dwindled and then vanished. It was said that the Noble Binah sent a mind message fierce enough to seal again that place which should never have been opened and blast into nothingness what had issued forth.

Kadiya could be quiet no longer. "And now this plague moves across the land, perhaps to this place known before?"

The Weaver glanced up at the girl. "It may be so."

"There was a plague then, also?" Kadiya persisted.

"There is no record of such."

The girl drew the sword and held it above the series of lines on the roll. A finger of light touched the weaving. It was the Vanished One's eye which had answered this time.

"Saa—" The Weaver jerked back from the spot of light and there were answering hisses from the others.

The light was gone, the eye near-closed again. Kadiya lifted the sword.

"I have no Power such as the Archimage," she said. "I would speak with my sister. The greater learning is hers and perhaps she can answer much. But I cannot reach her with my untrained mind. If you have such among you perhaps you can aid in this."

"We have only one under this roof—the one who has come to us for aid, Salin of the Uisgu." The First arose. "When she is rested let her try—have we not already witnessed her Powers? Weaver, let that be copied." She indicated the roll on the table. "For there may well be need for a guide."

It would seem that the records of the village had yielded all they would. Which was precious little, Kadiya thought. That the Uisgu wisewoman had Power, she had proved. However, if her Power had already been used up in seeking, then perhaps there was little she could do.

Kadiya returned to the quarters which had been assigned her. Once more she set about overhauling her trail pack. If she was to convey to Haramis the best information she could, she must see for herself this plague and where it led.

Cradling the sword in her hands, she attempted to use it as

she had the amulet. But there was no result at all — not even that vision of a swirling mist.

Weary measures of waiting passed before they gathered once more: Salin with her bowl before her, the others grouped in the shadows where only two lamps burned.

The Uisgu woman looked even more frail and trail-worn. But her hands were sure as she prepared the bowl. When the liquid within grew dark she spoke to Kadiya without raising her own eyes from that basin pool.

"One of Power, think upon she whom you would call."

Kadiya stared also into the opaque liquid.

"Haramis!"

Once more she called, fiercely, with all the strength she could raise, putting one hand to the amulet and one to the sword as she did so.

There was a haze gathering in the basin, a curling of mist. It wreathed around and around but it did not clear to show them any picture.

"Haramis!" Kadiya strove to reach out. Once more she struck against a wall which was not visible, with force enough to feel bruised as if her flesh had striven to break through stone.

Salin moved her hand out over the basin, her fingers crooked as if to scratch away that curtain. But to no purpose, the mist remained.

"There is something against us," she said slowly, as if she resented each word. "Power grows, and it is not of the light."

Kadiya let the amulet fall back against her breast but she did not loose her hold on the sword.

"Wisewoman, if you cannot reach my sister, can you see again the plague? Does it stretch still in the same direction?"

Salin brought her hands together in a clap over the basin. The mist was gone but the liquid therein had not cleared.

Instead it appeared to curdle and darken with shadows which then took on sharper form. Once more they looked upon a section of swampland where splotches of the yellow glistened like deadly slime. However, there was also something else: a black blot in the midst of that irregular patch of corruption. But that did not sharpen to allow them to see its nature.

Only for a space of a few breaths did it hold, then came a spurt of flame and the picture was gone. Salin drew back with a cry.

"Power . . . and Power which knows we spy upon it!"

11

"THAT PLACE I KNOW." ONE OF the First's Council broke the silence. "It is the Isle of the Sal Tower."

All of the women stirred. Once more that hissing "sssaaa" broke from the First.

She looked to the Weaver. "Unfold the waygoing for us now."

Once more a section of the table was cleared and now a square wide enough to have to be rolled at the edges in order to fit into the space was brought forward. Kadiya could see lines which wavered and as she blinked there was a flash of recognition. She was looking upon a map—the curve of the Mutar was plain.

The First smoothed it flat with her hand. "Summon Jagun," she ordered. "This matter is for a far seeker."

That a male of the clan be admitted to such a conference was plainly out of custom. There was a murmur of dissent from some of the women but the First looked to one of the lesser of the Council and the woman went reluctantly.

Salin had moved forward to stare down at the map. Now her hand came forward and she traced a line from one of the rolled edges to another point.

"Already it has spread so far!"

Though there was a map set upon the wall of the Great Hall at the Citadel Kadiya had seldom noted it. Fading lines of paint had so little meaning in her mind when compared to the living lands of the mires. Of that map now she could remember very little, especially in the western holdings of the Uisgu.

Jagun returned with the messenger, gave respectful greeting to the First.

"Hunter," she came to the point at once, "you have been to Sal Tower." It was a statement more than a question.

"Once. I met with Sinu of the Val Clan. He was well versed in that country since it was largely contained within his own. And the Sal Tower possessed certain legends which led me to wish to see it."

Now the First spoke to Salin. "Wisewoman, point out to us which way this plague has spread from its first appearance."

The older Oddling bent closer to the map and her finger traced a path from the west which led in what seemed almost a straight line to the point marking the tower. "So," she said.

Jagun had watched her intently, then as her hand drew back he put out his own finger.

"It would seem that the line runs so, but the Sal Tower may not be the end. If it continues in that direction it will cut deeply into Skritek country."

"Before it spreads farther," Kadiya said, "we should know more. Since your Power, wisewoman, cannot make it plain to us what we face, then we must view it for ourselves. One cannot fight any foe without knowing the nature of the enemy and what weapons it holds. This Sal Tower is a place toward which we can travel."

She refused to allow the memories of what Salin had shown them to come to the fore of her mind. Instead she held to another image—that of the sword in full strength when it had blasted forth with destructive power. It could be that if she confronted this invader, whatever or whoever it might be, she could so put an end to it.

The First rubbed a finger along the edge of the map roll.

"Powers, King's Daughter, can often not be measured until it is too late. This we know—that we do not know enough. You have some protection which is yours alone. If it is your choice that this be done, then let it be so."

Kadiya took firm grip on the sword. Well, she had offered; could she be sorry that her offer had been accepted? It was indeed far better, as she saw it, to track this creeping death to its source rather than to sit about a basin and watch it kill, knowing no more about it than that it could slay.

She turned to Jagun. "Shield mate, will you march?"

"Farseer, this venture is ours."

But Kadiya had already considered another problem. "Ours, only." She looked to the First. "Any large force could be easily discovered. With Jagun to pick the trail and but two of us, there is better chance to know without being known."

"We, also, One of Power." Salin raised her head to stare over the map at Kadiya. "This venture is truly mine, and I am sworn to it."

Kadiya would have protested instantly but somehow she could not speak. There was a confidence in this wisewoman which was like that of the First. She was one who was not used to having any of her wishes countered.

·   ·   ·

At least the monsoon had nearly exhausted itself. When they took to boat again—this time in a more substantial craft than that which had brought Salin and her grandson—there was not the heavy lash of rain to make their trip a time of constant vigilance and bailing. Their supplies were the best which the village could provide. Also, with the weather less against them they could better live off the land—or rather the water, for Salin's grandson Smail proved to be a master fisherman. Kadiya, who had long since learned the need for adapting to the trail, ate her shredded portions raw without protest.

Each night as they found campsites on some scrap of ground above water level, Salin would consult her scrying bowl. However, the clear results she had gained in the village no longer held. Shadows would appear on the surface but none of them sharpened into actual pictures. Twice she tried with Kadiya to reach Haramis, only to encounter that ever defeating mist.

Jagun guided them at last to a section of ground which was more than an islet. Here there was a trace of a ruin—a few blocks still piled one upon the other. He was able to spear a pelrik newly issued from its storm hibernation. By one of the stones Smail found some moss which had partially dried, enough so that its oily stems and minute leaves gave off a fraction of heat to at least sear their portions of the kill.

"From here," the hunter announced, "we must go on foot. There is an ancient way beneath the mud and growth which will give us a road . . . though we must sound the way."

In the morning's light, which was no longer as storm-sodden gray, he and Smail drew the boat well ashore and anchored it firmly, piling brush around it. Kadiya divided their supplies into three packs, for Salin needed her full strength, the girl judged, to use her staff and keep her feet upon this broken land.

Wary of patches, they moved slowly. In some places the fury of the rains had washed away soil and plants and Kadiya could see the blocks of what indeed might have been an ancient road. She was thankful that they had as sturdy footing as they did, for they were able to make better time than she had believed possible.

They came out into an expanse where there was little in the way of growth and wide uncovered stretches of the stone way.

" 'Ware!" Jagun's mind-flashed warning brought Kadiya instantly alert and she held her spear at the ready. A dart blower had appeared in Smail's hand.

Then it reached her also—a thrust of mind pain so intense it nearly rocked her. She heard Salin whimper and the Uisgu woman fell to her knees both hands to her head.

Out of the brush which walled the far side of the clearing there wavered a creature painfully dragging itself forward. It seemed to be hardly more than a heaving mass of puffy yellow, with stick thin limbs, catching desperately at any small hold to draw it forward.

The wind was blowing across it toward them and Kadiya gagged at a thick, putrid stench. In her mind that insane, never ending shriek of pain became harder and harder to combat.

"No—do not let it come near!" Salin cried out and caught at Kadiya as the girl moved a step forward.

It was Smail who raised his blow pipe, took careful aim and sent forth a dart that sunk in over its head in the monstrous mass of body. The thing shuddered, scrabbled vainly for a hold on the stones and then suddenly reared up and fell backward.

To Kadiya's horror that movement revealed what it truly

was. Half of an Oddling head protruded from the forepart of the loathsome mass.

"The plague." Smail's young face showed fear. He made no move forward to retrieve his dart. Salin pulled again at Kadiya.

"Do not go near it, take another path! It has sown the blight even as it crawled."

Though she wanted nothing to do with the dead, Kadiya forced herself to remember that she must learn all she could about this thing of terror. Shifting her spear to her other hand she drew the sword and held it up, the eyes turned toward the miserable, tormented body.

Freeing herself from Salin's hold she took one step and then another. Through the overcast of gray day shot a bolt of fire. All three eyes were fully open. From them streamed what appeared a twisted thread of radiance to strike full upon the body.

There was a brilliant flash of bluish light harsh enough to blind Kadiya for an instant. Then followed an explosion of fetid air. What was left was only a smear on the half exposed pavement.

A hold grasped at Kadiya's legs, moved up to her waist. Salin had so drawn herself to her feet.

"Use the Power, King's Daughter—cleanse our land!"

Kadiya staggered a fraction as the weight of the frail Uisgu leaned on her. She still gripped the sword and held it outward but now the pommel was dipping toward the ground. There was a weight dragging down her whole arm and inside her a weakness as if the fury of that burst of flame had drawn most of her energy from her.

Jagun had edged forward, near to that smear upon the stone, but he paused still a good way from it. Then his head turned and he looked beyond to where the tortured Uisgu had crawled into the open.

Kadiya could sight it, also. The brush wall was visibly withering, turning a ghastly yellow-white even as she watched. The crawler must have carried a dread contagion to everything it had touched.

And it was spreading, with a rapidity which was frightening. She could believe that it would soon contaminate all that wall of wet vegetation, perhaps encircle them.

With great effort she raised the sword a second time. Again she willed it to life, pointing it at those withering plants, those rotting vines.

Once more the light. This time she felt the draw as if all her strength, save that of will, was being pulled forth into feeding it.

The fire gave birth not to one major explosion but a number of minor flashes along branches and vine loops, opening a way ahead straight from the space in which they stood.

Kadiya fought to keep on her feet, to hold steady the sword. But she could not force it into further action. The light paled, was gone. The three eyes were once more lidded. She fell abruptly to her knees, too weak to remain upright. Jagun was instantly at her side.

"Farseer!"

"It—I can do no more—" Somehow she managed to get out. She was panting heavily as if she had run for a long distance, and her arms were so weak they had fallen by her sides, the pointless sword clanging against the stone pavement.

There was movement beside her, an arm around her shoulders.

"Smail! The drink of the foreseer!" That impatient order formed in the girl's mind. It was Salin who was supporting her now, rather than she the wisewoman. The Uisgu youth had taken off his pack to bring out a lidded phial. When it was opened another scent warred with the choking stench which still hung about them, the clean odor of some herb. Kadiya drank.

She was still too tired to move, but now warmth spread within her and she breathed more easily. Jagun had stood over her watching with concern. At last he nodded, perhaps to her, perhaps to Salin.

Hitching up his pack, he went toward the tunnel which the sword had blasted. With caution he edged to a point from which he could peer down it.

"It still dies ahead," he reported. "Yet, I do not think it wise to take this road, open as it may now be."

Kadiya wondered if she was able to take *any* road. She was more than a little frightened at this loss of strength. Well she knew that the use of Power drained one. She might hold in her hand the answer to cleansing the land — save that her body could not carry out that mission.

"King's Daughter, you can kill it!" For the first time Smail addressed her. "You can clear our land . . ."

Slowly Kadiya shook her head. "I have not the strength. I am not one of great Power." She picked up the sword once more. Yes, the eyes were firmly closed. Perhaps it was not only she who had been so exhausted. It could be that that which dwelt within her talisman had also been depleted for now. Or had it been drained past recovery?

She fumbled it back into its sheath and now leaned her weight on her spear, struggling to rise. Smail and Salin aided her to her feet and she stood swaying between them, as weak as if she had lain long ill.

That weakness awoke anger in her. She was no bower lady

to be so overwhelmed! The swamp demanded much from those who would walk it—and walk it she would! This was her free choice.

Kadiya licked her lips as her gaze swiftly passed the smear on the stone, the crumbling brush. She spoke to Jagun.

"There is a way forward, hunter?"

He pointed a little to the right of the brush which the Power had blasted. She could see no sign there of that yellow streaking, the withering.

"That way, Farseer, but slowly."

Somehow Kadiya found strength to smile. "Well must it be slow, shield comrade. I am one who must now take but a step at a time."

12

SINCE JAGUN HAD STEERED THEM away from possible contagion they found the going more difficult. Ancient masonry no longer underlay the skin of earth and vegetation. Jagun and Smail took turns to sound out their footing with spear butts. To Kadiya's surprise the isle on which they had landed appeared quite large, perhaps even greater than that which supported Trevista to the south.

Her strength gradually returned and after the second day she was able to keep a better pace. She did not draw the sword again, though she glanced at the pommel from time to time, always to see those eyes closed. At length she began to feel uneasy, wondering if she had indeed used all its Power in that blast.

On the afternoon of the fourth day they struck water again. The storms had swept heavily here, though the flooding had ceased now. However, the stretch of roiled liquid before them was as dark and thick as if the mud of a river bottom had boiled to the top. On the other side was a rise of growth as tall as any polder tree, yet this was a dark mass, caught and woven together by vines. And they were close enough to see that great thorns as long as the darts in Jagun's shoulder case sprouted within the branches of that brush. There was no mistaking the beginning of the Thorny Hell, the stronghold of the Skriteks.

Kadiya had passed through this twice but only upon the river, where the threatening thorny growth had walled the shores and did not have to be faced full on. Whether it could be pierced at all she began to wonder.

They rummaged in their packs and brought out leaf water-walkers, stepping into the thongs and making sure that they were well fastened to their boots. Jagun adjusted the sling for his dart pipe, so that he might lay hand on it in an instant. Smail followed the hunter's example after making sure the wisewoman's leaf walkers were well adjusted.

They headed on, the water-walkers serving them well. Kadiya continued to study the thick murk of the water closely. She had no doubt there were lurkers there; she only hoped that none were large enough to challenge the travelers.

As they approached the thorny shield of the rising land the girl could not see any possible opening, though she knew that the Skriteks traversed their stronghold with ease. However, the Drowners were practically water dwellers, having a liking for swimming under surface and attacking their prey from such hiding. Did they use some hidden waterways to take them in and out of that cover?

Still if Jagun was baffled by that barrier he did not show it. Kadiya tried hard, calling upon all the hunting lore she had learned from him, to spot any way of advancement. She did not expect to see him aim his spear directly at what appeared to be an impenetrable bush, work its head well into it, and then give a twist of his shoulders, exerting such strength as made his muscles stand visible under the skin where his jerkin had frayed away.

Smail slid forward on his own water-walkers and aimed his spear near Jagun's, then also bent to the task of twisting.

The bush they had attacked, which stood almost as high as one of the city's garden trees, shook. Kadiya saw a brilliant red snake drop from a top branch, appear to spread fin-like wings and so glide to another perch farther away. A cloud of insects, thick enough almost to veil Kadiya's sight, whirled upward.

Jagun and the young Uisgu only strained the harder.

Kadiya would not have believed their efforts possible if she had not seen the bush slowly bend to the left. Where it had stood there was a dark opening, a ragged path floored with black earth giving out a rotting smell.

Still holding the brush aside Jagun gave an order.

"In, Farseer, Salin."

Kadiya obeyed, gingerly placing trust in the hunter's knowledge, though she half expected to find herself wedged against those thorns, long and strong enough to impale her.

There seemed to be a tunnel through the barrier here but it had been fashioned for wayfarers Oddling size and Kadiya had to stoop to escape having her helm brushed off by the thorns and swinging vines. The latter she watched warily, remembering only too well her struggle in the city of the Vanished Ones.

Here was not only the usual fug of the swamp but she caught now and again a whiff of Skritek body odor. There was none yet of the putrid breath of the plague.

She squeezed to one side as Jagun joined her, ready to take the lead.

"This is a Skritek trail?" she demanded in a half whisper.

"It is a way—the only way we can take for entrance," he returned. "It is not long and it will bring us to the Sal Tower."

They put Salin in the middle, with Jagun and then Kadiya before, and Smail bringing up the rear guard. Kadiya's amulet was warm against her flesh. Glancing down she could see the golden light it cast through the near translucent scales of her mail shirt. But she did not need that warning.

Though there was no water here to hide a Skritek ambush, she could not be sure that the sharp thorned walling would not suddenly fall away to reveal a war party.

Jagun was advancing as if he knew exactly what he was about and the girl had enough confidence in his trail knowledge to hope that they could traverse this awesome tunnel without attack. It was true that the Skritek scent was not as strong as if there had been recent passage here.

She heard a sharp crack behind her and slewed around ready to confront an enemy only to see that Salin had broken a thorn from a near branch. It was not the sullen black of the other growth but grayish and now the wisewoman reached for another such. At her sharp tug that also parted from the parent wood.

"What—?" Kadiya began.

Salin was already harvesting a third. "Darts," the Uisgu woman returned. "Such darts will serve us well."

There was an answering grunt of agreement from Smail. However, he did not loose hold on his weapons to aid in the harvest.

As they worked their way on, Salin not only added to the store of thorns she was binding together, but here and there caught at a leaf of some vine or even a twist of evil-looking blossom which in Kadiya's eye too much resembled the head of a vibon viper.

It was humid and damp in this place. Sweat gathered under the edge of her helm, to trickle down her cheeks, even drip from her chin. Her hands were slippery on the spear and she found herself aware of breathing as if the act was an effort. There was no way here of measuring either time or distance and Jagun was continuing single-mindedly as if a strong will drove him.

When he did halt it was because they were faced by what looked to be an impenetrable wall of brush. He shrugged off his pack and movement from behind Kadiya testified that Smail was doing the same. Once more the young Uisgu stepped level with Jagun, though here they were crowded very close together by the walls of the hidden way.

Both spears thrust deep into the mass of the thorns as Nyssomu and Uisgu strained together.

There was no response except the whipping of the thorn branches, as if the vegetation had power to reason and repel. Kadiya slipped off her own pack. Though the slit in the living wall left her very little room in which to maneuver and she could not straighten to her full height, the girl pushed her own spear between those of the Oddlings, jabbing the point as deeply as she could into the mass. When the head caught and held, she added what strength she could in a united effort.

At last she felt movement. This time the tangled vegetation was not sliding to one side, but rather retreating as if they were pushing a cork out of a flask. The girl could feel as well as see the tension of the Oddlings and readied herself for a last assault.

That break came so suddenly that they all staggered forward, almost thrown off their feet. Light broke the gloom of the tunnel way. But with that came something else . . . the putrid odor of the plague.

Jagun and Smail edged forward very carefully. Ahead was an open clearing. However, they did not move as yet beyond the edge. Stones covered the ground to form a barrier against the rooting of the thorn. It was larger than they first thought as they studied it cautiously to find a way among those rocky blocks. Certainly there had once been construction here. On the top of one block, within a hand's distance of Jagun, coiled a brilliant red and black banded lenth. Warning was already on Kadiya's lips, but the hunter swung with practiced speed bringing spear butt down with smashing force which left the viper half crushed, though still wriggling.

Such crawling perils would find fine cover in this place, Kadiya knew. But now she was surveying the ruin studded ground for traces of another kind of death — the yellow leprous patches of that evil to which they could not as yet give any name, save plague.

She sighted one such at last, half in the shadow of what once had been a tower. Only a portion — the first story and half of the second — remained of what must have been an imposing structure.

Smail crouched by the stone where the viper had died and cut off the head, which he then pushed by knife point into a small pouch, fastening the string very tight. Lenth poison on the point of a dart formed a very deadly weapon.

Kadiya, swinging her spear before her, picked a careful way from one bare rocktop to the next in the direction of the tower. Well away from the brush wall through which they had come, she could better view that splotch at the base of the tower. It was not a large spot — apparently the lack of vegetation there had kept it from spreading. However, as she turned a little she could trace the rot back toward the wall through which it had issued—and a second line of slimy, putrescent splotches continuing on from the tower base, as if they marked footsteps.

She believed that the ruin must mark a stopping place, even a camp—if the thing they hunted was such that camped. In some places the infected vegetation had formed what appeared to be pools of liquid decay. About the edges of some of those, she thought she could see what might even be the skeletons of small creatures, some seeming to show phosphorescence in this cloud dimmed daylight.

Jagun had joined her on an adjacent perch among the rocks.

"It has come and gone." Apparently he read those tracks even as she had done.

She remembered the black blot which had appeared in the scrying bowl. This had certainly been the location of that scene. But where had it gone? The trail she could see crossed to the opposite side of the open space surrounding the remains of the tower.

Kadiya fingered the sword. Her talisman had destroyed the plague, brought a welcome death to that poor Oddling the foul blot had attacked. But if they must follow that noisome trail through the thorns, would the Power have renewed itself enough for her to cut a clean path for them? Jagun had known of a way to the tower, thus they had gotten so far without having to contend with the plague again. It was apparent now, though, that the tower had not been the final goal of what they must deal with.

Even as she stood there, the dusk grew deeper. They must find some kind of shelter—other than the infected tower—and rest out the night. A more unlikely camping spot she had never seen than this viper-ridden maze of rocks.

However, they dared not push on. All of them were tired from their march this day. Salin had sunk down on a stone, curling in upon herself, rubbing at her legs and ankles. The very droop of her figure was a warning that the wisewoman must be near to the end of her energy.

"A camp?" Kadiya hazarded, looking away from the ominous tower now and out over the ruins. The rain had stopped, though the air was dank and humid. Perhaps they could stay in the open and not fear the coming of another burst of storm.

Jagun was revolving slowly on his own perch—intent on the territory ahead and to their right. Now he pointed with his spear.

Three masses of masonry had somehow tipped toward each other to form a space which was half sheltered. The hunter dropped from his lookout point and padded carefully toward it. He reached the opening and stooped a little to survey what lay within. It was well away from the plague trail with mostly bare rock between it and that foul road, and therefore free from danger of pestilence.

At his wave, Kadiya (having again shouldered the pack she had brought out of the tunnel) reached out a hand to Salin, who dug her staff in between two stones, and with its support pulled herself determinedly to her feet.

They had not chosen too badly the girl decided after Jagun and Smail had clawed away some of the earth which had sifted around the three improvised walls and made sure there were no viper holes. The flooring was stone, and cold. Nor could they hope for a fire. But it was better than huddling in the open.

Their provisions were trail food, dry on the tongue, with only a few sips of the water they carried with them to make it chewable. Salin groped in the bag which hung from her girdle and produced some twists of dried leaf which she shared out and they chewed. The coarse appearance of these bits was deceptive. Kadiya found them refreshing as they mixed with saliva. In fact they were as invigorating as some of the reviving drinks she had known in the Citadel.

The wisewoman turned her bundle of harvested thorns over to her grandson, who was already busy with the smoothstone from his dart bag, working the hard pieces into straight lengths which he then passed to Jagun. The hunter was ready with a knife to trim delicately at the narrow tips, though the twilight had so far advanced that he must have worked more by touch than sight.

Kadiya sat cross-legged, her own hands slipping up and down the length of the sword. At her last clear sight the eyes had been lidded. Still, unless she deceived herself by hope, it seemed there was a warmth about the pommel which she could detect when she held a finger close to the lidded eyes. The amulet continued in its warmth though its light was limited by the mail coat she wore.

"Wisewoman," she asked, "has any message of Power come to you? Where does this thing of evil go? Can you scry and tell us?"

She could not see the face of the Uisgu woman but she was mentally aware that the other was troubled.

"One of Power, we are now in a country where others rule. Always the Skritek have been servants of evil. And evil has its own ears and eyes—yes, and senses beyond those. Should I raise *my* Power it may be a summoning for what we have not strength to face. However, there is another way...." She spoke hesitatingly as if she was not sure of the suggestion she was about to make.

Kadiya felt movement beside her and then a faint sound as if metal touched stone.

"King's Daughter, bring forth that amulet which you wear."
She spoke abruptly, almost as an order. Kadiya obeyed, wriggling the piece of amber on its chain out into the open.

Fingers closed about her wrist to draw her hand forward.
At the same time the light of the trillium-heated drop increased
so that she could see dimly the amulet dangling now over Salin's empty scrying bowl. The side of the basin reflected the
light almost as though they had a dim lamp in their midst.

"Power, King's Daughter," Salin ordered. "Give me of your
Power. Will it!"

Kadiya did as best she could, concentrating on the amulet
with a picture of Salin in her mind.

As the liquid had seethed in the other scrying so it appeared
to the girl that the light of the amulet began also to swirl. As
it had been when she held the sword to slay, so did she feel
her strength begin to drain down her arm, feeding through her
fingers into the amulet.

Now the amulet itself moved in a small, tight circle over the
churning mist of light. Below the center of that circle, there
formed a picture.

It was perhaps no larger than she could measure with a
finger's length, but for some moments of shock it was as clear
as if she were within the basin, a part of what she viewed.

Skritek, but with them another. This was no refugee
from Voltrik's destroyed army. Rather it was a caricature of
something else—one of the Guardians from the lost city!
There was no mistaking the features, twisted and fallen
away as they were, nor the body, though it was stooped
and shrunken, as if it were a glove from which the hand
had been withdrawn. She certainly saw one of the Vanished
Ones, save that this creature was the very embodiment of
death, rot, and despair. From that shrunken body there

shone the same greenish yellow as that given off by the victims of the plague.

The thing was marching, Skritek to either side but none, she noted, behind it, where on the ground it left patches of putrescence which might have oozed from its feet. These foul sluggish blotches seemed to take on monstrous life of their own, some uniting quickly and then flowing outward, seeking nourishment. There was a stiffness in its walk. As did Salin, it was using a staff, manifestly to keep itself upright. So might the long-dead walk from out a tomb, moved by some purpose which could not be denied.

They had a last glimpse of the marcher and his escort. Then light flickered in the basin and Kadiya's hand fell numbly to her side.

• • • ————————————————————————————— • • •

13

"WHERE DOES THAT THING GO?" Kadiya asked aloud, of herself as much as of those with her.

"We but follow a trail," Jagun returned, "the death trail it leaves."

"A Vanished One." Again the question formed in the girl's mind. "How could a Vanished One become so?"

"There were those who wove the Dark, even as their kin wove the light," Jagun answered. "Out of such weaving came the Judgment which changed the world. This thing is from that time, it is loosed and moves again."

Kadiya shivered, her hand again to her sword. Did she feel warmth there? She turned it over. The light was gone from her amulet and her hand was a heavy weight which she had difficulty forcing to obey her will. Cautiously, in the dark which had fallen when the amulet light had died away, she slipped a finger across the bulbous shapes of the three eyes. They felt locked shut.

"The forbidden Door is said to lie within this place of bitterness and death," Salin's thought came. "It can only be that this thing seeks."

"For what purpose?" Kadiya asked quickly.

They were crowded so tightly into this slight shelter that she felt the wisewoman stir, her small arm brushing against Kadiya's longer, mail-clad one.

"Woman of Power, this thing which leaves so deadly a trail appears ill unto death—yet it seeks some aid. There may be a core of evil which will give it renewal. The oldest tales tell that when the Vanished Ones saw the destruction their own warring had brought upon the land they withdrew to another place in sorrow. There was a doorway into that place and there they entered."

"But if those of good will went so," Kadiya countered, "why would something which is an embodiment of evil strive now to follow the same path?"

"For healing perhaps," the wisewoman said. "We cannot judge the thoughts of a Vanished One. We are wrought of their making, but it is not in us to guess what would move them or what Powers they hold."

Again Kadiya fingered the sword. This . . . this thing out of nowhere had poisoned wherever it passed. Even if it departed the land by some sorcery, the plague it had sown would spread, and though she had met and destroyed a very small part of that, she had not the Power to backtrail and burn out all which had been set alive.

If she could catch up with this walking death before it gained any strength or renewal she might just have a chance to destroy the foulness at its very core. This would be no battle as she had known warfare when she went up against Voltrik, or even against the Skritek. Those enemies were flesh and blood and could be killed. Even in dying this walker might win, its contagion spread. Yet there was no other answer. As best she could she must follow it, strive to deal with it as she had with Voltrik's general.

Her helm scraped against one of the stones which walled them in as she raised her head. She could summon no army now; she could not even reach out to her sisters—to Haramis who was supposed to be watcher and Guardian of Ruwenda. This was her own task; this must have been the reason for her headlong journey from the Citadel. She had not been drawn so to relinquish the sword—no, rather to take it up again, against a far more sinister foe than any invader of her own species.

"Jagun, Salin, Smail," she said, with all the authority she might summon. "This I must do: strive to prevent the evil from reaching its goal. But I do not ask any of you to come with me."

"Farseer, this is an ancient evil and we are a people linked with the day which must have shaped it first. Do not say that you walk this trail alone!" There was sharpness in his tone, a sharpness she had never heard from Jagun except on two occasions in the past when he had believed that she had endangered herself foolishly.

"King's Daughter," said Salin, "I chose to follow this trail even before we met you. I shall follow it to the end. The Power may not be as much mine as it is yours, but what I can summon I shall live to turn against this foul thing. Smail is of my blood and he is Oath-bound before the Elders to travel with me. We do not turn aside now."

Kadiya sighed. Jagun was tied to her by years of shared

memories and a mutual respect for each other's talents. He had become indeed her shield comrade and she would have felt inwardly bereft without him. The two Uisgu were not so attuned, but it was plain they had their own sense of duty.

"Then we follow," she said dully.

Sleep was fitful. Kadiya was sure in the morning that she had dreamed. Though she carried into waking the feeling that those dreams had been ill, she could not remember them.

Not only was there no rain this morning but a cloud-dulled sun shone as they left the rocks around Sal Tower. The signs of the path they were to follow were plain and they had to move with exasperating slowness to avoid the patches of spreading death, the putrid smell of which hung always about them.

Perhaps due to an underpavement laid to prevent deep rooting, the heavy growth did not stand thick here but rather opened before them. They went alert to any sign of movement which might mean a viper. One they saw but it must have touched a place of plague for it lay dead, its body half rotted away.

The openness narrowed again to a passage. Here were the remains of more pavement and it was easier to avoid the rot which could only attack some creeping vines and patches of fungi. Then, before them, stood a pole planted as firmly as it could be wedged between two blocks of stone.

It was surmounted by a skull—and not an ancient one, for there were ragged scraps of flesh still clinging to the bone. On the supporting rock there was a wide smear of blood, now a lure for insects and flying things.

Skritek markings. Kadiya had seen such before. So did the

saurians declare boundaries or set trail signs. A line of rocks behind this pole marked the wall of some long vanished building. They scrambled over to face water once again, a narrow tongue of it looping out of a lake of some size. Plain to see on the lake's edge was a stinking mass of what had once been water reed now brought down by the plague's touch—a clear sign that their quarry must have taken to the water here.

If there had been transportation waiting for that other party there was none for them. Jagun swung down to the water's edge well away from the tainted reed bank. Reversing his spear he used the point to dig into the reed screen. His vigorous thrusts brought out of hiding a form of craft Kadiya had never seen before.

Unlike the well-fashioned skiffs built by the Oddlings, this was a lumpy platform of heavy branches interwoven as tightly as the thorn brush walls. In fact as it came into open view through the hunter's urgings, the girl could see that it was fashioned from just such branches, interlocking thorns helping to keep it together. But those spikes which would have pointed upward and outward had been broken off and a matting of reeds plastered with mud covered it.

The lumpy raft looked far from journey worthy, and Kadiya wondered if they dared trust it. Yet having freed it from hiding, Jagun boldly sprung out on it, balancing himself against the sudden sway and dip, then sank his spear into the bottom mulch to anchor it while he jerked his head in a gesture for them to join him.

It was a craft far from comfortable or safe. They had to arrange themselves and their packs in the middle to balance it before Jagun and Smail used poles which had been half hidden in the mud to work them away from shore and toward the wider part of the lake.

As on each previous morning since beginning their journey, they took the precaution of greasing their skins against insect attacks. Here there seemed to be a new type of flying bloodsucker which was not banished by the usual method, yet they dared not move to beat them off because of the precarious state of their transport. Kadiya tried to be as stoic as possible against these pest attacks even as she felt and saw spots of blood on her hands, and felt those which must now speckle her face.

Their craft moved on with Jagun and Smail working hard to keep them parallel with the left bank. She set herself to watch for any sign of the rot there, to betray the passing of the one they hunted. As they went, the brush gave way to much taller vegetation which might have been called trees, save that they had not one trunk but several.

These trunks joined with drooping branches and reached out over the water to form crooked arches. At intervals they saw a stirring in the water beneath the widest of those which suggested that life lurked there. However, so far those spaces were, Kadiya deemed, too narrow to conceal any Skritek hunter.

Because they had encountered no guards Kadiya believed that the Skritek felt safe enough within their own territory not to take the precaution of placing a sentinel rear guard.

Continually tormented by the bloodsuckers, they pushed slowly on. So far there had been no sighting of any plague spot on the bank. Then Kadiya was suddenly deterred from her restrained slapping by a surge of warmth, stronger than the steaminess which appeared to issue from the dark lake through which they poled.

Though it had been inert since she had used it for the scrying, her amulet was again showing life. Cautiously she drew it out from beneath her mail shirt. The imprisoned trillium appeared almost alive as the amber glowed around it. Was it again a guide? It was tuned to Power and if there was some source of Power ahead now the amulet could well be answering.

She drew the attention of her companions to what she held and then edged a little along the center portion of the rude raft, aiming the amulet at the left-hand bank. For, if she turned it ahead or in the opposite direction, it immediately dimmed.

Here taller and taller branches swung out over the water. The arches formed by the roots were now nearly high enough for their heads to clear, though Jagun kept the craft well away from any such experiment.

No sign of the plague, but all at once the amulet moved in Kadiya's hold, and had she not instinctively tightened her grip it might even have leaped from her grasp.

"That way!" Kadiya pointed straight at one of those root arches, a tall and very thick one. The growth which it supported must have been very old.

Jagun alertly swung their raft left and a moment later they were under the shadow of the arch. Nor was there any sign of bank ahead. Rather they viewed more of the arching roots, forming a crooked roofing which led into true darkness. They might be entering some stream emptying into the lake at this point though Kadiya could detect no current pulling at the raft.

She stared ahead seeking the betraying slime patches. However, if those they followed had come this way that seeder of foulness had not touched anything which could carry the blight.

Now they passed under a fourth arch. With each the light had dimmed more, for overhead the tree growth had closed in to form a real roof, keeping out the wan daylight. There was the smell of muck and rank vegetation here but none of the putrid whiffs which had alerted them to danger before.

Jagun took to the fore of the raft, using the pole with the dexterity of long practice while Smail moved with care to the other side, bending and raising his own pole in unison with the hunter.

Somewhere ahead there must be a source of Power, of that Kadiya was sure. But for good or ill? The amulet would react to a strong emanation of evil as well as to the good which had fashioned it as a protection and guide.

At least its growing blaze gave them a spark of light as their unsteady voyage continued. About them, as it had in the thorn-thicket tunnel, the walls were closing in. However, it was not until later that Kadiya, having turned the amulet a bit, saw a fraction of one of those walls. Wall it was—ancient stone, dripping now with rank green water weed.

The amulet caught a glint of eyes. A length of the moss wavered, broke from a tuft and dropped into the water. So this place had its inhabitants also.

There was silence except for the sound of the poles being drawn forth and then reset to push on. Then Kadiya heard an exclamation from Jagun, saw in the glimmer of the amulet a sudden flurry as he drove his pole in with greater force to end their advance and anchor them in this underground streamway.

Kadiya pulled up to her knees and held her hand forward, reaching across the hunter's shoulder with that faint source of light. There was indeed a barrier before them—and such a one as perhaps was proper to see in eerie and forgotten places.

She had seen the intricate webs of the roxlin once or twice in the outer regions of the Golden Mire. But those had been small, the work of spider creatures no larger than her thumb tip. This web, as perfectly structured, filled the whole expanse before them from one dank wall to the other, from water's edge up into the gloom overhead to a point they could not see in this dark.

Nor were they thin threads which formed the perfect circle. The strands looked as thick as the cords on travel boots. And they were matted, some places in thick layers, with the bodies of unlucky insects—and other creatures. In one place was a lizard as green as the growth around them, surely one of the things she had seen take to the water. Its body was no light one, yet its weight hardly bent the cords which bound it.

The roxlin were avoided. While they could not suck the life from large prey, their bite was a danger, able to cause a wound very hard to heal. A roxlin of the size to have woven this would be a formidable opponent.

With one hand on Jagun's shoulder to steady herself as the raft rocked alarmingly under her feet, Kadiya held the amulet above her head. Neither wall showed any signs of a hiding place for a large creature. The Weaver could only be concealed somewhere aloft. But the amulet's light held as high as she dared reach picked up nothing. To touch that web would perhaps bring the roxlin into view eager to inspect its captured prey.

An attack from above would be perilous, perched as they were on such a frail footing.

Kadiya, still holding the amulet aloft, transferred it from right hand to left. Then she drew the sword. Under her fingers the eyes seemed shut, yet here no spear nor dart would do the job needed.

"Give me room," she ordered softly, fearing voice sound alone might bring an attack.

Jagun drew to one side and a little back so Kadiya could

inch forward, at once feeling the raft answer ominously to the shifting of her weight. She must be swift before it dipped too far. Having only two hands she would not be able to save herself if that happened.

Then an arm closed about her waist, steadying her. Jagun, though he still kept tight grip on the anchoring pole, was lending her what assistance he could.

Quickly Kadiya aimed a sword swing at the web. Though her blade lacked the point it did not go without an edge and that caught, for only a fraction of time, before it cut through the web. A second such swing and a third followed though she was tensely aware that any moment there might come an attack from the roxlin.

The rounded circles were in tatters, trailing into the water where swirlings suggested that something was waiting to feed upon the feast bound to the stickiness of the broken threads.

Kadiya was astounded that there had been no answer from the creature whose work she was now destroying with all the vigor she dared. That the trap had been deserted was hard to believe. Yet the more damage she wreaked upon that barrier the more she began to think it true.

The light from the amulet now showed a jagged hole, fully large enough for them to use. But suppose the maker was craftily waiting for their craft to pass beneath it before it made its move?

"Do we try now?" She depended upon Jagun's hunter's training, willing to leave the decision to him.

"Make ready!"

She dropped down into the same position she had held before, aware of Salin's fast breathing at her shoulder. She held ready the sword.

Jagun urged his pole free, reaching out to plant it ahead,

and the raft rocked, shipping a little water as Smail copied his swing. They moved forward at what Kadiya guessed was the best speed he could summon. Involuntarily the girl hunched her shoulders as they passed under the remnants of the web, still not believing that they would avoid reprisal from the Weaver.

Jagun's and Smail's concentrated efforts had them beyond the web in only breaths of time. She heard Salin give a small whistling sound and realized that the wisewoman must have been sharing her fears.

"There is this," Jagun commented as their voyage continued. "We can now be sure that those we hunt did not come this way."

Was that good or bad, Kadiya wondered. Had the amulet, answering to some other ancient emanation, drawn them away from the trail they should have followed?

Again she swung the amulet from side to side and caught glimpses of only stone walls, slimed and dark. Then suddenly the raft grated on an obstacle in the water.

Once more Kadiya steadied herself and swung the amulet forward, this time by its chain so that the limited light might reach farther.

Rising out of the water before them was an incline of the same stone as the walls. It was plain that they had come to the end of the streambed way. Smail crowded by her and echoed Jagun's leap to that solid landing place, uniting with the hunter in pulling their transportation further up on the shelfing stone.

Kadiya was quick to scramble out and push ahead. A moment later the amulet light caught the first of a flight of steps leading upward. There was no smell of the plague here.

She turned to help work the raft out of the water enough

so that it might not be swept away. Then she shouldered her pack as Jagun and Smail took up theirs. Salin, leaning on her staff, was not far behind as they turned to that stairway. Here Kadiya took the lead as the light of the amulet was all they had as an aid.

 ON THE THIRD OF THE WIDE STEPS Kadiya stopped abruptly. From below the water sighed against the landing stone, appearing to ebb and flow with a trace of current they had not noted during the voyage. However, now she caught another sound, faint, hardly more than a vibration, through the stone about her. The girl could not put name to it, yet it brought an inner chill.

Jagun's whisper hissed:

"Skritek!"

To continue to climb was perhaps the act of a fool, but in her hand the amulet glowed with an ever increasing fire. They were certainly drawing close to a very strong core of Power. The Drowners were thought to possess no wisdom, no weapons save their fangs, claws, and some crude spears and clubs. They accomplished their most successful raids mainly by stealth. Yet

she and her companions were now well into their home territory, and who knew what forces they could muster here?

It was not Salin's voice but the wisewoman's thought which
came now.

"These pay honor — they do not hunt."

The certainty in the Uisgu's statement made Kadiya accept
it. But whom did those scaled monsters honor? Some chieftain
or First of their own — or that thing which had spread death
in its passing?

There was no going back; they could only proceed with all
the caution they could summon. At least Jagun's senses were
well tuned for just such situations as this.

Resolutely Kadiya started on. Though she expected otherwise, the sounds did not grow any louder. In fact they appeared to fade at times.

In competition to the glow of the amulet, Kadiya became
aware of a second source of light on the stairway that increased as she took each step.

The light radiated from the top of that flight, but the beam
was broken as if filtered through patterns of small openings.

Kadiya allowed the amulet to fall back against her breast,
half covering it with her fingers. The heat within it was more
than mere warmth. It now approached a burning point, and
she had to will herself fiercely to keep her flesh pressed against
it.

That outer light increased suddenly and dramatically as the
stairway ended. Across its upper entrance was a barrier —
seemingly a screen which had been deeply carved, allowing
light to stream through curves and angled apertures.

She had seen something akin to this before! There were
passages within the walls of the Citadel of Ruwenda — part of
a system of secret and hidden ways. Many of these had been

discovered, and in Kadiya's childhood she had dared Haramis or Anigel to follow her into those forgotten ways. Some of them were hidden by portions of wall which were pierced by ornamental fretwork. From without, these appeared to be no more than fanciful decoration, but in truth they furnished light, air, and spying places for those lurking along the hidden ways.

They were faced now by just such a screen. From its other side the light was strong. Kadiya moved to the right to allow the others room on that ledge which topped the stair so that all might share her vantage point.

Beyond was a room. The walls were of the same time-resistant white stone as those in the city of the Vanished Ones. Placed at either end were hooks from which lamps swung by chains. Those burned smokily as they must have done many times previously as the walls were discolored with fans of black soot.

The surface they illuminated was as deeply carved as the one behind which Kadiya and the others stood. Perhaps it had once also been painted to highlight some of those carvings; Kadiya was sure she could trace dabs of red, blue, a touch of much faded yellow.

This was no picturing of any form of life. Rather the swirls and circling, the jutting rosettes, the meaningless, twisting lines, were eye-bewildering puzzles.

Those in hiding stiffened. Skritek jabber suddenly sounded. Kadiya closed her hand once more over the amulet, wincing against the heat of the amber but intent that none of the glow would be seen. How effective their screened hiding place would be no one knew but she was completely certain they must witness what passed here.

Through the door to their left, the only visible entrance into this windowless chamber, there emerged a strange company.

Jiggling from one clawed foot to the other advanced a Skritek. On its lizardlike head was mounted a skull which might be from one of its own kind, and yet was so much larger it suggested there had once existed a giant form of the species. The exposed fangs of this head gear were stained red and in the eyeholes were fastened the glow insects which served all swamp dwellers for lights.

Besides the skull which it wore as a crown the Skritek, after the customs of its kind, had little in the way of clothing. Its scaled shoulders supported twin belts drawn across the body, crossing on the chest and back. From them dangled bones strung close enough together to rattle as the creature walked. Around its paunchy waist was another belt. This was apparently of fur patched skin, which supported the sheath of a knife, almost long enough to be termed a sword, as well as a large pouch. In one hand the creature held a pole from which dangled another skull, this one obviously human in contour.

Reaching the center of the chamber the Skritek wheeled to face the wall. Raising the staff, it waved that sign of office overhead and brought the butt down against the stone floor in a steady beat which matched the harsh rumble of the mutter springing from its fanged jaws. It was, Kadiya thought, engaged in some kind of ritual.

The stench of Skritek was strong and speedily grew as two more of the creatures entered. These did not wear the skull headdress, and they carried crude spears instead of skull headed poles. Once within they moved back until their shoulders near touched the screen behind which Kadiya and her companions stood.

While the skull crested leader continued a rasping chant, there entered another. That shriveled, plague eaten figure Ka-

diya had seen in the scrying basin shambled into the full light
of the two lamps. Behind it, after a noticeable gap, were four
more spear-bearing Skritek.

The stench of their body odor, together with that foul efflu-
ence given off by the plague, would conceal any scent natural
to her and her company, Kadiya hoped—though that had been
well tempered by the herb paste they smeared on daily to ward
off insect attacks. At least the girl had caught no sign from
that foul company that those spying had been detected.

Having given a last and mighty bellow, the skull wearer
brought down the staff with a final vigor, then turned halfway
so it now faced the plague striken one. To Kadiya the latter
was a more fearsome sight than the swamp demons, for here
one of the fine bodies she had seen in the city statues was
eaten into a form of disgust and dread.

Nearly as bent as Salin, skin raddled and pitted with sup-
purating ulcer-like spots, its head resembling a skull covered
only with the thinnest shaving of skin, this was a nightmare.

Yet as it moved forward, the skull crowned Skritek not only
fell to knees but groveled, facedown before that monstrous
thing.

The thing halted, swaying as if it found difficulty in keeping
erect. One arm arose jerkily sending out drops of yellowish
liquid which spattered the floor as it gestured.

Pain exploded in her head so suddenly Kadiya nearly reeled
against the screen. Only Jagun's outflung arm steadied her. It
was as if there was a din, a discordant roaring in her head.
She bit her lip hard and fought to close her mind against it.

On the floor the prostrate Skritek writhed, perhaps expe-
riencing some of the same torment as Kadiya now fought. The
monster regarded its worshiper with eyes surrounded by great
wrinkles, so buried in loose flesh as to be hardly visible. It

. . . ———————————————————————————— . . .

made a movement with one foot, spurning the skull topped staff, and then lurched toward the wall.

With a visible effort it straightened. Both of those poison dripping arms moved out. Fingers, which appeared rotted to the bone, touched four places in the intricate patterning of the stone.

There came a sound as if the stone itself was protesting vigorously against what was demanded of it. Then a slit opened.

Out streamed a light as red as the flames of a vigorous fire. The creature tottered forward until those billows of light wrapped it around. Then it was gone.

The prostrate Skritek arose to hands and knees, saurian head up, turned to the wall into which both the flames and the thing which had summoned them had vanished. Then the priest—if priest this skull crowned one was—got to its feet and rounded on the guards, barking out orders which sent them quickly to the door.

However, the leader lingered behind, now moving close to the wall. In Kadiya's mind surged something more than that blast which had been the communication of the plague sower to his following. This Skritek was avid for knowledge, in a way resentful that such had not been shared.

With the point of that staff the Drowner touched the places which must release the lock upon that doorway, touched them first tentatively, and then with some pressure. But there was no answer. Kadiya's mind touch picked up bafflement and the beginnings of anger.

At length the Skritek gave up the vain attempt to solve the secret and left the chamber, thumping the pavement ill-temperedly with the pole.

Kadiya had to jerk her hand away from the amulet. The

heat there had flared too high to touch with her fingers. Not only that, but it was rising of its own accord. In her a need was arising...

A door — to open a door — to follow. . . . The remnants of her small stock of prudence argued against the urge.

"Jagun . . . Salin . . ." She wanted reassurance, some aid from them to understand this compelling impulse now possessing her.

"Farseer." The hunter's words were in her mind and she held to them as a defense against the need which gripped her. "This is a place of great Power."

"Yes," Salin agreed, "but, King's Daughter, it is neither of good nor evil. It will answer either call upon it."

"But will it aid or entrap?" Kadiya demanded. "There is something pushing me now. I will not be swept into that place beyond the wall." Her determination fought that pressure. Just as she had been driven through the monsoon to the lost city, so now there was eating into her the compulsion to go beyond the screen, to face that other wall, to follow the monster who had broken its ancient seal.

Kadiya edged along the screen, her will unable to still this other set upon her. Though none of the Skritek remained, there was no assurance that they would not return. Yet now Jagun and the others were following her, as if drawn in the same fashion as she.

When they sidled into the room beyond the screen the hunter and the Uisgu youth did not approach the wall holding that secret way but rather turned their attention to the entrance through which the party of the enemy had come. Smail had darts ready between his fingers, those made of the thorns and dipped in viper venom. Jagun handled his spear as one waiting orders to attack.

Step by step, her will overridden by her body, Kadiya was pulled on. The talisman still burned against her. Now she sensed something else, a kind of surge and retreat, then surge again, as if some force struggled for freedom, was baffled, then would attack once more.

With care she avoided those shiny yellowish spots on the stone floor which marked the path of the destroyer. Upon the wall carving she saw similar dots of glowing rot where those wasted fingers had touched. It was not in her to place her own hands in the same contact, unless she could burn off the poison with the sword.

Kadiya drew her talisman. Once more the blade below the pommel was warm, though it did not burn with the same bitter force as the amulet. She looked down to see that the lid over the great eye was lifting. Raising the weapon the girl attempted to focus that orb upon the poison marked spots.

But the blade fought her control. She could not hold it steady. The beam burst from the top eye, was joined almost at once by those of the other two orbs. However, though she clenched her grip to hold it, the sword twisted and turned as if she were indeed powerless.

The tripled beam shot forward right enough, but not at the spot where she had tried to aim it. It was choosing its own goals. Here — there — there — and there — that light pulsed forth to touch parts of the sprawling pattern — save none were the same the monster had chosen.

Once more there came that sound of a reluctant opening. Then the light flooded about her. This was no red of flame . . . rather it was sunlight bright. With it came something else: that fragrance she had known in the garden from which she had taken the weapon she had just now used as a key.

The goldenness engulfed her as the flames had engulfed that

other. In a breath of time the chamber in which she had stood was gone. Kadiya gasped; it seemed that she could not draw air into her lungs, that she was in a place with no air. There was another sensation—that of being drawn up and up, whirling as if a mighty storm wind had lapped her round to play with her as a monsoon tempest played with leaves and branches it tore from plants and trees.

As suddenly as she had been so lifted she was lowered, and fear caught at her. The force of the wind might well dash her to the earth. Her half strangled breath came only in painful gasps. That perilous descent began to slow. Her feet gently touched a solid surface. The force which had held her now steadied her until her balance was secure.

But the glare of the golden light was still blinding and she could see nothing, not even the sword which she knew she still held.

Kadiya blinked and blinked again. When she closed her eyes momentarily she could still see the savage brilliance against the lids. However, that was fading at last. Now when she dared to look again, the golden glare was dimming, breaking up, as might a thinning mist in the swamplands.

She stood in a chamber so large that the other end appeared nearly the length of a street lane away. The pavement under her shabby and water worn boots was patterned in soft colors as if a woven carpet had been laid over it. Those colors faded, joined, mingled in designs which seemed to ease her light dazzled eyes as she studied them.

The walls were hung with strips of soft stuffs which were white but carried golden symbols she recognized from the scrolls in the library room of the city—writings which she could not read.

A tendril of soft blue smoke, heavy with that flowery fra-

grance, curled toward her from the left and Kadiya looked in
that direction. There stood a block of stone inset with the blue-
green metal secret to the Vanished Ones. The block might be
hollow for from it arose a plant such as she had never seen. Its
sturdy stem was perhaps as tall as she herself, the leaves as long
as her arms, but what that stem bore was the true wonder.

There was a seeming giant of a three petaled flower like
those she had known all her life, the sign of her house, a
minute bud of which was sealed into her amulet. But instead
of black, these huge petals were golden, a gold which glistened
with an overlay of minute, colored specks as though it had
been rainbow dusted.

Even as Kadiya watched that magnificent flower moved on
its stalk to incline in her direction. Never in her life had Kadiya known such wonder and awe. Slowly she lowered the
sword. Without consciously willing it she sank to her knees,
but she did not bow her head. She could not; the flower itself
seemed to draw her eyes aloft.

There arose a trilling. From the flower in some fashion?
Kadiya could not tell, though in this place she would accept
any wonder.

She lifted the sword by its pointless blade, held it in some
vague idea of a salute. The eyes were all open now, but they
did not shoot forth any fiery rays.

"Great One . . ." Kadiya accepted that this was a thing of
Power. Perhaps not of intelligent life as she had always known
it, but life equal in its way to her species.

"Great One," she began again. "I have been called." She
still held the sword, one-handed now as she groped to bring
out the amulet as well. The amber appeared as a ball of gold
here, nearly equal in hue to the flower. Within it the Black
Trillium was stark.

Once more that trilling answered her. She was saddened that she could not understand. Had she any right to stand in this place? Was she being questioned? On the chance that she was, she spoke for the third time.

"Great One, I am she who is one of three in Ruwenda — in the great land of the mires. This was my birth gift from the Archimage Binah." She touched the amulet. "This," now she held the sword higher, "was won when I followed the geas laid upon me after Ruwenda fell to the evil ones. I strove to return it when my labor was over, but the earth from which it was grown refused it. And, Great One, it led me here when I trailed a new darkness through the land. I am Kadiya, King's Daughter, but I have chosen the swamps. Any evil which touches them is my concern. Great One, today I have seen this evil come before me through the wall gate — "

"Not so!"

Kadiya's head snapped around. They had gathered very silently — or else she had been too ensorcelled by the flower to hear. Three of them —

Her eyes widened. Vanished Ones! And no statues to be wondered at and dreamed over.

15

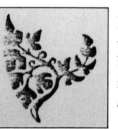 NEITHER DID THEY HAVE ABOUT them any of the misty clouding which had been a part of the One she had met before. To her eyes they were as much alive as she.

They were taller than she, even as she topped the Oddlings—the Oddlings! For the first time since she had won through the golden haze to the temple, Kadiya remembered her companions. A quick glance right and left showed her that she stood alone.

She set the sword point-down on the flooring, but kept her hand below the pommel so that the open eyes were still visible. In spite of the awe which held her fast she eyed these others defensively.

They were two men and a woman. Their garments were few and so finely woven that through them their bodies could be plainly seen. The men wore belts, one over each shoulder crossing on the breast. These flashed with white and green gems, and at that crossing was set a large gemmed medallion. Another belt at waist level, even more ornamented, supported a kilt not quite knee length. Covering feet and rising nearly to the knee were footgear which glistened with a silver sheen.

The woman who stood a little behind had a loose shift-like garment, fastened on the shoulders with broad brooches also gem set and belted with as complex a girdle as those of her companions. She wore also the high sandals on her feet.

The clothing was in contrast to their skins which were dark as those of the Labornoki plains dwellers who worked under the sun. Though the men appeared beardless their heads were covered with curling hair trimmed close to the skull. The woman's hair had not been so tightly cropped, locks falling to brush her shoulders.

However, it was their features which made Kadiya catch her breath. For of these three, two she had seen before — appearing carven in stone leagues away from this place. One she could even put name to —

"Lamaril!" He was the living embodiment of that statue which, hacked free of its armor of mud dried hard as iron, had pointed her way to the lost city when she had first sought it. Lamaril, who Jagun had said legend hailed as a great warrior against the Dark.

The woman she knew also, but not by name. Her likeness stood to the left on the fourth step of the garden stairway.

Certainly none of the three showed any signs of welcome. Both the woman and Lamaril were frowning. It was the third of their company who spoke.

"Who are you — what are you — who has dared the Gate?" His cold demand shook Kadiya out of her blank astonishment. Her chin came up and she faced the three squarely, yet one hand sought the amulet and the other tightened on the sword.

"I am Kadiya, King's Daughter to Krain who ruled in the Citadel of Ruwenda. It is set upon me to hold the mire lands against the Dark. We are those who came after your people departed."

"Mire lands," the man repeated. "You name a place we do not know, yet you have come through the Last Gate as one who has full right. And we heard your babble that you followed evil hither. There is no evil in this place!"

Now it was Lamaril who spoke. "You called upon my name, you who say that you are King's Daughter. Yet I have never seen you before. What mischief would you stir by naming me?"

His mouth set sternly, but Kadiya refused to be daunted by the coldness in his look.

"I have seen your likeness, not your person." She did not know what title of honor she should grant him and at the moment she did not care. "There is a figure of you on guard — though long ago it was mud buried and it was the enemy which chipped it free. Jagun of the Nyssomu named you to me then as a mighty captain who stood firm against the Dark in a troubled time."

His sternness of feature was suddenly gone. Now he showed astonishment, as one who might have heard a silent stone give voice.

Kadiya pressed what she felt was a small advantage. "And you," she addressed the woman directly, "I cannot name you. Yet your likeness, too, remains in the city of the fair garden, the Place of Learning. It stands guard on the stairs which lead to that same garden."

"Yatlan!" The woman pressed forward now. "Yatlan," she repeated and there was a soft note in her voice. She raised one hand, half extended it toward Kadiya. "You who have come, what is Yatlan now?"

"A city forgotten. No," the girl corrected herself, "forgotten by most. But it has its indwellers. They call themselves Hassitti and they have made efforts to hoard safely all which was left. There is the garden"—Kadiya raised the sword to hold it fully into view—"this was born of the garden. Binah, the Archimage, laid it upon me and my two sisters at birth to be the saviors of Ruwenda. She gave me a root which guided me to the city and there I planted it in the ever fruitful garden to become . . . this, and later the third part of a most powerful defense to save our country.

"Each of us found a part. Haramis, my mage sister who has become Binah's successor, wielded those parts into a mighty whole. Once that had served us well it separated again, returning to each of us that portion we had been geas-led to find. I was ruled by a great need to return it to the garden, but when I planted it again there was no change. Thus I knew that its task and *mine* was not yet accomplished." She had been speaking faster and faster, a desire to spill forth all forcing her to it.

"Archimage Binah!" The man who had first addressed her interjected. "She who chose to remain—you have seen her?"

"She set upon me the geas. But her rule was nearly done. Her last attempt to hold the Dark from the land weakened her too much. She chose my sister Haramis to come after her, then she died."

"Binah!" The man put his hand uncertainly to his head. "Her name—remembered in the wasteland!"

"You spoke of evil which you followed . . . here! Something which could not be true. . . ." Lamaril once more addressed Kadiya. "How did you find the Last Gate—and why?"

The girl flushed. His disbelief was very apparent, and some-how that realization brought bitterness.

Placing tight rein on the stir of her old impatient anger, Kadiya began her tale with the finding of the ancient mes-sage strip, the unease of the Hassitti dreamer. Step by step she covered her journey to Jagun's village, retold the com-ing of Salin and Smail, described what they had all seen in the scrying bowl. She was aware as she continued her tale that the three were listening very closely. When she men-tioned the western mountain country there had been a quick hand-to-belt gesture from Lamaril, as if he wished to free some weapon.

At her description of the plague, their expressions changed. There was horror in the eyes of the woman. But they did not interrupt and Kadiya brought her account to an end in a rush with the tale of what had happened in that strange room of the carven wall.

"So I came here," she ended.

Lamaril's hand lifted from his belt and reached out toward her—or rather toward the sword. There was a trilling as she had heard before. The great golden flower moved. From it drifted a wisp of rainbow motes such as embellished its petals. Those swirled outward and then down to lock upon her weap-on's pommel, bringing specks of brightness to the lid edge of each eye.

"It was red . . . this light which welcomed the diseased one . . . red." Though that did not have the inflection of a question, Kadiya answered the woman.

"Like flames from a fire which wrapped around, drew him . . . *it* . . . inward. But I did not touch the same key places," Kadiya repeated. "This"—she raised the sword a little— "chose for me."

"Into Varm's sanctuary," Lamaril said. "One of the sleepers
. . . but how awakened?"

"I do not know of any sleepers." Kadiya thought that question directed to her. "The Hassitti said that the Power which
Orogastus called upon could set askew the balances, that perhaps it freed some evil before he was destroyed by the talisman
of the Three. I have wielded a small Power, but I am not
learned in such things. I do not understand them even though
I was marked from birth by Binah to serve my people."

He might not have paid any attention to what she said, but
was rather thinking along another line. "With Varm, there is
Power and enough. We discovered that when we dealt with
him before. King's Daughter," now he did speak to Kadiya,
"from your account you have been sent, led, brought to That
Which Abides." He glanced up at the flower on the altar.
"That accepts you; we can no longer question."

Kadiya gave an inward sigh of relief. Now her thoughts
turned to the three who had not come with her. Had they been
indeed left behind in that Skritek guarded shrine, or . . .
dispatched elsewhere? She had so little of magical learning.
Jagun, Salin, and Smail had made themselves a part of her
quest; she could not leave them to death behind.

She spoke up boldly. "Those who came with me, are they
still in that place of doors and gates? Or have they been captured and taken elsewhere? They are my people and I hold
responsibility for them."

The woman shook her head. "They could not come with
you. Only because you held that from Yatlan"—she pointed
to the sword—"could you make entrance. They must remain
where they were."

"Jagun will not give up! He will seek to follow and perhaps
so be taken by the Skriteks. If this gate of yours has opened

once, surely it can again and let me back to my people. That monster I trailed is plainly not here and there remains the fact that it is *he* whom I hunt."

Now Lamaril shook his head in turn. "King's Daughter, we cannot open the Gate save when all agree and lend their strength. It remains locked."

That he spoke the truth Kadiya did not doubt. The awe — and the unease born from that awe when she had first sighted these strangers — was growing stronger though the need for telling her story had lessened it for a while. No way back? She felt the heat of the amulet, the vibration of Power in the sword. She was not ready to accept it yet. She could not return!

However, she went with them as they started down a long hall. Her sodden boots squelched across patterns and she was suddenly aware of the strange figure she must make in this place of light, order, and beauty with her stained and cracked shell mail, the battered helm covering most of her tangled hair. For such a shabby figure to proclaim herself a warrior against ancient evil was a farce. Kadiya bit her lip as she tried to match her steps with those taller ones who walked with such swift grace.

The lengthy chamber gave directly upon the open and Kadiya looked out upon a land under a warm sun where there hung no hint of storm cloud. Buildings of a clear white, over which played faint rainbow hues, were scattered about like a handful of carelessly tossed shells, rather than set in any pattern of streets as was Yatlan. Flowers and shrubs of brightly colored leaves covered the ground between.

People moved on small paths between the buildings. When they sighted Kadiya and her escort, they began to gather. All were Vanished Ones and they appeared to regard her with as much surprise as she had first looked upon those in the temple.

They were silent but Kadiya sensed what might have been a far-off murmur in her head, and she believed that they were using mind speech on a level she could not touch. The group gave way as Kadiya and the three came toward them but several fell in to follow. She searched each face as she went, wondering if she would be able to find among them others who were represented among the guards in Yatlan.

One such she did sight — another woman who joined the gathering company. They approached a second building, this nearly as commanding to the eye as that which the Hassitti had taken for dwelling and storage in Yatlan. However, here no vines covered the walls and the growth about the doorway had been tamed. The air was soft about her and there were fragrances carried by every soft puff of breeze. Her wonder grew. Much had been said of the Vanished Ones. It would seem that they chose to dwell in a place which held more beauty than Kadiya had thought possible for any land to produce.

The portal appeared to have no door. Laramil took a step in advance. Now he brought one hand against a shining plate beside the frame of that opening. A series of musical notes rose and fell in answer.

Kadiya saw only a solid shimmer of blue-green across the way. At the sound of that message the curtain of light — for so she thought it — split apart allowing them to enter.

Here was a hallway. Along it a number of doors opened, each curtained as far as she could determine with sheaths of light which shaded from deepest blue to a pale green. One of these, well down the hall, split also and then she was facing two who came from that doorway.

The Vanished Ones she had first met had been awe inspiring — but these two were true Power held in tight reserve. Kadiya stumbled, and then she went to her knees. The Archimage she had always sensed had been one to be given full honor. These two, woman and man, were such that Binah might have served. The Power which radiated from the newcomers was so strong that it could be felt, as one could feel the touch of the full sun at the height of the dry season.

In her hand the three eyes, now ringed with the gem-brilliant motes the flower had shed upon them, were fully open and staring, as if whatever animated the sword recognized a master energy to which they must respond. The amulet also blazed high. Yet Kadiya herself felt diminished, even though she had, she thought, made no false parade of what she was.

"Daughter of a land we departed," it was the woman who spoke, "why have you come to trouble us now? We had with-drawn as was right, for it was because of stiff pride and dark choices we were forced into exile. We left those whom we did not deal with fairly, those whose lives we arrogantly shaped, to live in peace."

Kadiya dared now to look straight at the speaker. "Great One, choices may have been made in the past, but the land is not free. One of evil who seems to be one of your race, though much disguised by a fresh ill, has sown such death across the land as those you left cannot defeat. It was he whom I followed and so came into this place of yours. Though I do not see how such can abide with you here."

"He does not," the man answered her. "That which is of Varm returned to his lord; the gate he entered was not ours. However, that one of Varm stirs — that is a thing of the Dark. Daughter of the new lands, take your rest and be at peace. We have much to consider now."

They were gone — gone as if they had been snuffed out can-dle-like, though she had been certain they were as solid as she.

Kadiya knelt, still staring at the spot where they had stood. This was the way the misty one of her first meeting in the garden had gone into nothingness.

There was a touch on her shoulder and she looked around up into the face of the woman who had accompanied her here.

"King's Daughter, come. Rest and refreshment await you. In truth there is much to be thought upon."

Kadiya got shakily to her feet. Some of the radiance of the amulet was spent; the eyes on the sword were half closed. That Power which had drawn them open might have left them so, though she now felt none of the usual exhaustion after their use. There was, though, a vast fatigue settling on her. She was aware it had been a long time since she had eaten, and her body's aches were now pressing on her.

The woman escorted her down the hallway to a doorway curtained in green which disappeared as they approached.

Kadiya had known the comforts of the ladies' bower at the Citadel, though at times she had been impatient with the need for such luxuries. Those were as nothing compared to what she was offered now.

She bathed in a shell shaped pool into which the woman dropped handfuls of powder, raising a froth of soothing ease to banish the discomforts of bruises, scratches, and all the other pains of rough travel.

While she relaxed in this pleasure the woman had seated herself on a stool. After she nodded briefly at Kadiya's thanks for such bounty she said abruptly:

"Tell me of Yatlan, far traveler. I am Lalan who was once of the inner guard there. Sometimes I dream of wandering along its streets, of the garden..." Her voice trailed away.

"The city has magic in it," said Kadiya. "From afar it seems to be in ruins as are all else of those places on the many islands. But within the gates"—she hesitated—"it seems to wait just as the Hassitti wait."

"The Hassitti." Some of the longing had vanished from the other's face, now there was a slight smile curving her lips. "Those little ones! They were always about and many were the tricks they played, bringing laughter even when the heart was heavy. What of the Hassitti now, King's Daughter?"

Kadiya once again described her meeting with the dwellers in Yatlan, going into more detail than she had earlier. She made much of the fact that they had preserved as well as they could what they considered to be the treasures of those who had left.

Lalan nodded. "So were they always . . . savers of things. Would that they could have come with us, for one misses their playfulness."

"You could not bring them?"

The woman shook her head. "The Gate would refuse any not of the blood. When we chose this exile we did so for the good of those others—those you call the Oddlings—and the Hassitti also. Those we raised out of strange seed and the time came that they must grow untended to become whatever they might be."

"The Gate did not refuse me." Climbing from the bath, Kadiya toweled her unruly hair.

"No, and *that* is a matter not yet to be understood," Lalan answered. She held out a garment of the same filmy material as she wore, not white but a gray like the mist rising in the early morning from a river. The shoulder brooches were of silver and set with stones shaped like bubbles of water, transparent but flecked with rainbows. Kadiya put aside the linked girdle laid by it, choosing rather her worn sword belt. She satisfied her hunger with food not unlike that the Hassitti had set before her—fruit and a bowl of creamy substance.

When Kadiya had done, Lalan who had shared her meal still asked questions concerning the swamplands. Perhaps, thought the girl, she had set to do this for a purpose and was not just moved by her own curiosity.

Kadiya had a question of her own. "Did the Great Ones in truth all leave Yatlan? I met one—or someone there—who spoke of knowledge to be gained. Was that real, or a dream, or did I hear a shadow speak?"

Lalan's amazement was manifest. "Tell me more of this." She spoke with the snap of an order. Kadiya obeyed.

When she had done Lalan drew a deep breath. "So—in that much did Carnot succeed. But for it to remain active for so long—" Again she gave a sigh. "He was the one of us who refused to believe that our day was truly past. Instead he swore that there would come after us some others worthy to walk our ways. Up almost to the last he worked with all his Power, and he possessed knowledge far beyond most. He strove to fashion that appearance which would be ready to aid such followers—if they were of the light."

She studied Kadiya closely. "And so his messenger appeared to you."

"Only once," Kadiya answered. "I hoped upon my return to Yatlan to meet with it again, but I did not."

"Power wears thin under the pressure of time. Perhaps making contact only once exhausted what Carnot left; he had little time for its fashioning, for he was injured to the death and was gone before our last retreat. However, perhaps it served well, for it did set you on the path which brought you here.

"Now—we have talked for long and you must be well wearied, Shadow Summoned. It is time for you to rest." As shadows deepened without she ushered Kadiya into yet another chamber. This was narrow, but with a window open to that fragrant breeze. In it, a bed which was fashioned of one puff of quilted material upon another, rather like the mats of the Oddlings.

With the sword still at hand Kadiya stretched upon that softness which yielded to and caressed her body. She gave a last murmur of thanks to her hostess and her eyes closed.

 RED — A RED AS OF FRESH SHED blood, like a hideous rain after some sky battle. Within the red moved things which that scarlet cloaked, just as there came sounds which were too faint to the ear to be heard as words, yet were of import.

The bloody curtain billowed unceasingly as if within it a force troubled air and life. Then Kadiya could see, no longer blinded by that spread of flame.

She gazed into a well of darkness where vast shadows hung heavy on three sides about a great chair. In that seeming throne was a limp figure, back bent, head on chest as if he lacked strength to lift it, hands outstretched upon the arms of the seat. There was no covering on his wasted body, save patches of yellow encrustation like wounds unhealed, the flesh gone rotten underneath.

Kadiya knew this to be the one they had trailed by the plague sign. Now so gaunt was his body the girl thought he might be dead.

The throne in which he lolled began to flush from black, as does a firebrand awaken once more to flame. Stronger and stronger grew that gleam, but the light did not vanquish the surrounding shadows; rather they drew in closer. On the burning chair the body writhed and twisted, the head came up and back. Eyes which did not hold any trace of sight were open, a mouth from which the lips looked to be eaten away grimaced. The creature might be shouting aloud in torment — but there was no other sound to break that which rose and fell as an undistinguishable chant.

The fire touch appeared to eat into the body. Now the yellow encrustations turned dark, were erased, perhaps burned away. The skeleton frame filled out, covering fully the bones which had been clearly etched under the skin only moments earlier. As the jaw relaxed the mouth closed firmly. Once more it was apparent the eyes could see.

Here sat now, straightening his back, holding hands before his face, as if to view their renewed life, one of the Vanished Ones. There was in him that same awe-inspiring Power which Kadiya had met in the two who ruled here beyond the wall.

But this was another place, well removed from the temple of the flower and the room in which she had fallen asleep. Although she sensed she slept, Kadiya was sure that what she watched was true.

A length of shadow dropped down upon the man on the burning throne. He caught at it, pulled it against him. Then he wore a corselet of scales like unto those the Oddlings fashioned, save this one was of glistening black which, with every movement of his body, showed a running of scarlet which was like the play of flames.

Once more he stretched forth a hand to the shadow, fingers crooked, and a portion of that dusky cloak loosed. Now in his grasp was a rod perhaps a third of a spear's length. Atop it formed a ball which lengthened and modeled itself into the likeness of a skull, such a one as mimicked in miniature that of the Skritek.

The eye holes of the skull glared as red as the chair when the man raised it high, his face a mask of victorious exultation. He arose, and the throne on which he had suffered that change began to dull, taking on the gray of spent ashes.

Now he held the rod in both hands. His head bent and he blew into the open jaws of the skull. With a quick turn of wrist he whirled it about. From the jaws into which he had breathed there shot a beam of yellow-green—that same color which had marked the plague.

Straight at Kadiya it shot. Had he sensed her there? However, the blow, if that it was meant to be, did not strike.

There was a flash of fire again and then dark. She felt the caress of a breeze as she opened her eyes. This was the room wherein she had fallen asleep. Beyond the window a quiet glaze of dusk laid over the world. Kadiya pulled herself up to see what might lay farther beyond. There was a section of garden serene in the twilight and suddenly she felt as if she must be free of walls, out into that place of quiet and beauty.

Quiet and beauty, far removed from that place of dark and flame wherein one had been granted new life and given a foul weapon to ensure power.

For she was sure that this had been a true dream as the Hassitti knew like unto the scrying of Salin. She had actually seen something which had happened afar.

So needful was it to seek cleanliness, freshness, and the peace beyond, Kadiya actually dropped from the window, instead of seeking a way out by door. Under her bare feet was the softness of thick turf; around her a wall of tall, flowering bushes, bending a little in an early night wind. She stood, taking deep breaths of that scented air.

That she must share what she had seen with those who now sheltered her Kadiya knew, yet she shrank from its telling. It seemed as if the very fact that she had been a witness in some way sullied her—that none could pass through that blood-flame, look upon the Power which wrought so mightily in that throne, without bearing some small stain.

Kadiya took a step forward. Even remembering made her seem to smell again the vile stench of the plague. She leaned forward to brush her face against one of the large blooms, drinking in its perfume. One of the fire spark insects she had seen in the garden of Yatlan halted for a second, perched on her hand, fluttering its gem bright wings.

"Yes," she spoke aloud to the night and the insect, "yes, this is . . ." She sought for a word which would encompass all she felt at that moment.

"Is what, King's Daughter?"

The voice startled Kadiya. Her hand went to the hilt of the sword she had belted on before she left the sleeping chamber. He had come from around a tall bush and stood watching her with, she believed, something of a challenge in his eyes.

"Lamaril!"

Soft footed he crossed the space between them. Before she might guess his intent, his hand was beneath her chin, raising her head a fraction so that he might look straight into her eyes.

"You continue to name me, King's Daughter. Would you

then bind me in some fashion? What do you know of the uses of Power?"

"Very little." With a twist she freed herself from that hold, her inner peace now fled. "I have no reason to bind you, warrior."

"Tell me of this likeness of me which you have seen."

She repeated in a few words how she and Jagun had come upon the mud buried mounds along the forgotten road and how the last one, freed of its rank covering, had been the statue pointing the way to Yatlan.

"Jagun knew old tales," she ended. "It was he who said that you were a mighty hero of a last battle."

For the first time she saw him smile, just such a shadowy lifting of lips as Lalan had shown when Kadiya had told her of the Hassitti.

"It is given few to know that they are so honored," he commented. "Though old tales are often changed beyond belief. So—the outguard still stands their ground even if they have been layered in mud. Now that gives one to think. Erous, Nuers, Isyat, Fahiel and I—the last of them."

"There are others—in the city, on the steps which lead to the great garden," Kadiya said. "Women and men—are they guards also?"

His smile was gone, but he nodded.

"Yes." He spoke softly and his gaze shifted as if he saw beyond her now. "There were many of us—and then few, few who won to the Gate. The land itself arose at the last and spewed us all forth, both Dark and Light together. King's Daughter—"

Kadiya interrupted him. "My name is Kadiya. If there is any Power lying in names, then I give mine in full exchange."

Again that small half smile on his lips. "Kadiya." He repeated her name as if he tasted it. "That name is strange, but you bear it proudly, Lady of Power. Tell me now, what of the old land? It must be far changed."

"First tell me," she countered. "Where is there a chair of fire in which a dying man may seat himself to be restored?"

Smile was completely gone; golden eyes narrowed. "What know you of Varm?"

"Nothing save I have heard his name mentioned here. But I have dreamed, and I believe, dreamed truly, even as one looks into a scrying bowl." She told him of what she had seen of that place of fire and shadow.

"So!" There was an odd note in his voice, as of weariness. "It rises again. Perhaps it is endless, this struggle. But Uono and Lica must know of this and speedily. Come!" His hand closed about her upper arm and he drew her along with him to a garden path and down that to the front door of the building which she had so unceremoniously left.

This time his fingers on the plate beside that portal drummed heavily and the sound which followed was deeper and more imperative, a demand for attention.

She had not tried to free herself from his hold for she sensed that this was indeed a matter of great import and she felt at that moment his presence was somehow akin to Jagun's, that he would stand behind her.

Once more she came into the presence of the two who had made her free of their hospitality. Swiftly Kadiya repeated the story of her dream, seeing man and woman exchanging glances as she spoke.

When she was finished, the man said with some of the same weariness she had detected in Lamaril:

"Once more — is there never to be an ending?"

"Can there be?" questioned the woman. "For each thing there is an opposite and the balance holds. Where there is light, dark abides, perhaps so the light can be better known. However, Varm's Power is awake and I think our battlefield lies waiting again. Save that the Gate is locked."

"That Gate opens for no one!" the man declared, but Lamaril interrupted:

"There are the Guardians."

"That is a task—" But the woman was not answering the Captain. Instead she was looking full at Kadiya, measuring with a stern weighing, so that the girl tensed as one facing an attack.

"It could be done." The man was musing, and he too eyed the girl.

Her initial awe of them had faded somewhat. Kadiya wanted to understand.

"Was I led here for some task, Noble Ones? And do you now hesitate to tell me what that can be? The mires I have chosen with my free will. Those are now riven with plague and perhaps other dangers. As long as this is mine"—she touched the sword—"and not drawn back to that which sent it, then I must follow the path it points."

Still they were watching her with that measurement in their gaze.

"You are of a people we do not know," the woman said slowly. "Yet it would seem that you have made the old land somewhat yours. If Binah dealt with you, then she found you worthy. Tell us more, King's Daughter, of your race and of the old land. For this is a matter which cannot be decided without thought."

The history of Kadiya's people had been impressed upon her in spite of her childhood resistance to spending time over the ancient rolls instead of wandering with Jagun. Kadiya strove now to put into order all she remembered of that teaching. Of how her people had come overseas and made the swamplands theirs, protected by the mountain barriers which kept them safe for so long, those barricades balanced on the south by the dense forests of Tassaleyo.

She told of the draining of the polders in the north and of the tilling of the water-freed land there, of their dealings with the Oddlings, of the fair for traders at Trevista, and how her people respected the swamp dwellers and between them there were often ties of friendship.

"We are not a great people," she said, though she returned their gaze as might an equal, "but we did well by the land. We served where we might, held fast against the Dark. The Nyssomu welcome us, the Uisgu see in us no danger. We do not intrude upon their lands except for trade, and they are welcome on ours. Only the Skritek we fight — but then all who live in the mire hold weapons ready against those."

Kadiya tried to paint word pictures of her father's court at the Citadel, spoke of the Archimage Binah's coming at the birth of the three sisters to bestow on them the amulets of Power.

Then came flooding the memories of blood, of cruel death, of horror, as she retold the invasion from Labornok, the cruelty of Voltrik and his cold master-servant Orogastus. There was her own quest, and that of Haramis and Anigel, which ended in a clash of great Powers, nearly tearing apart all they had known.

She talked for a long time, seated in that room. Twice Lamaril had moved from behind her, in his hand a cup from which she gratefully drank to relieve her parched throat.

Outside the windows, night deepened. With the coming of

the gloom, there had spread radiance from certain points high
on the walls so that she could see well the faces of those to
whom she told her story.

"Of my return to your Yatlan, what happened there"—she
touched the sword, an ever present weight at the shabby belt
about her waist—"I have already spoken. But what I have
said of the mires—that is what passes there now."

"Yatlan," the woman named Lica repeated, and there was
a soft note in her voice. "Yatlan, where we left our farewell
gifts in the everflowing waters." She raised one hand, half
extended it toward Kadiya. "You who have come, how is Yatlan now?"

"A city forgotten, but not despoiled." Kadiya remembered
the treasure of the fountain. "Your gifts lie undisturbed, Noble
One. It has its indwellers; they name themselves Hassitti and
they have labored to hoard safely all which was left behind.
There is the garden...." Now Kadiya raised the sword and
held it fully into view.

"This was born of that garden. Binah, the Archimage, laid
it upon me and my two sisters to be the saviors of Ruwenda.
She gave me a root which guided me to Yatlan and there I
planted it in the garden. Out of it grew what you see—the
third part of a most powerful talisman to save our country.
Nothing else did I take from there." She thought fleetingly of
the necklet from the fountain.

The woman stirred. "So much—so strange—this might be
a tale of another land than that we once knew."

"It is the truth!" Kadiya held the cup away from her lips
after another swallow. It might be water she drank so, but it
carried a faint taste she could not identify—tart yet comforting
to a dry throat.

"We do not deny that, King's Daughter. It is your truth,

which is the truth of now. But part of it relates another darker and more threatening truth.

"We were—are—a people who seek always to learn." The woman spoke slowly. "Secrets were wrested from the earth, from the fount of life itself. We could command rock, sea, land. We grew—perhaps we grew too mindful of the Powers we sought with such greediness.

"We meddled. Out of the life we knew we brought new beings: those you call Oddlings, and the Hassitti. We changed plant growth either to yield food stuff or to please the eyes. For a long time we kept ourselves occupied with such meddling and modelings.

"However, Power draws Power. Those who wield it are never satisfied—ever grasping for more. There were some among us who no longer worked with that which was of nature, but rather sought to create anew from other sources.

"Power rose against Power. Others awoke in time to see where these researches and acts led. There was a war—" She paused, and lines appeared about her mouth as if she chewed upon some bitter thing.

"We learned the Dark side of Power then. The land was riven apart, the waters released to strike and overwhelm. We were no longer the same country, for the mires had their birth in those days. Those most greedy for the Dark loosed experiments of their own: the Skritek, even plants which killed and feasted on their kills.

"Cities were overwhelmed and fell and still we fought, force against force, breaking new secrets loose from the earth under us and the sky above. In the end Death strode always with us. Some of the Dark who had loosed the worst of the Black Knowledge could not be slain. There remained a handful of them.

"Fleeing a last confrontation, they sought a refuge in the mountains. There they had prepared a place of last resource, for they had a mighty foreseer, one Varm." She nearly hissed that name. "But it did him and them little good, for our curse was laid. If they came forth from their hidey-hole all the ills of the world would strike them into rottenness.

"Into this hiding place they went, save for Varm and two of his acolytes. The others laid themselves in what were tombs, to sleep until the day that Varm with his foresight had assured them would come when they would rule again.

"Our striking force had been hot on their trail but when they reached that mountain hideaway Varm and his two were gone. However, they sealed that place of sleeping death with strong magic which by all their calculations would abide forever.

"Varm had his own place." The woman paused. "To one who does not know our learning this is hard to explain. You came through a barrier—a barrier which was of time and space. This place is not in your world and we who chose to come here cannot return. Varm also found such a refuge, drawing on his own Powers to reach it. But because he was of Dark instead of Light, he came not here.

"What we must now believe is that one of those death sleepers was freed from imprisonment, and that he sought Varm to gain from him that which would bring forth his kin once more."

Lamaril was at Kadiya's side. He touched her shoulder gently.

"Kadiya, tell now again your dream."

"I do not believe it was a dream," she said slowly. "I have not the farsight though I have scryed. But this, I swear once more, is what I saw in my sleep." And she repeated it all, trying not to forget a single detail, of that chair of fire and he who had occupied it.

Before any of her listeners could speak, Kadiya had a question for which she almost fiercely demanded an answer:

"You have said that you cannot return to the mires. Can this follower of Varm do so? Can Varm himself? We are still striving to heal the wounds of war. Must we face and fight an even greater enemy?" Not one question but many and she felt the old cold deep within her as she impatiently waited for an answer.

The man spoke first. "King's Daughter, our road and Varm's have long stretched in opposite directions. We accepted that there was no return. Perhaps he has sought to find one. Or else the servant he called to him can be armored to face return."

Kadiya faced them squarely—her awe of them had been overcome.

"Noble Ones, do you now say that there is no aid you can give us? Do we lose our lives and our land to that creeping plague of the Dark? I do not think that even Haramis with all her learning can summon up a weapon against that!"

"There is a way...." Once more she was aware of Lamaril beside her. "Were not the Silent Ones left ... perhaps for this very purpose? Here is one who may summon them if you will."

The woman's nod was abrupt. "This evil sprang from us. We cannot remain unminding that it spreads again. There was an Oath sworn once, Commander of the Sindona." Now she addressed Lamaril. "You wish to hold by it?"

"Lica, I do, and so do those others who swore it."

17

KADIYA SHIFTED FROM ONE FOOT to the other. Gone was her broken and battered shell armor, the dented helm, all her other travel-worn clothing. Nor did she wear the gauzy robe. Rather her shoulders were tightly clasped by chain mail fashioned from the blue-green metal from the storehouse of the Vanished Ones. And below that breeches of something as tough as well-cured leather and yet as supple as the finest weaving her people knew.

At her left side her arm curved around a new helm made with a forepart like a half mask. When donned it fitted down as far as her mouth, and she peered through eyeholes filled with greenish glass. It was encircled with an embossed wreath in the form of trilliums, but these were yellow as the great flower which, to her right, now moved slightly in its altar bed.

They had told her what must be done, but certainly they

had promised her little help in the doing of it. And the strangeness of the task seemed to make a matter of a bard's tale only to be marveled at. Still, those ranked before her believed and so she must accept that such a thing could be.

Six of them to the fore, with Lamaril at their head. Twelve ranked behind, and she knew each face there — these were the people of stone, the Guardians — save those she fronted were living and breathing.

All were bare of body, nor did they carry weapons. Would they find the armor, the arms they needed beyond the Gate? Among the scrap heaps gathered by the Hassitti there was certainly much. But weapons? Unless their weapons were far different from sword and spear.

The great golden flower swung, shifting into the air those rainbow particles. Uono and Lica advanced the far side of the altar. In the woman's hand there was a bowl of golden hue, yet near transparent. The man carried a flask of silver, wide-mouthed but no larger than could be easily fastened at a belt — a sword belt as shabby and stained as the one Kadiya wore.

A trilling of song carried from the flower to the company massed behind those who waited. Though Kadiya did not understand the words, she felt the swell of that invocation.

Trumpets might awaken her own people to battle. The shell horns of the Oddlings would sound harsh and rough toned here. This was not an urging on to victory, it was a farewell. There was a chance of return for those who waited, yes, but it was only that, and none could build upon it.

These were not her kind. She was not sure that she, no matter how strong the cause, could do what they were about to do. Her eyes kept going back to Lamaril. She saw not the one who stood before her, but rather that other, mud stained, footed in the muck of the swamplands.

. . . ——————————————————————— . . .

Three of their timeless days she had waited and twice he had sought her out. He had asked pointed questions, the inquiries of a fighting man about to order troops to battle.

Trust — they accepted her with trust. She had known the exultation of victory against odds when they had gone up against Voltrik and Orogastus. This moment was deeper than any she had known before.

They had told her that this was a place lifted out of time as she knew it. There was no past, the future did not matter; there was only the present. She must step back into time from a place which had enfolded her with peace far greater than even the garden of Yatlan had bestowed — for that garden was but a pale echo of what was known here.

The singing melded into the trilling, the trilling into the singing. On its altar the flower began to move faster. Lica stepped forward, set the bowl with precision at the foot of that swaying stem. Out of the heart of the blossom there arose a puff of golden particles, pollen shed by the flower's movements. The waiting bowl began to glow as the rain of tiny motes gathered within.

From the Vanished Ones the song soared. Perhaps they encouraged the flower to that shedding. When the bowl was half filled, the huge flower shuddered and drooped, its triangle of petals no longer so stiffly apart, its rich color fading.

Lica knelt before the altar. Her hands dug into the dark soil which rooted the plant there. Head flung back, eyes closed, lines of strain deepened about her mouth.

Kadiya could feel it! Just as her energy fed the eyed sword when she was using it, so was this woman of the Vanished Ones giving of her strength to feed the flower.

The singing grew softer, the trilling a mere scattering of notes. Lica slumped forward until her forehead rested against the edge of the altar. The flower straightened, its petals once more crisply apart, renewed.

It was Kadiya's turn now. She had been drilled in what must be done as a part of this alien ceremony which she did not understand.

She placed her helm on the floor and carefully edged along to stand beside Lica. Reaching over the woman's bowed shoulder, the girl took up the basin with both hands. What it held she knew was irreplaceable. She had been warned that such a shower of flower dust could not be summoned again.

Holding it breast high before her, Kadiya turned and descended the one step to the floor of the temple. Then she went forward.

Lamaril—he was the first. She was still not sure of what would happen, only that she must not lose hold on what she held, that which would bind those of this place to her, to what lay beyond the barrier she had passed to reach this place.

As she came before the Commander of the Sindona she raised the bowl a fraction. His hand came up, his fingers dipped to stir what rested within. A tiny spiral of the pollen climbed to wreath Lamaril's head.

Mist widened from that thread of gold, lost its rich sheen, became a cloud which descended to cloak the man from head to foot. An end of thread emerged from that mist, spun its way back to the basin. Lamaril was gone.

Kadiya swallowed, took firmer grip on what she held. To be told that this would happen, and then to see it—they were two very different things.

One by one they vanished as she stood before each and watched. Yet the bowl was no fuller, no heavier in her hand. This was magic such as she had never witnessed.

Once the last of those who waited was gone, Kadiya came back to the altar with the bowl. Lica was on her feet, although she drooped against the stone wherein the flower was planted. She was plainly still drained of strength.

She put out her hand and Kadiya delivered the bowl to her. Then Lica turned to where Uono stood, the widemouthed flask ready. Into that she poured the pollen, so slowly that it might be falling grain by minute grain. Uono fitted the top over the mouth. He moistened the forefinger of his right hand and held that up before the flower. Once more it loosed some of the rainbow dust, and Uono smeared it carefully to seal lid to container.

Once that was done, he held it out to Kadiya. The girl took a deep breath; her fingers closed about the flask. She hooked it to her sword belt, making very sure that the fastening was tight.

Having done so, she took up once more her helm. What farewell could she make? They had done what they could for the sake of a land no longer theirs. She could mouth words assuring them that she would obey orders, but that much they already knew. She had always been quick of speech, even as she was often rash of action. Now there were no words, perhaps not even thoughts to be offered.

The two by the altar did not seem to expect such from her. Uono gestured and Kadiya obeyed. She turned with Lica on one side, the tall fellow Councilor on the other. With them as escort, she came to face a wall.

Even now Kadiya could not be sure of what might happen and she believed that they shared her unease. She could only do what seemed right to her.

Kadiya drew the sword. Those eyes, the edges of the lids

still encrusted by the glitter of the plant's bestowing, were fully open. She held the pointless blade firmly and turned the eyes upon the wall.

There came that united beam of force, and she knew the familiar drain of energy. Where the beam struck the stone the light spread, clung to the surface as might a cloak plastered tightly there.

Kadiya keeping her attention only on that block of light walked forward. This was the test. There was no stone there. No. This was an open doorway which was ready for her.

She held in mind the picture of that doorway. Again followed that attack of vertigo, that feeling of being wrenched apart from all that was stable and known. She stood again in that underground room to which they had traced Varm's follower. Facing her, spear at ready, dart at pipe mouth, were Jagun and Smail, while behind them Salin's fingers wove strange patterns of power in the air.

There was no welcome for her. All Kadiya could see was a distrustful wariness. Then she remembered the masking of her new helm and quickly pushed it up, to reveal her face.

"Farseer!" Jagun's was a muted cry but one of excited welcome. "But —" His stare of astonishment was open. "You were gone. You come again. And now you wear new armor —"

"Come and gone — how long, Jagun?" She had the memory of days behind her, a hand's fingers of them. Had these three lingered here for all that time?

"As long as it would take to skin a borick — a young one perhaps," he returned.

"But — no. It was days!" Kadiya felt the chill of fear. What had those others said? That where they dwelt time had no meaning.

However, she was not the only one who might return here.

"The walking death, he of Varm—" she demanded. "Has that one also returned?"

All three of the Oddlings shook their heads.

"Only you, Farseer, and you have been away only a fraction of time—not days."

She looked over her shoulder at the wall through which she had come. So in this she had won a little time as she knew time. That other one had not yet returned.

"The Skritek?" Kadiya asked.

"They have not returned either," Jagun assured her. "Salin"—he nodded toward the wisewoman—"has set a warning, and nothing has come to disturb it."

Once more luck had favored them. She stroked the flask so tightly clipped to her belt. There was a long journey ahead, and to have to fight their way to her goal would mean delay—if not defeat.

"King's Daughter," Salin asked, "what did you find beyond?"

"Those who once ruled," she answered. "The Noble Ones."

"And they come also to our aid?" The Uisgu woman looked beyond Kadiya to the wall.

"In their fashion," Kadiya replied. "But they will not be with us in this place. And, it would be well to be away before that other returns. He carries with him a thing of black Power. We must go!"

She had already reached the end of the screen which concealed the secret entrance and, without further questions, the others crowded behind her. Once more they followed that staircase, this time back to the depths. There had been no trifling with the crude raft which had carried them here. Kadiya saw the nostrils of the three Oddlings distend and she knew that they strove to pick up any scent which might betray the Skritek. But if those creatures knew of this way they must not have used it for a long time.

Again they embarked on that clumsy raft and headed out into the open. Kadiya watched overhead for any movement which might betray the presence of the monster Weaver whose net they had destroyed. However, they passed the tattered strings unmolested.

Kadiya was still tense as they came out within the shadows of the tree root arches. This land of thorns and monsters still enclosed them. Somehow it was difficult for her to accept that they had passed even this far unchallenged. There were clouds overhead but no rain fell.

By that evening they reached the improvised shelter at the sinister ruins of the tower. They had not talked during the journey; all had been too much on guard. The uneasiness which burdened Kadiya was clearly shared by her companions. Still it was she who felt the greatest drive of all—the need to call into being the help they needed.

Before them lay a new danger—or rather an old one reinforced. That contagion sown by the follower of Varm had spread and they had to avoid patches of corruption with care. It was now deep twilight. Luckily those nauseous spots gave forth a wan purulent light in warning. They were being edged by that putrid growth away from a direct route. At last, they came to a place where they could not pass; the thorn hedge formed once more a barrier. Here the thorns themselves were diseased, covered with lumps like the pustules of incurable illness. Kadiya watched some break open and scatter minute flecks of greenish matter which soared and caught, to eat into whatever the breeze drove them toward.

She drew the sword. Though she well knew that what she would do would weaken her, she had no choice. The eyes had not closed since she had stood in the Temple of the Timeless Flower. Indeed, they appeared brighter, oddly more aware because of those sparking motes along the lids.

Kadiya hardened her will. Even as it had proved a key to the door wall, now the top orb sent forth a dagger of light which was joined by beams from the other two. That tongue of brilliance slashed at the corrupted vegetation before them as Kadiya swung it back and forth, her arm moving as if she were using the weapon against an armed enemy.

An answering burst of fire among the thorns spread as she advanced. The other three fell into a single line behind her. She could hear faintly a chant and then felt a touch on her shoulder. Salin had moved up beside her and from the wise-woman came a flow of strength in answer to her own need. That increased, once and then again. Jagun and Smail must have linked in turn.

The stink of death was half overborne by the odor of burning brush. Kadiya strove to push faster. This was betraying their presence and any roving Skritek would be drawn to investigate.

She stumbled once; half burned roots thrusting forth from the ground could catch the unwary. Still she used the sword, though her arm was growing heavy. She could not keep her original quick pace. The drain was continuous in spite of what the others gave to help.

Kadiya staggered again, caught herself. She could see that the beam of light she was wielding had shortened. Now it flickered once or twice. She bit her lower lip and pushed doggedly on. Her world had narrowed to that light, to the dark of the thorn wall immediately before her.

"Farseer!"

Not a vocal call, but a mind send, powerful enough to pierce her concentration.

"We have passed beyond the plague."

"We are not clear of the thorn—" she said aloud, too wary of using the least bit of inner strength in mind speech.

"This is for us, Farseer. Let us clear the way."

Jagun's offer might have been a spell. Her arm fell to her side, and, though she gritted teeth and struggled, she could no longer hold the sword upright. The glow of light touched the ground, flicked in a rhythm like the beat of a heart, was gone. Nor could she flog her will into raising it again.

Salin moved in beside her, pulling Kadiya's left arm across her bent shoulders, seemingly supporting them both with her staff. With the sword light gone Kadiya moved through a darkness close to blindness. She felt rather than saw the other two Oddlings push past.

What could they use to clear the road? she wondered dimly. She heard a crackling ahead, but not that of fire. Then Salin was urging her on, taking only three or four steps at a time. They did have a path, though it was very narrow and thorns reached out now and then to grate across that silk-sleek armor of the Vanished Ones, scraping but finding no opening to score the flesh beneath.

"On," Salin's mind voice came only dimly. "They use the passage knives, Noble One. It will not be far now—there is water smell ahead."

Kadiya wavered on only with the wisewoman's aid. She became dimly aware that the brush was no longer so tightly woven. She looked up. The eye holes of the helm limited her vision but she thought she caught a glimpse of stars in the early night sky where the clouds had parted. She doubted that she could keep on her feet much longer.

Dimly Kadiya was amazed at the strength of the wisewoman who not only was keeping her standing now but leading her forward as well.

Then she was no longer on her feet at all, but lying, to look up at a star through a frame of clouds. The weight of those dark clouds closed down upon her. Her last act was to grip the sword lest she lose the one weapon she believed hers alone to the encroaching dark.

 THERE WAS THE SOUND OF VOICES but Kadiya could not understand any words. As she opened her eyes she was struck by the full rays of the sun. Bracing herself on one elbow the girl looked about her.

The three Oddlings were together. Before Salin was her scrying bowl; on either side knelt the two males, all intent on what they were viewing. Salin's fingers moved in a pattern. There came an exclamation from Jagun and his hand dropped to the spear lying beside him.

Kadiya need not look at the vision the wisewoman had summoned. She felt the fear exuding from the three like the swamp mist. With effort she pulled to her knees.

They were on a hillock which gave root to some bushes, but none of these sprouted thorns. The girl could smell that rottenness which clung to the deepest swamp, but sensed none of the plague threat.

"What comes?" Kadiya found her voice. Moving brought back some of the feeling of drained weakness.

She had startled the three. Jagun's head jerked as he looked to her.

"Evil, Farseer." He was on his feet swiftly to come to her. His hands on her shoulders drew her up with a strength which seemed too great even for his wiry body. "Look you."

Kadiya found she could waver forward by his help to drop to her knees in the same spot where he had been crouching a moment earlier. She leaned forward to see the picture in the bowl.

Once more there was so real a scene that she might be watching it through a window. The background was plainly the thorny barrier through which they had fought their way. Here moved a squad of Skritek, armed with rude clubs and spears.

It was the one they escorted who Kadiya saw most clearly. This was the man of the flaming throne. There was no sign of the disease which had eaten him. Now he was tall, strong, as clean of skin and as forceful of aura as Lamaril. In his hand was the weapon rod. And, though the Skritek were plainly escorting him, they did not come too near, rather kept several paces before or behind.

The follower of Varm was pushing forward with great strides, looking ahead as if he sought a goal which he must reach in a limited time. Then, suddenly, he stopped, almost in midstep. The rod came up, his head turned right and then left. There was a seeking in his stance.

Salin waved a hand across the basin. There was an answering swirl of the liquid there and the scene was instantly erased. Yet still on the Uisgu woman's face there remained a shadow of fear.

"That one," mind speech flared to Kadiya, "knew he was spied upon!" She touched the bowl. "We dare not use this again."

"What if we use it to communicate with another?" asked Kadiya. "Would that also betray us?" She was thinking of Haramis. Perhaps her sister at this very moment could produce that which would arm them better. Knowledge could be more powerful than weapons alone.

Salin shook her head. "King's Daughter, each time I call upon this" — she now cradled the bowl in both hands — "there is a troubling of that which we cannot see. Such could guide that one to us."

"You have that. . . ." Jagun indicated the sword.

"I have more than that, but I must be able to summon it," replied Kadiya. "The Vanished Ones will join us — in their own fashion, and through our aid in return. Jagun, we must reach the road of the Sindona. Can you find that trail?"

Find it he did after a period of scouting. They saw the sun vanish. They spent the night on guard, another day. As her strength returned, Kadiya pushed the pace as well as she could, the flask rubbing against her side with every step, urging her on.

Those humps of brick hard clay stood even as she had seen them before, marking the forgotten road which led to Yatlan. At the head of that line stood Lamaril, the only one uncovered. Not quite as she had seen him in the place behind the wall, but as he might once have been in this world.

It was late afternoon when they reached that place. And certainly this was exposed territory. Kadiya hoped that that other party they had spied on would not be heading in this direction. Varm's follower had his own priority; time lashed at him even as it did at her.

"We must free these, all of them"—she pointed to the lumps of yellow, hardened earth—"as soon as we can."

They asked no questions. They had not since she had rejoined them. She believed at times Jagun still glanced at her sidewise in a faint awe. Now they set to work, chipping at the mud with spear and knife point. Kadiya worked as swiftly as she could with her dagger. The clay was hard baked and the work tedious, though now and then a lucky stroke of blade would set a large lump flying.

Twilight closed in, yet Kadiya and the others did not halt. Perhaps they, too, were now gripped with that need for hurry. Exposed as they were they could not start a fire to give them light, but Smail went away and came back shortly with a twist of reeds in which were some of those same light grubs Jagun had called upon for a lantern in Yatlan.

Limited as that light was, it still gave them a view of where to strike.

The yellow muck covering the old road, which the hidden statues marked, came alive with the dark. Creatures crawled there, though they could be sighted only by the movements of the surface. Salin stopped her pecking away at the mound she had chosen and rifled the journey pack for a small container. This in hand she circled the scene of their labors, shaking out a reddish dust.

In spite of her new helm giving protection against those minute flies which were a torment to the eyes, and that grease which all swamp farers used against the insects, Kadiya felt the sting of bites. Doggedly she continued her task.

Half free now was the statue of a woman whose face Kadiya

remembered from the assembly in the flower temple. Kadiya inserted her bruised fingers in a crack and gave a hard pull. A whole section of the mud fell away; the woman stood free.

Out over the muck there was a sudden glow of green light. Kadiya wheeled, startled. The light hung suspended for several breaths and then moved toward them. If it were carried by any creature it did not shine downward to show them what held it torch-like.

Nor was it now alone. Three other such burst into view. Smail stood away from his work. He had nearly freed another of the Sindona—a man.

"Ossfire!" Salin threw herself once more at the pack. This time she produced a jar into which Smail inserted a dart. His pipe was at his lips.

It was too dark to follow the dart in flight if it could be detected in its swift passage. There came a loud pop. The nearest of the fireballs advancing toward them was no longer a globe. Rather, segments of it flared out like sparks, plummeting down into the muck. Methodically Smail picked off the others.

Kadiya coughed. Her nose felt as if some of that fire had invaded it, and there followed a stench heavy enough to make her gag.

She leaned one hand against the second pillar she had set to work upon. Kadiya retched, bringing up the remains of the rations she had shared an hour earlier. Salin was beside the girl as she wiped the back of her hand across her mouth.

"Eat!" the wisewoman held between finger and thumb what looked like a wad of mangled leaves.

Doubtfully Kadiya obeyed. The stuff was sour. She wanted to spit it out, yet she had faith in Salin's knowledge of swamp-wise protection. When she forced herself to swallow the juice her teeth had drawn out of that mouthful, she discovered that she was no longer nauseous.

There was a moon tonight. As it rose its beams added to the grub light giving them a better chance to keep at their labors — though it was no easy job.

When the mounds had at last been cleared of the mud coating, Kadiya judged the time to be close to morning. Her shoulders ached and her fingers, bearing small cuts from the sharp edges of scraps she had pulled away, were becoming stiff and painful. But she was ridden by the thought that if she rested now she would lose the battle before it began — she dared not yield to any longing for sleep.

Salin once more came to the rescue with dressings for their minor wounds. Kadiya wiped part of hers away, afraid the slick stuff might impede the action she must now take.

The Oddlings withdrew as the girl slipped the flask free from her belt. With her dagger tip already dull from the use she had put it to this night, she pried up the cover.

The gray of very early morning surely was enough to give her the sight of the statues which she needed. Setting her teeth together with the effort she was making to hold the flask steady, Kadiya again wiped the fingers of her other hand across her breeches. Then she advanced to the statue of Lamaril. Between thumb and forefinger she pinched some pollen. Then reaching upward, the girl smeared it first on the forehead between those gem eyes. So much — now!

A second pinch of the pollen, this time for the lips.

She drew back a little. They had told her what to do, but it was hard to believe, truly difficult to understand.

The light of predawn was so dim. Had there been a change in the statue?

Then . . . That head, which had been for so many hundreds

turned in one direction, moved. The eyes looked down and around at her. That monstrous head which Lamaril had held in his stone hand as a warning was tossed aside, to go sailing out over the mud.

"It is done, well done—"

Kadiya looked to the man whose eyes met hers.

"Then I shall do it again!" she answered shakily, and stepped with renewed energy to the next of those they had freed from their mud prisons.

They lived and breathed, stood looking about them. Kadiya restoppered the flask.

"This—this—" It was one of the women who had been freed, and who now stood looking about her bewildered. "What is this?"

The sun was up far enough to give full view of that mud patched stretch which concealed the ancient road. Though in some places the swamp had a beauty all its own, this was a desolation.

"This is what has come," Lamaril said.

"Evil." One of the others of the Sindona moved a little forward to the edge of that yellow expanse.

It was Kadiya who answered. "Not evil," she replied. "This is of the swamp and not of that which the Dark has brought." If these who had returned saw evil in such as this, she wondered what they would say when and if they faced some smear of the plague infested land.

"The swamp," Lamaril repeated. "And time. Once more we must deal with time. That way then, and the sooner the better." His hand swung forward into the same gesture the statue had held, pointing out the path of the old road.

"The trail is more dangerous than it seems," Kadiya warned. "Jagun—"

With a start the Oddling came to her. He and the two Uisgu had been watching with awe those Kadiya had aroused into life.

Now he moved out, spear ready to sound for the steadiness of the way under the mud scum. They did not wear the water walking leaves but Kadiya trusted to Jagun's memory of how they had spanned this way before. She had her own memories of that way and they were dour ones. Death had trod the trail before her and left sickly evidence of its passing.

They crossed the open and came to that place of solid land where the brush and twisted canes and vines gave way to true trees. She was so tired—the night's labor behind her had been an added burden to the draining of the sword's power in the Thorny Hell.

When they were a little within the marching of the trees Lamaril touched her shoulder.

"There must be rest for you and those little ones who worked so valiantly." He nodded toward the Oddlings. "Though there have been ill changes, this way we know. We shall march and you follow. But first we encamp for a space."

At least there was a breeze here which did not carry with it too much of the swamp odor. She had nearly reached the end of her energy, Kadiya discovered, when she at last allowed herself to slip to the ground.

There was life here—birds twittered in the trees and there was a scurrying of a small furred thing up one curved trunk. Smail was busy pulling out a packet covered by leaves pinned together with small twigs. Kadiya began to struggle with the buckles of her own bag, only to have it pulled gently out of her grasp.

Lamaril knelt there. Others of his command struck out among the trees, but he waited while she drew out a packet of the dried and pressed roots which had so little taste but were enough to keep one going on the trail.

Kadiya pushed aside her pack. On the crushed mat of fern where it had lain she set down her share of what supplies they carried. Jagun added a bundle of dried strips of fish which smelled none too pleasant. Smail had way cakes made of reed root meal which were now crumbling into grayish pinches of dust-like crumbs. A small offering for even their own party, nothing to spread among all those now their traveling companions.

However, there was already movement from out of the trees. They were returning with food—fruit, small and sourish when compared to the bounty of the garden, but still of the same kind; some roots, dark earth still clinging to them; and then two of the party bearing silver scaled fish strung on reeds.

It was a strange meal—certainly no banquet—but they shared equally. This more than what she had already witnessed made Kadiya believe that she had wrought sorcery of a high order, though not by her understanding. Statues living, eating—and between bites looking about them wide eyed, searching—

"Nuers!" At Lamaril's call one of the others of the Sindona swallowed hurriedly and came to where his commander sat beside Kadiya.

"We move. Fahiel will guard until these are rested—"

Kadiya would have disputed that, but she knew that he was right. She and the Oddlings were not fit for the trail after their night's labors. Yet she was also needed in the city if their force was to be summoned in strength.

However, more might lie within those treasure rooms of

Yatlan where the Hassitti had packed away all they could find of what the Vanished Ones had abandoned. Lamaril and the rest would certainly need time to go through those crowded rooms. Thus she did not protest when the Sindona moved off, save for the one detailed to stay with them.

With him as sentinel, the girl felt for the first time that the full weight of responsibility had been raised from her. She pulled at the fern grass, crushing it. Discarding the mask-helm she curled up to sleep.

The sun was down far enough to have vanished from the sky, leaving only ragged banners behind to mark its going when Kadiya awoke. Jagun was already squatting by his pack, scraping the point of his spear with a honing stone. Smail sat up at the same time as she did, yawning widely, his pointed teeth showing. Salin still lay curled, but as Kadiya moved the wisewoman's eyes opened.

Their guard had been busy in his own fashion. A pile of vine lengths lay beside him and he had shredded a number, then braided pieces into a slender brown-green rope which he tested every few inches as he wove. When the Oddlings moved, he gathered the loops into one hand, revealing that the far end of it was looped into a noose.

Kadiya's hand went to her head. Her scalp was no longer sore where the vine trap had caught her. Yet what Fahiel fashioned suddenly reminded her of that attack.

Even though night was coming she had no desire to continue in camp here. The flask and her duty only half done pressured her on.

They passed that place of death where once she had granted release to a tormented Uisgu captive. There was no reason to fear any of Voltrik's scum now, though the Skriteks might be on the move.

They came at last to that tunnel which had first given her entrance into Yatlan. Kadiya had warned the Oddlings of what lay beyond and she knew that they swam well by nature. Certainly the Sindona, who had said very little during their journey, must also know of this way.

It was very near dawn. They had made good time she was sure, even Salin keeping the pace Kadiya had set without faltering. The footing had been secure where the old road was not completely covered.

Kadiya plunged again into the dark where she had once sought hiding. The water rose — she was swimming, with the sword fastened in her belt something of a weight. She had made very sure of the snug sealing of the flask.

Fahiel collected all their packs, fastened them together with his rope and took this bundle with him. He seemed so well aware of what he was doing that neither Kadiya nor the Oddlings protested.

Once more she emerged from the pool, though in the twilight the water did not shimmer blue as it had the first time she had come this way. Before her were the steps with their Guardian statues. Among those there was movement. For a second Kadiya tred water, holding off from exiting the pool.

Then the bobbing lamps showed her what — *who* — awaited them there. Hassitti crowded the steps and among them stood a much taller figure. The lamplight glinted from jewel bright mail but he wore no face concealing helm. As the girl found footing a little below him, Lamaril reached down to catch the hand she had unconsciously raised in greeting and drew her forth from the pool as easily as if she had been but a kotta blossom floating there.

19

 YATLAN WAS VERY OLD, THE SI-
lence laid by time had curtained it for so
long. Now lamps blazed in windows of
those buildings fronting on the pool, the
way to the garden. There were scuttling
noises of passage here and there. The
Hassitti, near hysterical with joy, were searching out all which
they could offer for the comfort of these who had at long last
returned.

Around Kadiya the glory of the night garden closed and
eased her, mind and body. One hand still rested on the flask
which was now empty. She had served the wishes of those
behind the far wall—there were no longer any statues silent
on the stairs without. Men and women of another blood busied
themselves in the buildings which had once sheltered them.
She was not sure what they searched for—armor such as La-

maril wore, yes, and perhaps weapons far more potent even than the sword which was hers.

In what could be a small breathing time of peace she drew to her all the quiet healing of the garden, watching with sleep-heavy eyes those flying lights weave their patterns from flower to leaf to flower.

The swamp had always fascinated her for all its murk and dangers. That place beyond the wall had been all beauty without any perils. This— Kadiya sighed. Even now when she had tried to let down all her defenses, put aside all her impatience, still she felt alien. Where did she by rights belong? She had arrogantly claimed the swamp when she had left the Citadel. No, the court was not for her. Anigel would reign correctly and proudly from a throne which was meant for a Queen. Haramis, in her northern mountains, would live for her learning, eager to grasp always more and more of that which would strengthen her inner Powers. When this peril was passed—if Kadiya did survive its passing—what then? Resolutely she pushed away that question.

Kadiya had tried a short time ago to once more communicate with Haramis, via Salin's scrying bowl, but there had been no response. Was her sister now aroused to danger also and on the move from her eyrie to route out traces of the Dark?

She lifted her head a little. Her hair was tightly braided except for the crown where the locks were still short from her shearing. Her skin was scratched, her body thin—though at least she had had the chance to bathe with what small luxuries the Hassitti could provide. It had been most necessary to refuse the jewels, the remains of fine robes, they pressed on her to wear. Once more she went in the mail which had been given her in the Place of the Flower.

. . . —————————————————————————————— . . .

A slight sound behind alerted her — one of the Hassitti come
to ask again, as they had for hours, what she wished?

"A place for dreaming —"

Though it came by mind touch, that speech was not from
any Hassitti. Kadiya looked back and would have arisen but
Lamaril would not have it so. He waved her back to drop
down beside her, his mail scraping the stone.

"Does it," she asked a question which had been with her
most of this day, "give you anger, sadness, to see Yatlan as it
now is?"

When he did not answer she was abashed. Perhaps in her
usual impetuous way she had invaded where she should never
have stepped. In this dusk light she could not clearly see his
face. This might well have been a place which he remembered
with joy and pleasure.

"You see deep," his message came at last. "These walls con-
tain that which is like a dream wherein one returns to childhood, seeking all that which was warmth and goodness then.
It is a shadow of something which was — But it is not well to
allow shadows to curtain what now exists. I knew the Yatlan
that was. This is a different Yatlan and one I must learn again
. . . if we are given the time."

"The mountains. . . ." She dropped hand to sword hilt.

"The mountains await us," he agreed. "Salin has spoken
with others of her kind. The dreamer of the Hassitti has had
some things to tell us. Yes, the Dark is returning to loose the
old evil. And evil it was."

"What must we do then?" She could understand a battle
with men, with Skritek, such as they had faced during the
invasion. Was this a time when she must summon Anigel and
Haramis, and somehow have them rewell the talisman into
one mighty weapon?

"They sleep. Five wait for the one who returns from Varm to awaken them fully. They are the lords of the Dark whom we could not slay at the ending. Thus we bound them — sealed them — with such forces as we believed could never be broken."

"Until Orogastus troubled and meddled. But if you could not put an end to them once, how can we hope to do so now?" Kadiya asked.

"In slumber they are powerless. We must stop that messenger before he awakens them. But, King's Daughter of another day, your part is already played — "

A small heat flared up within Kadiya. Was she now to be dismissed, like a child who had run some small errand but must not trouble her elders when they were about their more important business?

"This is indeed another day." She tried to tamp down her quickness of temper, to impress upon him without any show of what she felt. "Some tens of days ago I gave Oath to serve the mires — both peoples and land. Those of my race do not usually know the swamp ways. But from a child this water-logged land has drawn me. When I called the Nyssomu, the Uisgu also came battle ready — something they had never done for any of my blood, even Krain my father.

"What touches this land, what threatens this land is a matter for me, since this is *my* time. In this very garden was a weapon fitted to my hand." She had drawn the sword, held it out. The eyes were fully open, though they shot forth no vengeful fire. Rather it was as if they were truly using sight, studying her, even Lamaril. "As long as this is mine, Lord Guardian, then what happens in any mire battle is of my concern."

Again he was silent. Then he slowly nodded his head. "With your will so set, Kadiya, we cannot stand against you. But you

do not know what lies ahead. There can be such a Power unleashed that would scorch your talisman into nothingness. We cannot be sure that even we can stand against what will happen if the sleepers are summoned into wakefulness and armed by Varm.

"For long and long we have stepped out of time and been at peace. Though we have not forgotten old skills, still we have not put them to use. Weapons rust if they are not withdrawn from sheaths for the seasons. I would not have you believe that we are all powerful. In this time we can die as easily as one of your kind, or the little ones you term Oddlings." He suddenly caught at her empty hand and drew it to his forearm. Beneath her fingers his flesh felt as her own — there was nothing of the smoothness of the stone about it.

An insect fluttered near, settled on one of his fingers. He uttered an exclamation and flicked it away.

"You see even the flying things can sting us as they do you. We are vulnerable."

"But you are the Vanished Ones. This city was deserted and vine grown before my people came and we have been here more than six hundreds of full seasons. Yet you remember these streets and halls, you have walked them before."

"Time rules here. It does not beyond the Gate. Though my people are long lived, they do come at last to an ending. Did not Binah die? She chose to remain in the hold of time, and time lay heavy and heavier upon her. Yes, when you brought our inner selves through the barrier and gave us bodies once again, then we became answerable to time, just as we are answerable to death — and to another kind of life."

"So now we go to the mountains," Kadiya said. That the Vanished Ones were immortal was a legend of the bards. Yet

Lamaril said that they were answerable to death and time, and this they had chosen when they came for battle.

"At least we know the road even though we may not be sure what awaits us at the end of it. Kadiya, tell me of your people — you say you chose the mires for your own after the fall of this sorcerer Orogastus. When you did so, what life did you leave?"

It was true, she had chosen another life just as Lamaril and the others had chosen to return. She thought of the Citadel. Parts of life there she could remember as if they were bright flowers to catch the eye; others she shrank from recalling — those last hours of horror when Voltrik breached the walls and all which had been her safe and happy life had come to an end.

Now she drew upon those first memories: the life in the huge stronghold which must have also been built by those of Lamaril's blood, of the midseason festival of the Three Moon Feast, the arrival of flotillas of traders' boats bound upriver to Trevista, of hunting trips with Jagun, of the boring court ceremonies she had yawned her way through because she must.

Then she deliberately brought forth the horrors: the foul death dealt her father and his guards, her mother's body hacked with swords and war axes, of the escape through those inner ways which had led down and down into the very heart of the earth.

"Of the rest I have spoken before," she said at last. She found she was shivering, though the breeze in the garden was not chill. Did one ever wash blood out of memory?

Her hand was caught again, held not tightly but firmly with a warmth spreading through that contact which chased away the chill. Kadiya grasped at a thought, held it tightly as one might clasp a shield. With her two sisters she had a bond, yes, but a tenuous one — they were too unlike to do more than answer the call of shared blood.

With Jagun her tie had been that of battle comrade, but they were species alien to one another. That she could command his aid at all times, she knew, but she was suddenly aware now there was a void within her which had never opened even far enough for her to know it existed.

This one firm hand clasp was like the sword: a key, a key to feelings she had never owned to before.

No, she did not want to turn that key! The here and now was hers. She wanted no dreaming nor foreseeing. Kadiya withdrew from that hold almost roughly. She was quick with another question.

"The way to this mountain prison, it is far?"

"We cross the Golden Mire," he returned. "There are foothills beyond, a fringe of them. The way was blocked, hidden as best we could devise in the old days. It is no easy road."

Kadiya stood up abruptly. "Is any way within the mires an easy one? The rivers and streams can serve us but they do not run straight. Do we head for Mt. Brom or Gidris? Haramis is there. Her power — "

"No, we round the end of the Thorny Hell, strike then south through the country which is held by the Uisgu, and so to near that peak of Rotolo."

"What of the Vispi? Their country lies there. Will they not also be alert to this danger?"

Lamaril shook his head. "We think that the old barrier of silence holds. It would be to the advantage of Varm's servant who goes to awaken his comrades to keep it so as a protection against his return. Salin has been seeking and the small dreamer of the Hassitti has also done what might be done to try and discover some troubling of the mountain lands. But all he can perceive are the fear and horror of the death spreading in the mires.

"Already the Uisgu are traveling south, seeking to flee beyond its greedy spread where it turns all the land into a thing of rottenness."

"But you *are* sure of where this place of the sleepers lies?" She did not really know why she asked that question. Certainly he must be sure.

To her surprise he did not reply at once. "The land is changed," he returned slowly. "We have two among us who have the farsight. What they see is a wasteland of plague and that must be pierced."

Kadiya thought of her sword. Would what she could summon be enough to clean a path for them?

"Fire"--he might be reading her thoughts though she had not felt the mind touch—"will cleanse in part. That we can manage—if he who seeks the same place does not summon some other weapon."

The Vanished Ones were all powerful; legends ingrained in her from childhood declared that was so. Yet his words were not calm reassurance; they left her with a prickling of doubt. Perhaps there was never any core of true safety one could seek—not this side of that door. However, this was her land and she was set to live in it.

Their party made an early start in the morning. To Kadiya's vast surprise, there were six of the Hassitti waiting when they assembled. Their bedraggled remains of rich robes had been discarded, though some still wore bejeweled chains. Each had a pack. The two to the fore Kadiya recognized—Tostlet, the healer, and Quave, the dreamer.

They had arms of a sort—long knives, which, because of

their diminutive size, would serve as swords, and rods with
thongs waving from their tips, not unlike whips. Their use the
girl could not guess.

That they had added themselves to the company, had been
allowed to do so by the Sindona, was a primary puzzlement
to her. Still Lamaril and the others appeared to take their
presence as a matter of course.

They left the city through the gates which held illusion and
cut out westward away from the Thorny Hell. Here there was
a goodly amount of stable land and the bogs were not to be
feared. Though Kadiya could follow mind send if it were directly beamed in her direction she could not follow that which
was in use now—save to be aware that information passed
continually among the Sindona and perhaps the Hassitti.

She kept pace not with the Guardians, but stubbornly kept
to her own comrades—Jagun, Smail, and Salin, the latter
holding to her walking staff though the speed Lamaril had set
was not taxing as yet.

Jagun and Smail cut away from the main body first. Kadiya
knew that the need for scouts sent the Oddlings ahead, even
though none of the Sindona seemed aware of the necessity.

They were well away from Yatlan when an Oddling mind
warning struck Kadiya and she hurried ahead to Lamaril.

"Skritek! A full raiding party, Jagun has crossed their
tracks!"

One of those who followed the Commander had also turned
to face the west. It was Lalan, the woman Kadiya knew,
though her face was masked by the helm. Her pose was that
of one picking up a wind-borne scent.

"A rear guard." Her mind send was cast this time such that
Kadiya could pick it up. "Varm's creature is moving fast, and
the scaled jaws are following to his command."

"There are Uisgu," Kadiya had a fresh send from Jagun. "They flee the rot. Smail goes to warn them."

Lamaril only nodded abruptly but he lengthened stride. Now Kadiya, though she disliked it, fell back to help Salin — for, as willing as the wisewoman was, she could not hold to that pace.

As the two dropped back, the Hassitti closed in about them. Kadiya was sharply elbowed aside and looked down in surprise to see that Tostlet had come up beside the Uisgu woman to offer support.

"We shall do well, Noble One," the Hassitti's assurance came swiftly. "Go you where the Power will be needed."

Several of the Hassitti had put out a burst of speed, scuttling along at a rate which brought them along with Kadiya as she rejoined the head of their small force.

"Thus be it!" Lamaril drew from a sling at his side, where a sword might have ridden, a narrow rod. The tip of it appeared to quiver. Kadiya staggered. There was a driving pain behind her eyes. A hand reached forth from the Sindona she marched beside and lowered her helm, for bothered by the limited sight through the eye holes of the face mask, she had pushed it up on her head.

Instantly the pain was gone. She had drawn her sword and now she felt the growing heat of it in her hand. The eyes were open, and on impulse she held the blade a little higher as if those orbs could really see and thereby understand what was happening and what might be asked of them.

The Sindona broke the tight formation they had held since leaving Yatlan and moved out into a curving line which still advanced steadily, resembling the move of hunters driving game into the nets as Kadiya had seen Nyssomu do on a large island near Trevista.

All of them had rod in hand now, and, though Kadiya could no longer hear that stupefying sound, she was sure any not helm-protected were suffering. Yet it did not appear in any way to affect the Hassitti who still scrambled on, sometimes even threading ahead through the Sindona line.

They had almost reached a growth of brush, the first real obstruction they had come across after leaving Yatlan, when the branches began to writhe furiously. Out into the open staggered a Skritek. Greenish foam dripped from the corners of its open jaws. Its eyes gleamed red even as Kadiya had seen when the blood lust was raging in them.

However, if this one had ever been armed he had dropped his weapons. Instead both hands were pressed to the sides of his long jawed head which shook from side to side. His plunge out of the brush carried him to his knees and he seemed unable to rise again in spite of wild struggles.

Those eyes were pits of rage born in pain and Kadiya could feel the heat of the hatred he held for them. One of the Hassitti scuttled up toward the furious creature and Kadiya started forward, sure that a single snap of jaw would end that small life. Then Lalan's arm dropped like a barrier before her.

The Hassitti had reached its goal. The whip-like weapon it carried fell in a vicious snap across the scaled features of the Skritek. The Drowner reared nearly to his feet, swinging out a clawed paw at his attacker. But the Hassitti was well away, watching as its enemy fell forward again, facedown, body twitching.

The Hassitti's feet shuffled back and forth for an instant in what might have been a small dance of triumph. What blow that whip stroke had delivered Kadiya could not guess, but it was undoubtedly effective. None of the Sindona nor the Hassitti spared another glance at the Skritek as they moved on, though plainly the creature was not yet dead; Kadiya could see the body moving with labored breathing.

They were at the edge of the barrier of thick brush and there they halted for a moment. Lamaril snapped off a twig of the growth, rolled leaf and stem between his fingers, and then held up the mashed bit to the edge of his helm mask. He was plainly smelling that which he had harvested.

Dropping the mauled stem, he ran his finger slowly up the length of the rod weapon, a gesture which was copied by his followers. With their rods now outheld, they marched confidently on as if no barrier existed. Nor did it. Leaf, stem, heavy branch were . . . gone. The air about was filled with a green mist as heavy as a thick smoke. Kadiya waved her hand back and forth as she tramped immediately after Lamaril and felt dampness on her skin, saw it turn green as if from a stiff coating of Uisgu body paint.

The disappearance of the brush revealed five more Skritek, now rolling to the ground, their weapons laying useless. Once more the Hassitti, joined by two of its kind, went into action reducing the creatures to helplessness.

Only one did they have to pursue, for he was doggedly crawling, his head wagging from side to side while clacking his fangs together as if he were tearing apart some prey. Around his scaled throat was a chain of black metal from which hung small gray bones — finger bones. This Kadiya recognized as a hunter of skill, one who bore the right to leadership. He slewed around on the ground to face them.

His head went back and up, like that of a creature howling its anguish to the skies. Kadiya retreated a step. Just as that sound the Sindona had used as a weapon so did this screech strike — it was raw emotion, a hate so potent that it might have been poison spewed into her face.

Three of the Hassitti closed in upon him but they were showing more wariness. The Skritek leaned heavily on one arm, swept out with the other. His extended claws nearly scraped the plated breast of the nearest Hassitti. The other two sprang as Kadiya could not have thought possible, given their short legs and heavy bodies. Their whip weapons fell almost at the same moment across the head of their prey.

There came a last burst of overpowering rage — then nothing at all, though the still jerking body lay in their path and they had to detour around it.

20

THEY CAMPED THAT NIGHT ON solid land and Kadiya watched Lalan, her wand weapon pointing to the earth as she made a circuit of their dumped packs. A golden spark followed the drawing and Kadiya realized that they now had protection, an invisible sentry on guard.

Already the mountains showed a fanged fringe against the sky, and with them so close Kadiya made one more attempt to reach her sister. Salin and she sat on either side of the scrying bowl watching the dark mirror steadied there.

The girl linked hands with the Uisgu wisewoman willing the basin to show what she longed to see. At a sudden movement Kadiya leaned further forward.

Within the bowl, a shadow grew out of mists as white as the snow curtaining the high peaks.

The cloaked figure became clearer.

"Haramis!" Kadiya projected a mind call with all her strength plus that added energy Salin fed her.

Her sister turned to face her squarely. Haramis had her staff in hand, that potent source of Power which was aligned to the sword across Kadiya's knee. However, there was no welcome on Haramis's face, no answer. Instead she showed a questioning which became uneasiness. Haramis's hooded head turned from right to left, her eyes seeming to peer in search.

"Haramis!" If mind send could shout perhaps Kadiya's call reached that point. This time her sister's lips moved as if she spoke.

"Haramis!" For the third time Kadiya put all the strength she could summon into that call.

A mere whisper came, so faint she could hardly distinguish a few words.

"Sister . . . evil . . . barrier . . . have not yet knowledge — "

The rod in Haramis's hand lifted from the snow bank on which she stood. As if she held some pen suitable for only a giant's hand, the sorceress drew symbols in the air. They were in the form of whirling snowflakes but Kadiya could see them, could even feel their effect. They were warding Powers, Haramis's own — both warding and warning.

The airborne patterns blurred. Then all was gone.

"She is right." Kadiya started from her half trance, roused by that voice at her side. Lamaril knelt, gazing into the now unrewarding bowl.

"There is a barrier," he continued slowly. "That which we go up against was very strong in its day. We defeated it, yes, but we could not wipe it from the earth. For it is of the earth — even as is that we can command."

Kadiya shivered — those whirling flakes from afar might have cloaked her for a moment. Haramis, who had taken on

Binah's age-old powers, had been thwarted — and Kadiya's belief in the might of the Sindona was shaken by their leader's admission.

"If we can keep the seeker from the sleepers — then we are victors in the here and now. He is armed, certainly well armed, with the best Varm could give him. He must not awaken them!"

Now he addressed Salin. "Wisewoman, how far can you range this night? Can his trail be picked by your scrying?"

The Uisgu did not answer for what seemed to Kadiya a very long moment. Instead her long thin fingers wove air patterns back and forth.

"Noble One," she replied at last, "once we tried — when that one was going for the aid he needed — and he felt us! There have been times — of these I have had warning through all my use of this talent — that death itself can strike the viewer when those spied upon are strong and knowing."

"True — yet that one is alone at present, and we are more than he would want to face. That which he carries to renew the sleepers he will not waste. He dare not — his master will have made sure of that. But we must discover his path. The closer he draws to that which he seeks the narrower our margin of victory becomes."

Salin's hands once more fell to the sides of the bowl. Her large eyes were still on Lamaril as he turned to Kadiya.

"King's Daughter, old links are stronger than new in this. You have worked with Salin before; you have seen this one we search for. Will you focus for us?"

Kadiya remembered the fear of her dream, of the Power she had felt released into the one they would spy upon. There was warmth on her breast: the amulet was alive. She glanced down at the sword. Now it seemed that those eyes were all seeing, and what they fastened upon was her.

"Yes," she said—one small word to bring within her a cold wavering. Let him sense that, she would still hold by her word.

He moved until his hands fell on her shoulders, and behind him she sensed others moving—the Sindona were linking touch, one to another.

Kadiya's tongue tip swept over lips suddenly dry as she said to Salin:

"Now!"

The Uisgu woman began a hoarse chant, her head bowed as if some great weight pressed her. Kadiya felt the pull, far greater than it had ever been before. There was another movement. Someone had come to stand behind Salin, but Kadiya dared not let her concentration be broken. In her mind she strove to set the picture of the man on the throne of fire.

The liquid in the bowl bubbled this time instead of swirling as it had always done before. The vessel could have rested on open fire. Fire—there was heat in that basin, spreading to her hands and Salin's as they once more clasped.

That which bubbled thickened. It was not like a mirror of dark glass now, but more a scoop of something viscid and vile. The surface smoothed and there was a picture. It wavered for a moment and then sharp enough for her to see indeed that one who served Varm.

He stood on a hillock and before him blazed a fire of sullen flames, each of which were edged with black. Around that fire massed Skritek. Even as Kadiya watched they raised a bound captive who struggled frantically, piteously, to fling it into the heart of the fire.

She was sickened; bile rose in her throat. Now the swamp monsters were dragging forward a second captive—an Uisgu girl hardly out of childhood. They played with her as they did so, leaving her unbound, flinging her from one to another.

Now they held her directly before the man of Varm. His face — Kadiya fought to shut her eyes against that face, but this was inner sight as well as outer and she could not.

Almost delicately he lowered the rod tip of the weapon he held and from it shot a thread of flames. Back and forth across that trembling body, arching it in agony, he drew that trickle of dark Power as he might use the lash of a whip.

The Skritek let the charred body fall forward, this time into the full of the flames. Somehow the picture in the bowl grew larger, the leader ever more its center. There was a moment when his face appeared to fill the whole of the mirror they had created.

His eyes narrowed, he was *aware*!

Then they were away from him. They looked upon the Skriteks, upon the outer fringes of that mob sweeping about. Kadiya, even as she was pressured to do this, realized what the Sindona needed: some landmark, some hint of where lay this place of destruction and pain.

She was given very little time. The picture twisted, began to darken around the edges as if eaten by fire. Sudden, searing heat on her own hands was too much to bear.

Lamaril's hold on her tightened, dragging her away so she broke contact with Salin and the scrying bowl. She was able to raise her eyes from the liquid turbulence which was now beginning to subside. But every small movement brought an answering ache from her body.

The leader did not release his grip on her. Rather she was drawn closer to his body. Into her flooded new strength from that contact. But nothing could wipe from her mind what she had seen.

"That place I know." Smail of the few words spoke. Kadiya had not even been aware that he and Jagun had returned from their scouting. "They are at the Fangs of Rapan. It is near the Nothar."

Lamaril gently released her. "Rest, Kadiya." His words came softly. "This night you have wrought as a battle hero. You also," he spoke to Salin.

Lalan had knelt beside the wisewoman, her hands on either side of the Uisgu's bent head. Kadiya guessed that she was doing for Salin what Lamaril had done for her—giving renewal.

Now the leader of the Guardians was already smoothing a space of earth and on either side of that had set two of the glow-grub lights. With dagger tip he drew lines on the ground.

"It has been long; there are many changes," he commented as he worked. "Young warrior, can you show us where stand these Fangs of yours?"

"The Nothar runs so, down from the heights where Mt. Gidris holds caves of ice, or so they say." Smail knelt beside the drawing and was now pointing with one long finger.

"Yes, there are caves to the north of the Nothar; that is where we seek. But the Fangs?"

"Stand so!" Smail stabbed a point to the west of the river. "Noble One, the plague has eaten far thereabouts. Those of the clans have fled southward. It is death to hunt that trail. We have spoken to scouts, who say safety can only be sought so." Now he trailed a finger farther east. "That which was Noth, the hold of the Archimage, is ruins now, yet there is still some virtue about it as the plague has stopped and spreads no farther toward it."

"And the one we hunt is there." Lamaril considered the markings. "Does the plague-sown land hinder him?"

He might have been asking the question of himself. For he did not wait for an answer but instead asked:

. . . ———————————————————— . . .

"The mire, is it solid ground for our road?"

"Not much, Noble One, but we have spoken to the scouts. There will be those who join us at sunrise who know hunters' paths. Also it is the custom for clans to keep their river and pond crafts concealed near any needed crossing and those who come will know much of that."

Kadiya wondered they could see by so dim a light, but they spoke positively of distances and possible ways which might well delay them too long. He who they sought had the Skritek as well, and those skulkers in swampland were a formidable enemy.

"We do what must be done." Nuers joined the group about the crude map. Next to him was one of the Hassitti. The little creature had squatted close, even as if it would sniff out the lines with its long nose.

Then it straightened to its full height and pointed, not to the map but westward voicing its eerie chatter in some state of excitement. Lamaril listened to that rapid click-clack of speech and then said:

"This is Quave of the dreamer line. He asks that we let him farsee for us tonight. Wisewoman," he added to Salin, "there seems to be a need for certain herbs. This one, the healer Tostlet"—the other Hassitti had appeared from the shadows — "has not a full supply. Will you share with her?"

At Salin's quick nod, the Hassitti joined the Uisgu woman and together they burrowed into the pack. Tostlet held at last a hand cupped about a bundle of twisted leaves while Salin watched with attention.

However, Kadiya wanted no more of farseeing. Inside, the nausea which had been born of what she had witnessed grew stronger. She could not raise her share of a ration trail cake to her mouth, though she made a pretense of doing so. When she curled on her sleep mat, she held the sword unsheathed and tight to her breast, its eyes pointed outward as if to stand guard.

Mercifully she was not visited by any dreams that night. And with the precautions the Sindona had taken to fortify and guard their camp, she felt no responsibility. Sleep came swiftly and was not troubled.

There was a chittering, and Kadiya felt a touch on her hunched shoulder. She opened her eyes upon the gray, mist-veiled dawn of the day. Tostlet was beside her and even as Kadiya looked up the Hassitti's hand stroked the girl's face.

Coolness spread in the path of those claws. The Hassitti was holding in her other hand a cup of thick greasy stuff. Unlike that with which the swamp dwellers usually anointed them-selves against insect attack, this smelled fragrant and imparted invigorating freshness to the skin it covered.

"Healer," Kadiya shook off the last bewilderment of sleep, "my thanks to you." She sat up smiling at Tostlet.

"The wise one, she had some things; I had others. Together we make the winged biters fly away," the Hassitti explained with some complacency. "Also it does not insult the nose with bad smells."

Kadiya laughed. "True, Tostlet, and that is a comfort in this place."

She had awakened for the first time with a feeling of con-fidence. They had much on their side in this battle. For all of Lamaril's warning, she was certain that the Sindona could summon such Power as her own kind had not dreamed of — perhaps far more than even the potent talisman of the Three could command.

As she rolled up her sleep mat to stow in her pack she saw that she was one of the last to do so. Most of their company were eating, not only of the trail rations, but also of gorba which had been freshly grilled. She saw Lamaril licking his fingers, a sight which would banish much of the awe in which his race was held were it to be witnessed by those from the Citadel.

Having roped her pack Kadiya moved toward the fire which was now smoldering and accepted the last remaining gorba impaled on the twig which had supported it over the flames.

"Bright the day, fair the journey." Lamaril's greeting was formal and she made answer as best she could.

"Let it be so for all here!" She waited for the fish to cool a little as she asked:

"The dreamer?"

"Dreamed," Lamaril returned. There was no lightness in him, and Kadiya's earlier feeling of good fortune was somewhat quenched by that. "We must travel fast and far."

Jagun and Smail were not to be seen. The girl guessed that again they were scouting ahead. Their packs she did see, slung on two of the Sindona's shoulders along with those the guardians already carried. Lalan flanked Salin as they started out, though she was watchful only, not giving any physical aid to the wisewoman whose staff did not seem this morning to be so much of a crutch as a badge of office.

They were soon off the hard ridge of earth which had supported them for so long, and the pace slowed as they wove a way through bogs. Twice that morning they faced stretches of water and each time they discovered one of the swampland's craft waiting. There were no rimoriks to draw these; rather the Sindona stood to the punting poles and ferried the party across.

They moved now through the tall golden growth which had given this part of the mire its name. Although the monsoon had beaten off the seed tops, it was thickened by new blades from below. The Sindona took turns, the Hassitti often beside them, in swishing spear lengths through this thick matting and sending the dwellers within scuttling away. Twice Kadiya saw Hassitti bend forward with outstretched hand-paws and arise holding writhing vipers which they spine-cracked with precision and tossed away from the path.

The party could not stop at noon—though they had slowed their pace—for there was no stretch of ground firm enough on which to rest. Salin was using her staff now, and Kadiya kept beside her, ready with a hand wherever the footing was suspect.

There had always been rumors that there were lost ruins in this wilderness of golden bog; certainly the Uisgu had brought treasure to trade at Trevista which had come from this land. But they had not encountered any such sites through the day's travel.

Jagun appeared in late afternoon when they had come at last to a rise of ground on which they could crowd for a rest after battling the mud banks and drifts. He was accompanied by three Uisgu, their faces heavily painted with designs Kadiya recognized as those of the war trail.

The news he brought sent their party angling westward, the newcomers as guides. Before sunset they reached a stretch of island land. There were even some trees standing and their coming sent spiraling upward six droski—those birds whose rainbow hued feathers were greatly sought by traders. The shimmer of the iridescent peach-orange against the sky was eye catching. But there was no sweet singing to match that beauty, only the birds' hoarse croaking. Beautiful as they might appear droski were carrion eaters upon occasion and had habits which belied their appearance.

On the other hand they were extremely shy of any large ground moving creatures, so to find them nesting here meant that the travelers had reached a camping place which was not in use by anything large enough to be an enemy—certainly none of their own kind.

The Uisgu were mustering, was the message the newcomers brought. The plague seemed to have halted its continued sweep across the land, though it had infected a good quarter of their territory. Their healers and wisewomen had been working hard to find a remedy—something to clear the leprous land once more—so far to no purpose.

There were Skritek loose, invading brazenly as they had in Voltrik's day. A skirmish had already been fought, resulting in a draw with Uisgu deaths. But the Drowners seemed eager to go west—mountainward—and though trailed now by Uisgu warriors they did not attempt to turn aside from the path they had chosen to wreak any more damage on the already suffering land and people.

Also, the Uisgu had noted that now they could travel even across the diseased land without apparent danger, though they detoured when they could to clean territory. Perhaps whatever granted them safety did not hold for long.

"We cross the Nothar," Lamaril announced. "Then turn west. The land is better there and we can move faster."

"The one of Varm?" Kadiya asked.

"He moves on this side of the river, or so it was dreamed."

"How swiftly?" the girl demanded.

He did not have time to answer that. There was a squalling cry which seemed to split the sky above them. Kadiya had never heard such a noise before. It was menace given voice, hunger, rage—

They were on their feet, the Hassitti huddled in around them, weapons swung up and out.

The screech tormented their ears for a second time. Kadiya had been looking skyward since it seemed to come from that direction. Now there was a wavering of the brush on the far side of the island on which they were camped, vigorous enough to be clearly seen through the dusk.

21

THE THING SPRANG OUT OF HID-
ing with a leap. It did not tower over
them but the width of its body made it a
monster such as Kadiya had never heard
described by hunters, and the mouth
which gaped wide to give vent to another
screech was nearly as vast as a doorway.

Rolls of warty hide almost hid the red eyes, which were well
to the top of its vast head. And there gushed forth from it such
a stench as was an assault in itself.

The two forelegs were bowed outward and it plopped to a
stand, its gray paunch barreling out between them. Those forelegs ended in huge webbed paws.

This was a nightmare—the more so because Kadiya now
recognized its origin. There were dwellers in the water rooted
reeds, no larger than her hand, which resembled this monster.

Out of that cavern of a mouth snapped a rope of tongue,

thick and patched with slime. It shot straight for one of the Hassitti and would have trapped that little one, save that Lamaril moved with the speed of a trained swordsman and swung his rod so that it struck full against that menace of a tongue.

There was a flash. The tongue jerked high. Down its length ran a fiery ribbon of green-blue.

That fire struck the monster's face only a finger length away from one of the eyes. The whole body of the thing tensed. Kadiya had only a breath of time to throw herself to one side, carrying Salin with her, before it rose for another leap, one which would bring its giant weight down upon the whole party.

There came a scream from the sky overhead. Then Kadiya was sent flying by the huge paw which scraped against her as the monster landed. She fell facedown, dazed. A din arose behind her as she scrabbled in the moist soil to bring herself up and around.

What she saw through blurred vision was a battlefield indeed. Not only was the toad monster in action but from the sky over their heads voor were zooming in. They were not huge, but even voor of ordinary size were able to raise and carry an Oddling, bearing off any such captive to tear at it as they flew.

She fumbled for the sword. Without a point, it was of no use as a blade. Her hope was that the Power would come making it a potent weapon.

But it did not warm in her hand; there was no life in it — the eyes were near closed.

Flashes from the weapon rods of the Sindona laced back and forth. The toad thing bellowed, raised a foot high, and crashed it down. Kadiya stiffened in shock as she saw it beat one of the Hassitti into the mud.

Then as sharp as a battle shout a word struck into her mind: *"Illusion!"*

She had scuttled out of range of that foot. The tongue hung in a limp loop from the creature's mouth, though the end of it wriggled like a serpent's severed length.

"Illusion!" Again that imperative signal.

How could there be any illusion to this? She could see one Hassitti leg still protruding from under that paw. There were darts in the monster's skin—and from the sky another voor planed down, its deadly talons ready for a strike.

She sighted Lalan with three other of the Sindona. They were making no effort to avoid that strike from above. Were they indeed captive to some illusion?

Kadiya found voice at last: " 'Ware—voor!"

None of them raised head to look at that attacker. The thing had winged close enough now that its claws were closing about Lalan's helmet. Though the Sindona might be too great a burden to bear skyward, the voor's talons could kill.

"Illusion!" For the third time that mind word.

Kadiya clenched her hold on the useless sword. The voor's claws had closed about Lalan's neck. The foul thing was beating its wings heavily, striving to rise with its prey. Yet the woman's hands did not raise her rod to beat it off, nor did she move.

Illusion? Kadiya's one hand went to her breast. The amulet! She tugged now at the chain, dragged it out into the open, and held the amber drop to her forehead, lifting the mask helm. Why she did so she could not have told save that it seemed she must.

There was a sudden rending pain as if the amulet had the Power to cleave its way into her very skull. Her sight blurred and then cleared.

The sky was empty, Lalan stood free of any clawed hold. Kadiya gasped and looked toward that other monstrous enemy. There was no rounded warty shape as large as a trade boat. Lamaril stood over one of the small reed dwellers she had long known. He stooped to prod at its puffed body, which deflated under that touch.

Illusion—all illusion! It was still hard for the girl to believe it true. She crawled to the Hassitti who lay facedown where that powerful leg had felled her. . . . Tostlet . . . No!

As the amulet swung back and forth on her breast, Kadiya used both hands as gently as she could to turn over the small scaled body. There was an impression in the ground; she had not imagined that. And Tostlet rolled limply beneath her touch.

Kadiya's fingers flew to the Hassitti's throat, searching for a sign of life. How could one be slain by an illusion—or could belief in it be the real weapon?

"Tostlet?" She sought for mind send, for reassurance that the healer still lived. "Tostlet, it was all illusion!" Even as Lamaril's word had reached her she strove now to reach the Hassitti mind.

The long nose quivered. That funneled tongue showed a tip and the small eyes opened.

"It was an illusion, Tostlet!" The girl had drawn the small body up against her, the scales rasping her skin unnoted. "An illusion—look!"

Kadiya supported Tostlet so that she could see the lumpish reed dweller which Lamaril was still examining.

The healer gasped, uttered a chittering cry. One of her hands closed on Kadiya's arm as she turned her head upward to see the girl's face. Kadiya nodded to enforce her mind words.

. . . ——————————————————————— . . .

"A trick, Tostlet, a trick to set us against ourselves."

"True." Salin hobbled over, sank painfully to her knees, still gripping her support staff. "But such a strong one"—she shook her head from side to side—"this is indeed of the great Dark."

"Who?" Kadiya still held the healer. "What Power?" And why had the sword failed her? She shivered. Had she come to depend too much on *her* Power, that which in truth she did not and had never understood?

Lamaril at last turned away from the toad thing.

"Again it is the old pattern: the land turning what it holds into a weapon." There was a twist to his mouth below the edge of the helm. "But this is a game for those unknowing. How could Varm's creature believe it would hold against us?"

"Because it did—against some of us," Kadiya returned bleakly. "I saw death—and Tostlet felt it. The belief held us, if not those who follow you. Can he know how full our Powers may be? Even my sword failed."

"But that which you wear did not," Lamaril returned.

"Only because of your warning," she said stubbornly. "Otherwise . . . I think these illusions would have indeed brought us death. Is that not so?"

For a moment he gave no answer.

"Is that not so?" she demanded a second time. "I am not of your race, nor are the Oddlings, nor these little ones who cherished your memory so long. If we cannot read illusions sent upon us by one who is a master, then cannot our deaths ensue?"

"Yes," his answer came at last. "But such illusions have now been revealed for what they are and we are warned—"

"Warned so that we must mistrust all our eyes see, our ears hear. This is a land which is already against us in part. Every bog and muck patch can be turned into traps now."

His nod was one of agreement and Kadiya shivered again. She had wanted more from him, reassurance that this was not so. She had known fear—but always before it had been real, issuing from some confrontation she could understand. Now she was helpless.

"King's Daughter—Kadiya." Lamaril moved closer. "We are what we were born to be. You have wrought much in the past. Do not dwell upon what you lack, rather look to what can be done. If the sword failed you, your birth gift did not. You are not without resources."

She hoped his mind touch could not sink deeper and release to him the whirl of her feelings, the doubts which arose like black shadows to lessen her confidence. Always she had been termed reckless, one to take chances without proper thought. Now—now thought was blanking out her courage, showing her a chasm which she might never be able to cross.

"I do what I must do," she muttered and was very glad when he turned away in answer to the summons of one of his command.

Tostlet sat up straighter within the girl's hold.

"Noble One—"

Kadiya winced. "Please, Tostlet, you can see that I am not of the company of these great ones. My name is Kadiya and I would that you would call me also 'friend.'"

"Friend," the Hassitti repeated. "Yes, there is goodness between us, Kadiya. But also you are not less than we have called you. You wear Power." She had wriggled around in the girl's hold and now held her hand toward the amulet but did not touch it. The glow of the trillium, caught forever within the casing of the amber, was steady—warming even—to look upon.

"Do not lessen yourself in your own eyes, friend," Tostlet

continued. "We go to match Power with Power, each of us has something to offer. When a worker in metal fuses one kind with another he creates a stronger weapon. We shall be such a weapon as can free this land."

If illusions had been sent to delay their march the mage who had summoned them was not well served. They pushed on following that encounter at a pace which was even faster, the Sindona taking turns with the scouts to seek out any more such traps.

Whether their enemy wished to lull them into carelessness might be a question, but they were not so involved again during the next two days of march. On the second day they took again to boats, but these had come to meet them. They were not only Uisgu-manned but also harnessed to rimoriks, giving them speed which Kadiya had thought beyond their hopes.

They proceeded up this lesser branch of the Nothar and now the sun sank behind the towering ridges of the western mountains. Uisgu scouts came in twice to report that the Skritek were in force and mountain-bound. But on the south side of the river there was another army assembling — Uisgu, with Nyssomu of the northern clans.

Many of these Kadiya recognized from the gathering which had joined against Voltrik. Twice she asked to be set ashore to speak to commanders of clan forces, warning them against illusions.

The Hassitti dreamer was nearly frantic with frustration. All the talent he knew could not prevail over a cloud of darkness which closed in the north. Nor did Kadiya dare to try to reach Haramis again.

On the third morning after their struggle with the illusions the stream was already among the foothills. The water had lost the peat hue that it carried in the swamp and it had turned chill, so that one cringed when trying to wash in it. This stream was born of the everlasting snows of the upper heights.

Also the warmth of the swamp was gone. The Oddlings wrapped themselves in woven reed cloaks and offered the same to their companions, though such garments were far too small to clothe the Sindona. Kadiya gratefully accepted one, discovering that it was less of a protection against the probing of mountain winds than she had hoped.

Those Uisgu who had brought the rimorik-drawn craft regretfully reported that they could no longer ask their water living companions to travel on. This chill was not for those who were at home in the swamp.

Thus their party took to the slower pace of land travel once more. But the foothills were beginning and the footing continued firm.

For the first time Kadiya saw the wind twisted trees of the heights. The air was so crisp in the early mornings that it seemed to burn as she drew it into laboring lungs. Lamaril used his rod weapon in an odd fashion when they broke camp the morning after the Uisgu boats deposited them on the west side of the river. Standing a little ahead of their company he had balanced that length of gleaming metal on his flattened palm and stood watching it with complete absorption.

Kadiya had taken to wearing the amulet on the outside of her mail, depending on it for warning. It had glowed for days now, and was always warm, the sign they were nearing some source of Power.

On Lamaril's palm the rod moved, swinging a fraction toward the south. Once more he set it straight and watched, until again it made the same move. So it was in that direction that they started off.

They entered a valley between two of the foothills. Underfoot gravel marked the bed of a vanished stream—or perhaps one which only filled at certain times of the year. The lush growth of the swamp was gone. Here was a tough grayish grass which had a sharp edged blade as Kadiya discovered when her foot turned on one of the water rounded stones. She grasped at turf to steady herself, only to have to lick drops of blood from her fingers.

Their going was not silent; now and then there was the clatter of a weapon against a boulder where the valley narrowed. Once they heard a scream from above and saw the spread of lammergeier wings as the huge mountain-born bird swung down as if to closer inspect these invaders of its country. Lammergeiers were in the service of Haramis. If there was only some way of communicating with this possible sentry. . . . Kadiya watched it wing away. But surely her sister knew that there was trouble and such a sighting would alert her.

The streambed was now walled in by slanting rocks which grew taller as they advanced. There was no longer any sight of vegetation—only ancient water markings on those walls to show the rise and fury of the water which had once battered a way here.

Before them there was a sharp turn—and their way forward was blocked by a towering sweep of stone, the gray surface of which was streaked with wavering flashes of dull red and a pale yellow. Crystals of a sort, Kadiya saw as she viewed them more closely.

The course of the streambed was to the south here. But Lamaril had not turned away from the barrier which fronted them. Instead his rod pointed to it.

Kadiya gasped. The weapon sped from his open hand—certainly he had not hurled it—and struck against the rock where it remained horizontal, as if the point had pierced the stone. At the same time her amulet flew forward, the chain which anchored it rasping against her neck. It, too, hung there until she grasped it and fought for a moment to tear it from some invisible grip.

On the surface of the stone those streaks of crystal glowed. Now the girl could see they appeared to form patterns, not unlike the weavings of Jagun's people, or the characters in some of the ancient books of Yatlan.

Lamaril put his hand to the rod and pulled it back. For a period of several moments the glow of that inscription remained and then was gone. There was a shifting among the Sindona and Lamaril's lips now set in a grim straight line.

Kadiya was aware of an uneasiness which was not active fear, but rather that which might follow direct disobedience of some old command, as it had been with Jagun when they had first taken the road to Yatlan forbidden to his people by very ancient Oaths.

Lamaril swung left. But no stream had worn this way—it must have been long dammed by the wall of crystals. This was a tumble of rock, looking loose and dangerous to the footing. It showed as a sweep from above where the wall had seemingly given way.

They shed their packs and lashed them together in bundles. Their cloaks followed, as they stripped for the ordeal of that climb. Kadiya looked to Salin—could the frail Uisgu woman do this?

However, the wisewoman showed no uneasiness. She had slung her staff to her back and stood now, her hands outstretched before her, flexing her fingers as if to prepare them for finding proper holds.

The Hassitti had already clustered at the foot of that slide and now the small ones started to test holds. Their clawed feet and forepaws proved to be highly fitted to the task and they went up eagerly, followed at a slower pace by Jagun and the Uisgu. Twice they froze tightly to holds as loosened rocks gave way to thud downward.

Kadiya made sure her sword was well fastened in its sheath and left her short spear with her pack.

How good a climber she might be she could not tell until she put herself to that task, but perhaps she could still aid Salin. She motioned toward the coiled rope on a Sindona pack.

"Together—" she thought to the wisewoman.

Lamaril, though she had not aimed the mind send at him, turned sharply. But he did not object. Rather he took the rope from his comrade and held it out to the girl.

At first Salin shook her head and drew back. But Kadiya, without warning, threw a loop of the rope about the little Oddling and had it knotted before the wisewoman could slip away. Resolutely the girl turned to the slope. Behind her Lamaril stood ready at the fore of the larger and heavier Sindona.

 KADIYA HAD NEVER TESTED HER strength against the raw stone of such a climb before. There were no heights in the swamplands. However, she knew better than to look anywhere but straight at the wall of rubble before her. There were cracks enough to afford finger and toe holds, but whether they might support her weight was another matter. She was only too aware that some had shifted under the passage of the smaller and lighter Oddlings.

It was a slow matter, this testing as best she could of each grip before she trusted her full weight to it. Her fingertips bruised and her nails broke against the stone as she fought to find crevices large enough to take the toes of her boots. But advance she did.

And so did Salin. The rope between them did not tighten; so far the Uisgu woman was able to match Kadiya's climb.

Then, under the girl's right boot, a stone moved. Frantically she dug her hands into an upper hold which held her spread-eagled against the treacherous rock slide.

Fingers gripped her ankle; she could feel the determined force of the hold even through her foot covering. A moment later her toe was slammed into a space where it held steady. But she was shaking, and chill as was the breeze which lapped at them as they climbed, she was sweating. Drops ran down her chin from under the edge of her helm.

She held where she was, trying to steady her nerves, to find the courage to hunt out new holds above. Somehow she was able to do so. Finger hold, toe hold, she fought upward. Then hands reached down to fasten about her wrists, steady her, and lend strength to bring her, belly down, over the rim. Still on her hands and knees Kadiya scrambled away from the drop and felt the pull of the rope about her as Smail and one of the Hassitti closed hand on it to draw Salin also onto the dubious safety of their perch.

Perch it was for they had not reached the top of the cliff. Here was a ledge where they could get to their feet and stand backs to the rise, the battered scree up which they had made their way almost at their feet. Once erect Kadiya could see whence that slide had come. This ledge had been much wider but there were cracks across it, plain evidence that most of its width had broken off to cascade to the dried streambed.

There was something else. Kadiya raised her head higher, her nostrils expanded, as she strove to catch that odor. Faint, but still it was! And it was death!

"The plague!" She set the danger into words as well as sent out a shaft of thought. There was no blighted vegetation here, no form of life the fungus could have fed upon, yet there was no mistaking that wafted stench.

Those beside her made room as Lamaril swung up to the ledge. He must have been right behind her. She wondered fleetingly if it had been his hand which had reset her footing.

Their perch narrowed where the worst of the fall had occurred and they edged along it with their back to the wall, taking the same care the climb had demanded. The larger Sindona needed to venture very close to the edge to travel at all. And over all was that stench of plague.

Yet the ledge must be their road for it ran on past the crystalline barrier above the dammed streambed. Lamaril and Fahiel of the guard scraped by the others, steadied by those they passed as they went. Before them scuttled the Hassitti. There seemed to be a new eagerness among the small ones from Yatlan, as if they were engaged in a race.

The barrier was wide and the ledge narrowed even more, until those leading them dropped to the top of the barrier wall itself. They could see ahead; the streambed still lay there and there were water marks high on the walls as if the dam had once created a small lake. Here and there were patches on the dry stone which Kadiya first thought were flowers, so bright did the color appear against the rocks. Then she saw that they were small beds of yellow and red crystals such as studded the wall.

They reached the end of the barrier. Now they needed to descend again into the streambed as that narrow upper way could not offer footing. The packs which had been drawn up were relowered. Then the Sindona held fast the ropes while the Oddlings, the Hassitti, and Kadiya descended.

One by one the Vanished Ones followed, until only Lamaril and Fahiel remained above. Both of them went to their knees and turned their rods point down against the surface of that wall. It was as if they used the rods like the drills Kadiya had seen employed by boat builders. The slender lengths settled into the stone.

Looping the rope about them, Lamaril and Fahiel swung over the edge and slipped down almost as one. When their boots thudded into the gravel of the ancient streambed, they pulled at the rope and Kadiya heard at very high range a whistling.

She could see the rods twisting, loosing from the stone. Then they flipped upward into the air and dropped so that their owners made quick grabs to catch them.

Lamaril rubbed his fingers along the length of his strange weapon-tool. Kadiya could only see that gesture—not his features below the helm mask—but she felt an uneasiness which she was sure emanated from him and Fahiel, as if in some way they had diminished the Power they could summon. If so, they accepted the fact quickly for the Guardian Leader turned almost at once to the rest of them.

"We go so—" he pointed ahead. "But 'ware touching the crystals. They are guards of a sort, and we know not how long their Power has lasted, how strong they still may be."

Thus warned they threaded their way single file, watching the ground and angling around one brilliant patch after another. The plague scent was still in the air, yet it was not as strong as it had been when Kadiya had faced the loathsome traces in the swamp. She kept a careful lookout, not only for the dangerous crystals, but also for any kind of vegetation which could support contagion. So far she had seen nothing but sterile stone.

The streambed was sloping upward and, in spite of the high walls on either side, ahead they could sight the dark bulk of the mountain country, while the wind which whistled down that hollow was snow and ice chill.

The daylight, already cut somewhat by the walls, was dimming. Close to evening they had discovered no place where the land was free enough from the crystals for any camp. Yet rest and eat they must—at least, thought Kadiya, must the Oddlings, the Hassitti, and she. Perhaps the Sindona did not need such refreshment.

As it grew darker, the crystals began to glow. The light they emitted was enough to mark them so they could be avoided. However, as far as Kadiya could see ahead, there was no end to them.

As far as she could see . . . Suddenly the girl realized that there was a misting, a clouding before them on this path, not unlike the mists which clung in the swamp country. Yet here was no water to give them birth.

A curious thickness seemed to roil within the outer parts of that mist. Also the smell of the plague was stronger. Kadiya slowed and mind sent a warning which she hoped would reach all their company. Yet the Sindona did not slacken pace.

"Lamaril!" She strove to match the longer strides of the leader. "There is rot ahead—"

"There is no other path, King's Daughter," he returned.

She wanted to halt, to hold back the Oddlings, the scurrying Hassitti. The plague might appear to be a lesser ill to the Sindona, but she had seen it.

Slowly Kadiya worked her sword free. Her exertions in the cliff climb appeared to have forced it more tightly into the sheath. There was a small glow of light—the eyelids were half open. From them beamed a subdued radiance. They were alive, those strange orbs, and they had indeed burned plague sores on the ground into nothingness—but could they withstand a long demand on their Power?

The mist was now a dark curtain, looking so thick as to be

tangible, and the path they wove toward it was growing shorter. Kadiya kept testing the air. So far the putrid smell had not grown any stronger.

Lamaril's rod swept forward. A spear of light no larger than the girl's forefinger shot out against that curtain. He was actually slicing at it, moving the rod up and down as he might a cutting knife.

The dark shrouding did not dissipate. Instead it curled outward in long ribbons, reaching toward them. Another illusion? Kadiya did not think so. But neither did she believe it to be some ancient guard that the Vanished Ones had left, even though Lamaril was so briskly dealing with it now.

One of those strips of dark reached toward the left. A Hassitti—Quave—crouched closer to the stony ground and wriggled backward. Lalan raised her rod as one might use a whip to bring the unruly to terms and struck at a wandering wisp.

As if part of a sentient creature it recoiled, but a stone it had touched showed a point of glistening slime—a bubble of rottenness from which puffed forth that telltale odor.

Three other of the Sindona moved up beside their leader. Their rod tips were now pinpoints of bursting light—a light which leaped at those writhing tatters of curtain.

Fire ran along it as it twisted and spun, as might a living thing being destroyed in a furnace. Then it was gone and they could see ahead. Yet there were stinking spots on the ground, spattering the way before them. Kadiya swung out the sword, aiming the eyes toward the first drip of slime.

But her will brought no answer from the triple orbs. It was one of the Sindona who burnt the patch to nothingness.

Shaken, Kadiya stood holding the weapon she had so long trusted. The eyes were open and she could look at them, into them: the greenish one which was like that of an Oddling, the brown flecked with gold which might have been lifted from her own skull, and the bright and larger one whose like she could see in any Sindona head.

Watching—they were only watching—or waiting. For what? Preserving their strength for some trial to come? Her jumbled thoughts could supply answers but who knew whether they were true?

However, she kept the blade unsheathed in her hand as she moved forward behind the Sindona leaders, accompanied by the Oddlings and the Hassitti who had now fallen back. The mists were gone; she could see ahead.

There was the ancient streambed continuing on and on, but to her left there was something else. A narrow stair cut into the cliff wall, leading up. And there were markings on the steps: dim patches dried and chip-like, but yielding still the putrid stench of the plague.

Lamaril's rod was at the ready. Light washed over each step as he started to climb, cleansing the way as he went. They were steep, those stairs, and plainly intended for the feet of the taller Vanished Ones. The Hassitti were using both hands and feet to aid their ascent, and Kadiya could only take a step at a time, sideways with her back to the wall, so that she might aid Salin. The wisewoman seemed even more frail and shrunken, yet she made no complaint, only drew from a belt pouch what looked like a half handful of dried leaves which she packed into her mouth and chewed upon determinedly as if she expected some aid from that endeavor.

Dusk had caught them, but the dark did not seem to deter the Sindona. Perhaps through some talent night seeing was theirs, but Kadiya, keeping resolutely from looking down over the unprotected outer side of those stairs, found this now nearly as great a trial as the ascent of the rubble had been.

There must be an end to this. Had they passed from the foothills into the true mountains? She shivered from the bite of the wind, though luckily it was not strong—not strong enough to pluck them from this stair, at least.

They came out at last on a flat stretch of stone so smooth it might have been pavement. The fore of that gave on a space well open to the winds of fast coming night; the rear was another rise. This of rough stone unworked, creviced here and there.

Lamaril and the others who had flanked him in the battle with the mist curtain went directly to the stone wall. Once there they held out their open palms, rods pointed to the surface. Again the rods began to move of themselves. Lamaril's left his hand to strike horizontally at a point a little above his helmed head. Those of his companions flashed a few to each side.

Kadiya saw those weapon-tools move again, Lamaril's first right and then left, drawing a thread-thin line of light across the rock. The other operated in a similar way to draw two vertical lines. What they outlined was an oblong which might mark a door.

However, those lines of light winked out almost as soon as they had first appeared. Lamaril quickly touched the rod but did not try to release it from its hold on the stone. Once more the lines showed and then were gone.

Now he set his hands to the rock within the frame the rods had drawn. Kadiya watched his whole body tense. Two of his companions moved in behind him, one reaching for the Commander's right shoulder, the other for the left.

Power! Kadiya caught the backwave of what they were expending. It was plain that the Sindona were attempting to force some opening.

The backlash of energy was increasing steadily. In Kadiya's hands the sword twisted in protest. She saw the eyes there close as if in pain.

Another surge of the Power. Still Lamaril and the rest faced an unyielding wall. The lines had flickered out this time not to return.

"Sealed." Lamaril stepped back, having plucked his rod from its point against the rock. "Sealed as it was left—but it does not answer for us."

Resheathing the rod at his belt he once more faced the wall. Now he set the fingertips of both hands against the rock surface, sending them back and forth in sweeps, keeping within the section the lines had outlined.

"There is darkness here—woven darkness!" The mind speech had not come from Lamaril, rather it was Salin who stepped forward now. The wisewoman's face showed both disgust and an underlying fear.

"Darkness," she repeated as Lamaril turned his head to look down at her.

"The work of Varm's chosen!" Lalan stared. "Then he has won here before us!"

"I think not," said Lamaril slowly. "If that were so this way surely would have been opened since he wishes what is within to come forth. Caskar set the final locking—and he was not of Darkness. Nor was Binah, who watched that setting that she might keep full guard. Kadiya," now his mind touch reached the girl, "you have told us of this Orogastus who meddled in the forbidden. What manner of man was he?"

She tried to think of all Haramis had told them. But she also knew that there was much concerning the sorcerer which had been private to her sister and never shared, even though Haramis at the end had stood against Orogastus and brought him down with the Power of their combined talisman.

"He knew much, but he was strange and from another land. We never knew whence Voltrik brought him as an advisor. Only we were certain that Voltrik moved to his bidding thereafter, whether the King knew it or not.

"Haramis said that — though he knew much — he was thirsty for more and that he believed that he would find hidden secrets in the mire ruins. He was certainly one of the Dark and he sought always to master Power."

"From another land . . ." Lamaril was thoughtful. "And Power draws Power. This might have drawn him."

"His own place was here in the mountains," Kadiya added eagerly.

"A seeker who meddled, and perhaps set a lock so that his meddling would be safe until he could come again," Lalan hazarded.

"Perhaps — yet one escaped to reach Varm. And it could be *his* sealing which bars us now. So." Lamaril looked back to the wall. "We can do the same. When he reaches here he may be so delayed." He turned his full attention to the Uisgu wisewoman.

"What know you of sealing Power?"

She settled herself cross-legged on the rock of the wide ledge, moving with difficulty. But at her gesture Smail brought up their pack and worked loose the ties for her.

"What I have, Noble One, is small. I farsee, I foresee . . . a little. I have arts of healing to some degree. What I have of protection is for the hunter, the far traveler, or one troubled with ill dreams —"

"Dreams! That touches the Hassitti," interrupted Quave,

padding to the side of the Uisgu. "Dreams I can deal with. But of what use are they here?"

Salin had been raiding the pack and now laid out three small packets and a metal plate no larger than Kadiya's hand.

"Perhaps they are no use as yet, small one." Lamaril rather than the wisewoman answered Quave. "But all aspects of the Power have use."

Kadiya tightened hold on the sword. All aspects of Power —

Salin crumbled a small fraction of dried leaf onto the plate and added pinches of powder from each of the other packets.

Though it was dark now, the plate before her gave forth a glow and the rods were like candles as their bearers moved in around Salin, leaving open only the side toward the mountain.

"This is the greatest ward I know, Noble One." The wisewoman brought forth a small splinter and touched it to the plate. A spark sprang into the mixture, and there rose from it a curl of smoke phosphorescent enough to be seen. Salin waved her hand and that vertical thread of smoke became horizontal, probing out to the wall.

Lamaril had gone down on one knee, head turning from Salin to the wall and back. Even in this poor light Kadiya could see his nostrils expand. She had also caught the scent — acrid, teasing, such as might come from some steaming highly spiced dish.

"Zarcon — yes." His helmed head nodded. "Your song, wisewoman?"

Still holding her hand to direct the smoke Salin put her head back as if she now sought to address something unseen in the air above them.

From her lips there came a strange quavering, not a song such as Kadiya knew. Salin's eyes closed. Smail had moved to kneel behind her. He brought his palm up and slapped it down on the rock, bringing forth a regular rhythm. Kadiya could hear the sound fit itself into the guttural quavers of the wisewoman.

Now Lamaril was on his feet again. In two strides he was at the face of the cliff. His rod out, he reached down toward the thread of smoke. The end of that encircled the rod and, when he raised it, he drew the wisp along.

With a sweep of arm he sent the captive smoke toward the hidden doorway. His rod flared brightly as he passed that weapon back and forth. On the rock face lines showed again — this time thin and gray — smoke lines being woven into a tight web.

23

IT WAS JAGUN WHO DISCOVERED a way from the ledge into concealment. The web, having encased the doorway, had disappeared, but Kadiya was certain that it was still in existence. Now they worked their way along the ledge toward a break in the cliff wall that could not be seen from their original position.

Here a crevice formed a chimney-like stair to a higher point of the mountain. The Oddlings, Hassitti, and Kadiya found it easy enough, but the Sindona had to scrape their way in and up. The girl heard the rasp of their mail against stone.

Luckily the climb was not long and it led them into the narrow throat of a greater break, one which widened out into a pocket of valley. It had been occupied in the past, for they stumbled into a mass of dried branches, grass, and unidentifiable material which made up a vast nest. They had come upon one of the lammergeier lairs.

However, Jagun and two of the Uisgu, having made a careful search, assured them that it had been several breeding seasons since this had last had inhabitants. As the giant birds always returned to the same nests each season, this must have been abandoned for one reason or another.

They set about clearing one mass of rubbish—which when stirred gave off faint foul smells—from a space large enough for them all to crowd into though these were very close quarters.

That they were awaiting the coming of the Dark One Kadiya knew. If he, on his escape, had indeed set up the barrier to protect his helpless companions, then he might be delayed on his return by the net Lamaril and Salin had spun.

It was not until the girl subsided in the small space she could claim, and was gnawing on a hard hunk of trail ration, that she surrendered to the fatigue which was the result of their day's exertions. The persistent ache of strained muscles wore at her. Kadiya had believed that she was hardened to the trail after her exertions of the past days, but now she knew the full cost of such a one as that just ended.

This night the Sindona drew no protection circle, nor did they light any fire, though the materials of the old nest were dry enough to make a good one. Plainly there was to be no use of magic or light to warn off their quarry.

Kadiya wondered if the man she had seen arise jubilantly from the iron throne would be easy to face. She had no knowledge of the extent of Power either the Sindona or he could produce at will, but she had become sure from Lamaril's attitude that the Vanished Ones considered this ancient enemy of their own blood a formidable opponent.

Luckily the walls of the crevice shielded them from the worst of the night wind but she felt the shivers of Salin crowded against her, the shudders of Tostlet on her other side. They shared with her such reaction to the chill, which the mire-born had never known before. Their reed cloaks, meant to shed the wet mists of the swamp, allowed these gusts of air nearly free entrance.

Kadiya was too tired to sleep and she had to fight against gloomy thoughts of what might lie ahead. Had the Sindona not failed at the doorway below, she would not have such active doubts. Having all her life believed in the supreme Power of the Vanished Ones, to accept any limits for them was to shake all her confidence.

The girl wished that they might have tried to reach Haramis again. Here in the very mountains where her sister had chosen to establish her new home surely there would not have been the barriers they had met in the mires below. But the ban against any use of sorcery held for their own protection.

At length her weariness wore out all her inner questioning and doubts, and she slept without any dreams to trouble her.

The sky was barely the gray of dawn when she awoke within their cramped camp. The form on her right had stirred and was sitting upright. And against the sky at the edge of their crevice perch Kadiya could see the silhouette of two helmed heads, Sindona already alert and at watch.

"King's Daughter—" It was the merest thread of mind touch, then a clawed paw-hand touched her gently. Tostlet.

"There is trouble?" Kadiya shook the last of the sleep from her mind, aware now of something else—that the sword hilt against her arm was a spot of growing warmth.

"There is—a secret..." That last word was tentative, as if the Hassitti healer was not quite sure.

"Where?"

"Beneath us."

Tostlet had pushed and pulled away the flooring of the nest, the powdered stuff which had coated the stone when they had cleared the coarse tangled mass. Now her claws scratched faintly on the stone. Kadiya could not see, she could only guess what the Hassitti did in the abiding gloom. But she put out her own hand, felt claws close about it to bear her fingers downward.

There was stone, but also something else. Surely the smoothness of metal! And it was tightly affixed to the stone, set level with the rock. With Tostlet's guidance the girl traced an angle, what might be the corner of a larger piece.

As she had leaned forward to answer the Hassitti's pull the amulet on her breast came to golden life, swung out over that portion of the rock under them.

"Kadiya!"

Lamaril's mind touch. She could always easily recognize it.

"There is something here. It is of Power."

Those about them stirred; the mind touch must have awakened them all into action. Some drew aside as the Sindona leader joined Kadiya.

By the glow of the amulet she saw his hand held out over that spot palm down.

"Power." He echoed her own conviction. "Let us learn more of this."

There was not much room in which to work, but those around them drew back as far as they could. The dusty deposit encrusting the rocks gave forth a faint unpleasant odor as they scratched it up but it was not that of the plague warning.

With their hands and the use of some of the brittle bits of wood, they scraped clear a space to discover something which was indeed metal. As the daylight advanced they could see more detail than the amulet light had shown. What they had uncovered was a grating inset in the rock. The narrow open strips which made up most of it formed a frame clogged with dust. There was no sign of any method of lifting it; the metal seemingly had been fused to the rock about the edges.

"It is of the sleepers' prison." Lamaril settled back on his heels.

"It is also guarded," Tostlet commented. "Noble One, this is a mighty guard—from the ancient days."

"Indeed. Yet it may serve us. The find is good—"

What more he might have said was swallowed by a thrust of warning which overrode all other mind speech.

"Someone comes from below!"

The chain of Kadiya's amulet moved as her talisman swung to the left, pointing now toward the outer edge of the crevice. Kadiya tensed. Her eyes were for her sword since she was too far from that vantage place and there were too many crowded in between to see what was happening. The sword had come alive, there was no dull withdrawal in the orbs on the pommel now.

There was a scuttling sound as Jagun dropped from above into the back of the nest crevice.

"Skritek above gather on both sides!"

They were trapped in part by the narrow cliff in which they had camped. The Sindona moved back along the way which had brought them here. Their rods swept beams of light downward across the debris of the nest while the Uisgu fell back to the walls of the cliff to give the others full room, dart blowers in hand. The Hassitti took position among the mire people. Kadiya, perforce, had to do likewise for the moment, the large bodies of the Sindona choking the chimney descent.

She was studying the cliffs on either side. The rock widened out so that this cut was wedge shaped and they were in the narrowest portion. Lammergeier were huge birds, able to bear riders—she had seen Haramis so mounted. So the downsweep into this deserted nest was certainly large enough to admit the smaller voors.

Fire was the most effective weapon against those deadly raiders. But to fire this nest mass would be to also condemn themselves to roasting. The stuff was too dried and brittle to keep flames from roaring up quickly.

In the gray sky flapped wide black wings—certainly voor. What had drawn them here? The cold air of the heights was surely not to their taste—they must somehow be under the control of the follower of Varm. Not only the voor cruised the sky above; a waft of air down the cliff brought the stench of Skritek. The Dark-led party must have discovered this cliff and spread out to come upon them both from below and above.

There was a roar from overhead followed by a rock bounding from the top of the cliff against which Kadiya and a good part of their company sheltered. It struck the opposite side and rebounded straight at them! It hit again, near enough to Kadiya to make her cringe. The Uisgu closest to that point threw himself to one side quickly enough to escape.

That was but the beginning of the bombardment intended to either crush them where they stood or drive them down into the chimney. They were surely in a trap. A voor planed down. Then it twisted and screamed. The Oddlings might be under dire attack of a new kind but they were not so fearful as not to be ready. The creature was falling, turning over and over, and as it crashed into the mass of the ancient nest, Kadiya saw two darts in its body—recognized them for those envenomed thorns Smail had fashioned during their questing.

The rocks continued to fall. There came a scream which resounded through Kadiya's head. One of their beleaguered company had been struck down.

The voor they could sight weaving back and forth overhead did not try a second attack. But there was no end to the rocks sent to pin them in, if not crush them. Nor was there, that Kadiya could see, a way to reach the attackers on the crest above. Jagun had climbed there earlier, and descended to bring his warning. But to try a second ascent was to face rolling rocks at too great a risk.

They would be safer below. Kadiya mind-touched and those lining the walls began to obey her, moving slowly to the opening down which they must climb.

Now she tried mind touch with Lamaril. What did he and the Sindona face below?

For a moment or two it was as if she looked through his eyes. Skritek were striving to reach the ledge before the curtained door, only to be picked off by rod flashes. Yet still they came, and now she could hear their yammering cries even over the crash of the rock bombardment.

The mind touch snapped as if there had never been such a link. Lamaril? But if he had fallen how had the enemy reached him? She had seen no Skritek get past the edge. Kadiya struggled with all the force she could summon to link again, only to meet a forbidding curtain. Lalan — she pictured the woman in her mind, strove to hold that picture. Dark wiped it out, closed down.

Dead! Were they both dead? She could not believe that — she dared not.

Salin had Power, the Hassitti dreamer had Power of a sort, but now her sword might be their only defense. She must not let the others make that climb down, perhaps into the waiting talons of the Skritek.

At her command—though Jagun and Smail stood firm against her until she shook the sword before them and they gave back at the sight of those open glowing eyes—the Oddlings and Hassitti drew back to let her go first.

She needed both hands for the descent, but she must also have the sword at ready. Kadiya set the blade between her teeth, gripping it as tightly with her jaws as she could. The weapon was growing ever hotter and it fretted the corners of her lips. She held on grimly, putting her mind on the handholds and footholds which would take her below.

Kadiya was into the chimney halfway down, when the Power force reached her. It came like the surge of a monsoon-mad river. She clung to the holds, fighting for the strength to keep from falling.

That punishing force changed from a surge to a steady pressure. Continuing down was like lowering oneself into a vast pool of energy which she expected any moment to flatten her against the rock as crushingly as one of the stones the attackers had been flinging.

That pressure made each movement a struggle. The sword between her lips grew more and more like a coal of well-nourished fire. Still, stubbornly Kadiya fought on. Though when she did at last reach firm footing, she clung for a moment or two to her last hold, the Power force so strong now she wondered if she could long stand before it.

With that a-play Kadiya knew better than to again try communication with those she sought. Power might flood along any path of communication, know and seek her out. The sword— Shakily she put up one hand and freed the sword from the grip of her aching jaws. Power attracts Power . . .

But there was no way she could control the output of either the sword or the blazing amulet on her breast.

The girl turned away from the wall and edged toward the open. The weight of the force out there was intense. Surely that must signal that the Sindona were still alive, fighting — or were they prisoners of the same pressure she felt?

Now she could look out upon the ledge. The backs of Sindona who were erect, at least still alive, faced her. She had to twist a little, without venturing out of the shadow of the fissure which hid the chimney climb, to see Lamaril.

He was positioned a fraction ahead of the others, his rod agleam. Facing him was that other, the one she had seen in the sanctuary. Cloaking him was a strange shimmer as if he did not wear armor but rather a force flowing from within his body. His head was unhelmed, and his face plain to see.

There was a smile on his lips. His eyes held small center cores of red. There was no hint of the ravages of the plague about him. Rather he stood with the confidence of one totally in command of himself.

Mind speech — she was sure they were using mind speech, they stood so still in that confrontation. Kadiya wet her sore lips with her tongue tip. Dared she try to pick up what they said? Or would that move somehow disturb the scales — attract attention in the wrong way?

She could not just wait on results. She must know. This had been her battle from the first. These others had taken it on, but she was not to be denied her part in it. The mires were threatened by that shimmer-clad stranger — befouled as even Orogastus had not done. Kadiya reached, seeking the level on which the enemies spoke.

"... there was said this day would come, fool. Your spells broke in the end — I stand here proof of that!"

"But not by you were they broken, Ragar That Was. There was meddling in the mountains, but that meddler is no longer to be called upon. You summoned him, did you not, Ragar?"

"How clever of you, Lamaril. You seem to have become more astute while you lolled about in that paradise of yours all these many seasons. Yes, the one named Orogastus could be touched, even by a sleeping mind. Dreams are very powerful—and dreams a sleeper can use. He could not be controlled, of course—our bounds would not allow open contact—but we fed into his mind that there was a secret hereabouts which was worth the seeking. And he was a most curious little meddler in what he did not understand."

"Except he did not bring your full release. Rather his action set the pattern for others, Ragar."

"One needs only a door unlocked, Lamaril. Which now moves me to action—behind you is that which I locked and now would open. He who sent me is not one to practice patience and he has waited overlong."

"The sleepers sleep," Lamaril returned calmly. "You shall not disturb them, Ragar."

One side of Ragar's mouth moved in a way which made his smile a cruel grin. "*Shall not?* Such words to me?"

With a flash of brilliant fire he swung his own rod point out. The flames were dark, the red of drying blood, with no honesty of real fire about them.

They met a golden wall raised by the Sindona's weapons. There was dark smoke and the red flames bored in, darted in flashes from place to place. Twice red fire bore back the gold, only to have the barrier straighten. Kadiya reeled under the backlash of the Power. But somehow that which beat inwardly in Lamaril reached her as well. The Sindona held—but they could not raise a counterattack. Into the other weapon Ragar had poured a raving hatred which was energy in itself—a fuel supplying ever more force. Ancient bitter rage which had been honed through countless seasons, meant to be used when the opportunity arose.

There was even a low keening from that meeting of flame against flame, like that given by some beast not to be robbed of its prey.

Then—a thrust of the flame, a flicker of gold. The flame hit through the gold barrier to the wall of the cliff behind Lamaril. The Sindona on the Captain's left buckled at the knees—Nuers fell forward.

Ragar screamed his triumph. The dark flame clung to the wall. Even though the golden light flashed back, shutting off its source, it remained to crawl back and forth across the stone.

"Not yet, Ragar, not yet." There was Oath-grimness in that. Nuers did not move. The rod he had dropped, had snapped and lay as might a dead branch.

"Soon, soon, Lamaril—very soon!" There was a heady confidence in that, like a blow in itself.

24

 THE LIGHT WALL OF THE SINDONA continued to hold. The crawling flame on the rock remained alive as well, though there was no sign of the door. A scream shattered the drive of flame energy.

A voor swept down at those on the ledge. It was the largest of the species Kadiya had ever seen and it swooped straight at Lamaril. Without thinking the girl raised her sword, setting the eyes on a line with that diving death.

From the great eye on the pommel shot a finger-wide beam which caught the head of the bird of prey. The voor uttered no more cries but twisted in the air to fall as heavily as a stone.

Into the battle of red flame and gold light hurtled the plummeting body. There followed a flash of brilliant fire, strong enough to blind Kadiya for the moment. Then she heard a cry of triumph, not mind sent but uttered aloud. The line of golden light had broken, the red flame licked out avidly at Lamaril.

Again Kadiya, without thought, turned the sword against the attack. This time there was no answer. Lamaril had gone to his knees and the light of his rod dimmed. That attacking fire flared high beyond him, straight for the hidden door.

"Out — away and out!"

The cry rang in her mind. Kadiya held the sword in both hands. Her bringing down of the voor had caused this, broken through the Sindona defense. She could see them only through tearing eyes, for the burst of fire still half blinded her.

If that door opened now — if those within came through — Lamaril and his people would be caught between two attacks, crushed. . . .

She pulled farther back. There was only one slim chance, so slim that she could not count on any success. Still, she knew she must take it.

Kadiya turned her head. Crowded tightly behind her were the Hassitti and the Oddlings, some of them still clinging to the walls of the chimney because there was no room to move out below.

Did the rocks still crash down up there? Perhaps that which she must seek would be entirely buried — yet there was a chance, a chance. . . .

"Jagun." She sighted the hunter among those packed so tightly behind her. "I must go back —"

The others picked that up quickly. She heard murmurs, the chittering of the Hassitti.

"If there is another way into the place of the sleepers, we must use it and attack!"

They were moving in the chimney, reclimbing, to clear the way. She saw Jagun swing to a newly vacated spot and reach for a handhold. Kadiya squeezed through — Salin and two more of the Uisgu, the Hassitti somehow giving her room. Once more she took the sword in her jaws, withstood the heat which held in it, rising to a greater level with every passing moment. So she climbed.

Those who had proceeded her were once more plastered against the walls of the crevice. The hail of stones had stopped, but there were piles of them across the stretch of the nest. And surely there must be lookouts above to make sure their quarry did not venture here again.

What she sought lay in the open, plain to the eyes of any watchers above. Yet she had no choice. Kadiya took the sword by its blade and surveyed that broken mass before her desperately. The grid — it must lie . . . there!

Something pressed against her from behind, and she heard a loud, impatient chittering. The Hassitti had followed her up. She nearly fell as the first of them shoved past her.

Kadiya tried to warn it out of the open with her other hand, but it had fallen onto its belly and was skittering out into the nest makings, burrowing into the pile of stuff they had swept aside earlier to uncover the grid. There was a rise of dust, the scent of the ancient foulness of long dried droppings.

Stones? Kadiya's upward glance searched the edge of those cliffs. No sight as yet of any Skritek on guard.

She went to her own hands and knees and then even lower, crawling, wriggling as had the Hassitti out toward the grid. The dust whirled about her. She dared not cough, for once more she held the sword between her teeth. Always she listened for Skritek yells of triumph, the sound of falling stones.

That these did not come was almost a matter for fear. She could not believe that the creatures had abandoned their perch above, were not ready to deal again with any of the party daring to return.

She crawled onward. Then she was in the open, hunching in upon herself as if such a clear target could somehow be made invisible. She grabbed the sword so quickly from her mouth that there was a sharp pain and a trickle of blood marked her chin.

They had cleared the grill when they had found it. Now the Hassitti, who had beaten her to this goal, was running claws about the meeting of stone and metal, plainly striving to find some crevice.

"Back!" Kadiya's thought was a sharp order. The Hassitti — it was Quave she saw now—obeyed.

A clatter sounded above: a stone coming. Kadiya cowered. If it was going to hit— She flopped over on her side and saw the thing strike.

It was close enough to send grit and dust puffing into her face. But she saw something else: Jagun and Smail climbing up the walls. Around both of them thickened a strange and quivering envelope of dull green into which they disappeared from sight more and more. It was also turning grayish, fading into the stone behind it. Power—but whose? Kadiya had no time to wonder.

She turned again and held out the sword, striving to banish everything from her mind save what must be done—to feed into the weapon she held the utmost strength she could summon.

The sword heated still more, the pain in her hands was a rising torment. Now the three eyes blazed down on that grid. She shifted the focus so the light moved slowly back and forth across the metal. Pain was rising to the point where she could have screamed and she fought it bitterly. This must be done!

There was a shimmer on the grid—or was that her eyes betraying her? No, even when she moved the sword there remained a glow across the metal. With all her remaining strength Kadiya continued to lace that plate even as Lamaril had laced the door below. But this was not to seal a barrier. It was a key to open one — if all the forces of Light would will it so!

The Power was so draining! A second Hassitti had joined the first. That the grid was glowing with heat did not appear to trouble them at all as they clawed in and around those shimmering metal bars.

A harsh ripping sound — The Hassitti, working together, had suddenly thrust downward and the grid had given!

What the aperture had sealed was now a dark hole. Kadiya crawled forward once more. She had no time to waste.

Trying not to think of crashing rocks though wondering for a second why those had not come, she sat up and held the sword over the hole. The eyes were near closed. They gave no light to see. The amulet! Would that serve instead? Kadiya clawed the chain from around her neck and dangled it down. As the amber passed the surface where that barrier had been it did indeed give light. At least enough to show a large space below, and that the drop to the floor was not beyond her powers.

Her mouth hurt too much for her to grip the sword again. She managed to anchor it to her belt where it could be quickly to hand. Then Kadiya swung over to let herself drop, moving away just in time as two of the Uisgu followed, and then a third.

The chamber which they entered thusly was not a rough cave. Its walls had been smoothed; they reflected a little the gleam of the amulet. Piled about those walls were coffers of metal such as Kadiya had seen in Yatlan.

There was nothing else. But as she turned slowly, the amulet in hand, she glimpsed a dark patch on the far wall which was so much in shadow she could hardly distinguish it.

Toward that she hurried, the Uisgu after her. They had been joined by Salin, as well as the Hassitti who had scrambled through the hole to drop what was a much longer distance for them.

As she approached the far wall Kadiya could see a door there — or rather an opening across which there appeared no barrier. Yet, as she stepped toward it, she came up against a wall she could not see, though it was firm under the hands she put out to feel across that invisible surface.

There was only one key she knew of, one which had served her faithfully in the past. She unloosed the sword and held it vertically to face the unknown.

From the pommel streamed a light indeed, but very faint — from one eye only, that which resembled her own. Back and forth she swept it, as she had cleared away the grid.

Kadiya felt with her other hand. The way had opened, yet she could not see what lay beyond. The amulet's gleam appeared almost as if it were thrown back upon itself.

Nevertheless the girl moved on, the others close on her heels. And once beyond that portal the light did indeed wax — enough so that she did not stumble on two steps leading downward into what was a space her poor light could not reveal in its entirety.

Sword ready in one hand and amulet in the other Kadiya moved cautiously. Under her worn boots the flooring was smooth. Thick dust lay there and it was disturbed enough by their passing to set them all coughing.

Then the dim light caught on something looming out of that dust. Kadiya saw another coffer but this was as long as one of the Sindona was tall. The sides were of the blue-green metal of which their race had made so much use. However, the top gave back, even from so pale a light as the amulet emitted, glints of brilliance. As the girl came up beside it she saw that the whole of the lid seemed to be one massive slab in which crystals were embedded, point-up.

Salin joined her.

"A sleeper," the wisewoman answered Kadiya's unasked question.

The Hassitti who had left the circle of amulet light now scuttled forward. "Three more which are sealed—one broken by fire," Quave reported.

Kadiya went to see for herself. The Hassitti was right. The crystal encrusted lid of the farthest coffer had been broken and blackened as if from fire. In fact most of it lay in jagged pieces on the floor.

From the interior arose a fetid odor which reminded Kadiya strongly of the plague scent.

"Do not go near it," she warned quickly as she turned back to view the other coffers.

If those Sindona who held the ledge had failed, if—if Lamaril was gone, then what these held would be summoned forth to do the will of the Dark. And, she thought grimly, they would do it well. Perhaps they would spread the plague to rot the mires still more. The peril would reach across Ruwenda to send death across all the lands she knew, and perhaps even beyond.

These who slept here . . . there could be only one answer. They must not wake!

"Salin, Quave." She sought the wisewoman, the dreamer. They had Power of a sort; she had more. But might those strands be woven together to do what must be done? They must! And it would be a race against time. Their skills had locked the outer door, but the Dark Power lay now both over and under their spelling — two sides might well crush the middle! And the Sindona might be even now falling just as she had seen Lamaril go down.

The short Uisgu, the even smaller Hassitti, now flanked her one on either side.

Kadiya pointed to that coffer next to the one which had been broken open. "What lies within must not awaken."

"Kill!" The Hassitti's demand was swift.

"King's Daughter, we have not the Power to keep it sealed. The little one is right — the sleeper must be destroyed."

"But first we must open this." Kadiya doubtfully eyed the lid with its coating of jagged crystals.

Those Uisgu warriors who had followed her were closing in now. They looked frail and small against that coffer, but one was already feeling along the top edge, seeking some lock or fastening. Then three of them moved in together and Kadiya joined them. There was enough of an overhang of that lid to give them finger room for a grip and now they all exerted strength to lift.

The solid weight or perhaps a restraining spell was against them.

Kadiya strove to insert the pointless end of the sword — but with no result. Then Salin drew her hands along that sealed line between top and sides.

"There is a Power-lock," the wisewoman reported.

One set by the Vanished Ones long ago, Kadiya wondered, or one placed by that dealer of death who fought without, to protect his kind until he returned? Either could be beyond her hope of breaking.

She had only the sword — But not to try was to admit failure, and that Kadiya could not do.

. . . ——————————————————————————— . . .

Once more she turned to Salin. "Will you link—you, and Quave also—" What inner strength the Hassitti dreamer might be able to summon the girl had no way of measuring, but surely there was Power behind those dreams.

Salin moved closer. Her hand touched Kadiya's shoulder, and the Hassitti was quick to link by touch in turn with the wisewoman. Kadiya drew a deep breath and called upon the sword, aiming the now open eyes at the edge of the coffer.

The light beam answered. She saw the light center on the edge between lid and side. Then, though her hand did not move by any will of her own, the sword tilted so that the spear of light now moved across the top of the lid, waking to fiery light the many points of crystal with bursts of brilliance strong enough to be nearly blinding.

Those points of crystal took on the full fury of flames. Kadiya thought she could see them outlined in a haze as if they were really burning. Back and forth the light swung—she was now subject to whatever had taken control of her weapon.

She was dimly aware of a disturbance at her back, that the Uisgu warriors had gone in that direction, but she held to complete concentration as best she could.

There came a shattering noise. Bits of the crystals exploded outward. Kadiya flinched as a line of pain split one cheek from edge of helm mask to chin. The lid broke in a frenzy, throwing parts in all directions. Draining energy had drawn her some steps forward and now those splinters of glass flew so that she threw one arm across her face, a moment later feeling pain as if many Oddling darts had pierced her skin.

When Kadiya dared to look she saw that the lid had broken across. Parts of it were missing, either thrown outward by the force of that breaking, or fallen within the cavity which had been concealed.

The sword was dimming. For all the extra energy had added to her own strength, it was still plainly near exhaustion. Kadiya realized that her own will was spinning.

She was wet with sweat from the effort, worn but still able to keep to her feet. Now, with her free hand, she caught at some of those loose chunks, jerking them free to hurl to the floor. Salin and Quave joined at the work.

For the first time Kadiya was mindful of something else: a high, ear-tormenting keening. She looked over her shoulder toward the wall.

There, even as she had seen it on the ledge outside, showed the outline of a doorway—but not marked in the golden of the Sindona searching, rather in the sullen red controlled by Varm's liegeman.

Setting her teeth Kadiya turned back to her own task. The Uisgu warriors were waiting, blow pipes in hand facing that wall. That they could hold when the Sindona had gone down she doubted. But that door was as yet closed.

She looked down into the coffer. There was a misty veiling there, as if the box were filled with sluggishly moving liquid. Still, she could see the outlines of a humanoid form within, one as tall as the Sindona.

That any dart, any spear, could put an end to what slept here, she doubted. The moving swirl about it was rising, and from it puffed the foul odor of the plague, so foul that she felt some offal had been thrust into her bleeding face.

Sword fire had defeated the traces of the plague, sword fire was all she could summon now. Kadiya felt once more the touch of Salin, and an added small but steady surge of Power which must have been from Quave.

Kadiya raised the sword horizontally over what lay in that muck. There was light, but not from the large orb which crowned the three — rather it fed from the two beneath. And it was only a thread compared to what she had earlier been able to summon.

Yet she stood as steady as she might, sending that double beam down into the mass within.

The light hit the surface of whatever coated the sleeper, spread outward. There was a small flickering — not quite fire, but still something which moved. Then, as might a fire when blown upon, it flared up and coated all the length of the sleeper, blasting outward with the stench of death.

Deep in her mind Kadiya heard a thin, anguished cry. Did she or did she not see that shrouded form beneath the fire writhe?

The sword eyes closed. She must accept that what they had to offer had been given. However, they had cleansed but one of those coffers. Only one!

Desperately she regarded the three which remained. She could not do it, but she must! Leaning against the edge of the one wherein the fire was smouldering, she glanced back apprehensively at the outline of the door.

It was more than just an outline now; the wall within those lines had begun to glow. Yet it seemed to her that the dull red was not so dark, that it had in some way been diluted, lessened. Perhaps the Sindona's fire had sapped the Power of the enemy. Yet Kadiya was certain that, even in a weakened state, what that other could command far surpassed anything she might summon.

She stood away from that coffer they had plundered and wavered on to the next. Salin had reached the side of that before her, and Quave's arm about Kadiya's waist was supporting her with a strength she would not have thought possible in the smaller Hassitti.

"Power of the mire," Salin said, "Power of your kind, King's Daughter. Perhaps only Power of the Old Ones does not hold here. If it *is* Power of the mire—"

Now instead of just touching Kadiya she reached out and covered the girl's sword hand with her own, while Quave stood between them, a paw on each.

"Now!" Salin made that word a call to battle.

With an effort Kadiya lifted the sword. She willed— There was a stronger surge of force into that blade than she had felt earlier. Now she knew what to do, and, with the Uisgu helping to hold the weapon, she traced a pattern across the crystal back and forth as quickly as she could.

Once more that shattering—and Kadiya saw from the corner of her eye a bloody line open on Salin's shoulder, felt a peppering of broken crystal against her mail. Again the light from the two eyes alone ate at what lay within.

Kadiya kept her feet with difficulty. Her sword arm was growing so heavy she feared she could not hold it aloft again. She did not wait to see the fire finish the second sleeper. Instead she staggered with Salin and the Hassitti to the next coffer. Two more—could they do it?

The door on the wall was fully aglow, heating so that the Uisgu guard were forced back. But now it bore a golden tinge. The Sindona? Could it be that they were not totally vanquished? Lamaril—thought flinched from her memory of him. She thrust his image away from her, buried it. Only one thing mattered now—those two coffers yet to be emptied.

Salin tottered beside her. Once more they linked, and, with the Hassitti feeding them, they wrought against the crystal. This time she was cut along the throat by the flying shards, though luckily the helm kept her eyes from danger. Again the light brought fire and an ending to what lay beneath.

They turned to the last of the coffers. Kadiya was doubtful if she could keep her feet long enough to reach it.

Sound — not the shattering of crystal which they had not yet attacked, but a deep rusty note. Before their eyes the lid of the last coffer began slowly to rise.

... ——————————————————————————————— ...

25

THE THING WHICH EMERGED MOVED slowly as if with great effort. From it the form-shrouding liquid rolled away reluctantly; it was viscid, like the heavy slime of a bog snail. The thing flung out both arms, hands curled about the edges of the coffer to pull itself upward.

Now its half shrouded head turned. Kadiya saw only the eyes in that face, eyes which held the dark fire of Varm's burning.

Instinctively she retreated, her companions with her. She swung the sword up between them and that thing levering itself out of its age-old bed.

Greenish liquid which was like a distillation of rot splashed on the rock as it gained its feet. One arm swung out and droplets of that stuff spattered near them. A long leg swung over the side now and the thing was almost free of its bed.

The sword— There was no gleam from the top orb. That was glassy, lifeless. But from the other two broke pencils of light, joined to form a line hardly thicker than a reed-net thread.

Kadiya aimed, knowing even as she did so that she might have made a fatal mistake in gauging the weakest point of this sleeper. However, she centered that lesser beam at its rounded ball of head from which the slime was still sloughing. It struck full on and the creature jerked back, flung up one arm in an attempt to deflect the beam.

At the point where that light struck grew a spark of fire, as if a single small twig had been ignited. This new fire was neither the red of Varm, nor the golden radiance the Sindona commanded. It was green, the fresh green of newly sprouted river reeds.

It struck and seemed to root, and from it sprung tendrils of even finer girth which writhed around the head. The creature's cry was not for the ears, but rather a raw pain in Kadiya's mind. She might have reeled back but the Hassitti, with a surprising show of strength in his small body, steadied her.

The head of the awakened sleeper was now fast being enclosed in a green net. Its second cry came from the throat—a scream in which rage sounded even greater than pain. It threw itself forward, hands outstretched as if to embrace all three in one swoop of attack.

Death! Like its fellow, it carried death in its touch. The opened coffer behind her was now a wall against which Kadiya half cowered, knowing that there was no escape from that vindictive attack.

On her breast the amulet was an orb of fire in itself. It swung from side to side though she was not willing that movement. And there was a shrill din in her ears, a crying as if a hundred, a thousand voices of the mire, Oddlings, all manner of creatures—perhaps even plants—were uttering battle shouts, standing steady in defense.

The head of the sleeper was now completely enfolded by the winding of the light save where those coals of eyes showed. It might be that the hate blazing within was what preserved its sight, that it might bring down its enemies.

Both arms raised higher, dripping the foul moisture in which it had been immersed. It tottered on. In Kadiya's hands the sword hung heavy. All three orbs were now glassily inert.

A dart flickered out of the air and its point sank deeply into one of those red eyes. One of the Uisgu behind Kadiya had found a target.

The creature did not react. Yet the girl was certain that the Oddling had shot one of the poisoned darts. Perhaps this thing was such poison in itself that venom could not enter what ran in its veins for blood.

It lunged. At the same time there came a new sound in that now foul smelling chamber—a call:

"By the Blossom—stand!"

A puff of golden dust burst from behind her. When it reached the gleam of the amulet, it put forth colored sparks as if it were fashioned from shards of crystal. A glittering shroud drifted over the awakened sleeper. The green of the web light waxed until the head and shoulders of the creature were curtained. Kadiya could no longer see the mad red sparks of its eyes.

Its hands smeared down the sides of the other coffer only a palm's width away from where she had leaned. Kadiya was pulled back against the support of a tall, strong body. The relief of her escape was so great that the whole of that dusky chamber whirled. Nausea gripped her and she fought it, so caught in that struggle to control her body that she was hardly aware of being lifted, carried out of the putrid air of that place into the open.

She blinked up at a cloudless sky, felt the warmth of the sun. Dared then to turn her head to see who had carried her. He lowered her onto the stone of the ledge now criss-crossed with black traces of angry fire.

"Lamaril!" But he had fallen when the weapon of his people had failed. . . .

"Varm's man?" She turned her head slightly to look.

On the stone was a wider stain — evil, black, like a shadow in the form of a man crouched in upon himself, suffering from some great wound.

Lamaril leaned back against the stone cliff. The door to the sleepers' chamber was now an open mouth.

Kadiya raised a shaking hand to her face. She could taste the sweet stickiness of blood. Her fingers slipped across the smarting wounds the exploding crystals had made.

"It is over then?" She was so worn now that it was difficult to shape either words or thoughts.

"Varm has no longer any doorways into this land. The old terrors are laid, Kadiya. The strings which tied the past to the present are broken at last — which is as it should be. We were remiss in not making an end in the old days. But it was not in us to slay out of hand those who were our captives. Better though we had taken blood guilt on us then. Almost he won. Had it not been for you and those of our creation we would have failed. To us that is a thing we must always remember. We are not almighty, victors though we were in the elder days. We are but men and women with other talents, but we can taste of death and know disaster."

"The mire lands are safe." She did not make a question of

that, rather held to it as a fact, something which would perhaps be a comfort in days to come. Why she would need a comfort Kadiya was not sure now — she was too tired, too overdriven.

She looked down at the sword. There was blood on her hands where she had gripped it so tightly that even its dulled edge had been able to cut her flesh. The eyes were tightly closed. That glitter which had edged the lids was gone. She could sense a difference through her whole body. The Power which had come to her summons was exhausted to the full at last — there was no life left.

Her hand went to the amulet. Under a touch which left smears of blood on the breast of her mail the amber was cooled. Lifeless, too? Perhaps.

She had not Haramis's will for Power. What had been lent to her she had used as best she could; now it was gone. Kadiya stared dully ahead, past that smear on the rock which marked the end of Varm's liegeman. She shivered. The winds which had begun to sweep the ledge were mountain cold.

"Where now?" she was asking that of herself more than of him.

"We go to Yatlan." There was a chill, a kind of withdrawal, in that mind touch.

Kadiya remembered what a return to Yatlan would mean. Those she had summoned out of time would return into timelessness.

"King's Daughter!"

Kadiya's head jerked. Jagun was coming toward her. One of his arms was in a sling across his chest. He limped, one of the Uisgu steadying him.

"Jagun!" Then a moment later she added, "Smail?"

The eyes of the hunter blinked. "The healer cares for him. Three of the Skritek he bore down before the fourth tried to break him against the rocks. The Drowners fled when the death cry of Varm's minion sounded. However, few escaped dart and spear as they went."

"It is well." Against all the will Kadiya could summon her body was relaxing in a manner she could not understand. Her eyelids seemed weighted. She could no longer fight this weariness; it was as heavy as one of the rocks which had rained down into the crevice of the nest.

Darkness lapped about Kadiya with the soft comfort of sleep robes. Sighing she surrendered to it, seeking the forgetfulness of healing.

How long she lay so cocooned the girl did not know, but at length there pressed upon her a summons she could not elude.

"Kadiya—" Her name from a far distance, demanding.

She strove to shut ears and mind against it.

"Sister!"

That was too sharp, too close to be denied.

Where they stood in meeting Kadiya could not tell; perhaps this place had no existence as she knew reality. Haramis was but a face looming out of veiling shadows.

"What has troubled the land?" That demand was peremptory. "It has been shrouded from my seeing these many days. What has come upon Ruwenda?"

"An evil out of time," Kadiya's answer came draggingly; the overpowering weariness still held her fast. Yet somehow she held on to her sister's face and knew that Haramis listened.

The plague, the discovery of that other place where the Vanished Ones had gone, their return—the trek into the mountains to the battle—all which had happened in these past days.

"Lamaril tells me," Kadiya ended, "the land is now cleansed. He and his will return to that place beyond time."

Haramis's mouth twisted. "Guardian I was said to be—yet in this I had no hand."

Kadiya could almost taste the bitterness she sensed in her sister. More than Haramis's pride had been bruised; that which she honestly felt for her land suffered.

"I do not know why this was given into my hands," Kadiya said wearily. "I do not hold any great Power." She remembered the burnt-out appearance of the sword, the vanishing of the fire in her amulet. "Now—I believe I hold none at all. Perhaps it was that I could reach the Great Ones the easier. Haramis, I am done with Power—and it is done with me."

"Be sure, sister," Haramis returned, "that I shall find a means whereby such will not happen again. Binah knew so much. I have had so little time"—she paused—"and part of my learning was tainted. Orogastus was of the Dark and strove to draw me with him."

"But you did not yield," Kadiya reminded her. "And you are great of purpose, sister. Lamaril and his people will go—but there will be remnants of learning in Yatlan. I may not be able to comprehend it, but I shall guard it until you wish—without Power if that must be."

Haramis regarded her steadily for a long moment. "Little sister, you are far greater than you guess. And," now her eyes had the look of one who foresees, "you shall be more. Until we meet again, dear one."

Once more the soft dark, the oneness with nothingness which was a rest for mind and spirit.

When Kadiya roused again it was not into any place beyond the boundaries of the real world. She looked up to traceries of greenery against a clear sky, smelled the scent of fast growing things which follow the monsoon. She was lying wrapped in reed cloaks within one of the light craft. Before her, an

Uisgu tended the guide reins of a rimorik and they were speed-
ing along.

"Noble Lady—"

Kadiya edged her head around to face the speaker. She still
felt as drained as if she had awakened on a bed where she had
fought a dire illness. Salin was there, with Tostlet.

"Where are we?"

"You have been long asleep, Noble Lady. The Great One
said that you must be carefully tended, that we must do all we
could, for you gave too much of your strength to the Power.
Now we are riverbound to Yatlan."

She tried to think. Already riverbound . . . there was a long
trail behind them then.

Salin spoke again, softly. "The Sindona of the outer guard—
they who follow Lamaril—have gone as it was set upon them
to return to their own place. Those from Yatlan travel with
us. Not all survived the struggle, King's Daughter. There were
five who passed into the Last Flame. For the Dark One was
mighty. Had he awakened the sleepers and brought them
forth, none of us would be alive."

Lamaril had not died; Kadiya dimly remembered him on
that ledge. But gone . . . Kadiya knew a strange hunger, not of
one who craved food, but rather as if she sought a missing
part of her inner self.

There had never been one who had filled such an emptiness:
she discovered that now. Her mother, her father, they had had
their place in her life, and she had known grief tinged with
rage at their stark deaths. Haramis: she and her elder sister
had had little in common except their blood; she could not
enter into what fueled Haramis's life. Anigel: she felt again the
faint contempt which had been born of her sister's union with
the son of their enemy. As Queen, Anigel was already buried

in a life which Kadiya would find as confining as a prison. But Anigel had been born to wear the crown. Jagun? She could not think of days without him—but he was an Oddling, of another race with thoughts and beliefs of his own into which she could not enter. Salin? The girl looked now directly at the wisewoman. Salin was also a friend, and one she hoped she would never lose.

But . . .

Kadiya settled her head back in the blanket nest. She—would—not—think— She could not think! To him she would be as an Oddling—as the Hassitti—a strange creature with no touch of common life. He was already gone, back to leave his likeness to stand guard on the way to Yatlan. Already he must have vanished beyond time.

She fought her battle lying there—fought and knew she could not win. Wounds healed, but there were scars always left behind. When she had been with him she had never truly realized this change in herself. It was only when he had faltered under the attack of the Dark One, when she believed him gone, that the truth had come upon her, to be strengthened and rooted deep now as she lay in this craft upon the river.

Well, she was no weakling; Kadiya believed she had proved that. One can live even with painful memories. Time passed—and she was caught again in the flow of time.

The other Guardians—those of the stairway—were gathered on two other Uisgu craft which swept along before the one which carried Kadiya. They made no attempt to speak to her when they camped, keeping to themselves. She wondered if they were not already half withdrawn back into their timeless paradise. Nor did she seek out their company, for even eyeing them made her aware of the ever thickening barrier between them and the people of the swamp.

Strength returned. Kadiya ate what the healer urged upon her, listened to the Uisgu reports of how their clans were now hunting stray Skritek back to their own noisome territory. Perhaps the Drowners had suffered such a defeat that they need not be a danger for some time to come. But that did not mean that scouts and patrols would not prowl along the borders to check on them. That they would always be a peril, Kadiya accepted.

When their party had to leave the boats she was well able to march cross country. To her inward relief they did not take the road of the Guardians. She never wanted to look again upon Lamaril's likeness frozen forever into mud-daubed stone.

As they entered Yatlan itself the Vanished Ones lengthened stride to a pace which left the rest of them well behind. They passed along the edge of the pool quickly, but Kadiya trod determinedly at their heels. Though she no longer had any touch with them, she felt that she must see the end of the magic she had been given to work.

They shed their armor on the steps, leaving it in a tangle as if they had kicked it aside, unwilling to ever see it again. One of the helms rolled and fell to the lowest step near Kadiya's feet. The Vanished Ones fitted themselves into the same stance from which the trillium pollen had awakened them.

Then—the life was gone out of them, snuffed as if a lamp had been blown out. They stood, even as they had for centuries, though they were nothing but the likeness of those she had seen alive only moments earlier.

Hassitti scurried about her, swarming in upon the discarded armor, then trotting off again, carrying bits of it as insects might dismember a dead thing, stripping it to the bones.

Kadiya came forward slowly. On each step she turned left and then right to face the Guardians. She tried to remember

names, but some she had never really heard, those which had
kept themselves more aloof from the Oddlings.

The blank eyes made her shiver, yet she forced herself to
look at each. Yes, they were gone — all of them — and she was
very sure that they would never return. The world ravaged by
their mighty war so long ago was rebuilding itself in another
pattern, one which would mean nothing to them. She remembered that rich and peaceful land beyond the wall. Ruwenda
had been like that once, but there was no returning, any more
than she could again fit herself into the person of a daughter
in her father's vanished court.

What she was now, she must discover. Kadiya thought that
that was going to be a long and painful task. She had almost
arrogantly claimed the mires for her own — and thus she took
on responsibility. Foresee — Salin had that Power, a little. Kadiya shook her head. No, where there was no immediate danger she would not ask foresight from the wisewoman. Let each
day bring what it had to offer and she would meet it as best
she could.

She slipped the sword from its sheath. There was no life in
it. The orbs were as sealed shut as if they had never been
open. This part of her life was indeed finished. The amulet
hung like a pretty bauble on her breast. She could see the
black trillium within but it had no spark of life-fire.

Kadiya took off her own helm, left it on the steps. The mail
still clothed her, but the Hassitti would have other clothing
more in keeping for one who was no longer a warrior.

She crossed between the columns and came step by step
down to the garden. It was beginning dusk — the spark insects
were starting to weave their patterns about the flowers whose
heady scent thickened the shadows.

With the sword in both hands Kadiya once more came to

that patch of barren soil. She raised the blade high enough to give force and drove it down. The fact that it lacked a point did not deter its entrance, the ground seemed eager to accept it.

She sat back on her heels waiting. There was a glow, faint at first, deepening, concealing blade and hilt.

A flower was being born—such a flower as she had seen in another place, another time. No black trillium this, but one of gold, completely encasing the sword. It moved as if some breeze touched it lightly, and pollen shook free in a rainbow shower.

Kadiya gasped in awe. And then she stiffened, for there fell a weight on each of her shoulders. Hands—

She turned slowly and looked up. He was kneeling, too, but his greater height made him loom over her.

"Lamaril!" Her lips, suddenly dry, shaped his name even if she did not utter it aloud.

His masking helmet was gone and she could see the whole of his face, all so plain. Her breath caught almost painfully.

"But—you are gone!" Kadiya protested.

He shook his head. "There are always choices given us. I made mine very willingly. No stream of time shall lie between us, heart planted one. See"—he had drawn her into his arms and now he turned her gently to look upon the golden trillium, so firmly rooted—"this is the answer—for us both. Yatlan is dead, the world it ruled is gone—but many seasons of what is new lie before us. There is much to be learned, much to be done—together."

A breeze gathered up the gem pollen of the trillium and carried it toward them. Kadiya sighed. The enfolding of those arms about her was better than any foresight. No—*was* a foresight!